COURT OF ILLUSIONS

BLOOD LEGACY SERIES BOOK 4

ELISE HENNESSY

Copyright © 2021 by Elise Hennessy

All rights reserved.

No part of this book may be reproduced in any form or by any electronic or mechanical means, including information storage and retrieval systems, without written permission from the author, except for the use of brief quotations in a book review. This book may not be redistributed to others for commercial or noncommercial purposes.

This novel is entirely a work of fiction. The names, characters and incidents portrayed in it are the work of the author's imagination. Any resemblance to actual persons, living or dead, events or localities is entirely coincidental.

Flutterbye Trail Press
797 Sam Bass Road #2541
Round Rock, TX 78681

First edition

Editing by Red Loop Editing
Cover Design by FrostAlexis Arts
E-book Chapter Art by Real Life Design
Published by Flutterbye Trail Press

ISBN: 978-1-7345137-8-3 (E-book)
ISBN: 978-1-954582-01-9 (Print)

Feedback: Encounter a problem with this book? Let us know at elisehennessyauthor@gmail.com

Books by Elise Hennessy

Books in the Altare World

GRYPHON RIDER ACADEMY
Second Chance
Chosen
Storm Front
Wild Flight

ROYAL SPY INSTITUTE
The Crown Heist
Five & Chance

Also by Elise Hennessy

BLOOD LEGACY SERIES
Dream Walker
The Winter Key
Queen's Return
Court of Illusions
Shadow Dance
Rule the Night
Dhampir's Wish

Blood Curse
Blood Legacy: The Complete Series

Court of Illusions

Blood Legacy Series Book 4

Elise Hennessy

Neala felt like she was about to break something, and by something, she meant the ancient, dangerous fae standing right next to her. They were deep in the darkness of a cave in Ireland, at the back of a tourist group as a guide flashed a light over the ceiling.

"This is an outrage," muttered Izell. "Turning this beautiful cave into something for tourists. *Fah!*"

Neala elbowed her to be quiet. The fae was hiding under a glamor, her magical disguise making her look like a perky brunette, while on the inside, she was as salt and vinegar as always. Many of Neala's friends liked to keep company with Izell, something she struggled to understand since she disliked the fae's abrasive personality.

While most of Neala's companions, vampires and fae alike, were looking quite bored under their own glamors, one man was listening attentively to their guide. Cedric was half-fae, half-human, and as far as Neala knew, he was coming on this mission to play his enchanted lute and look pretty. He turned to her and whispered behind his hand. "What's a straw?"

The guide's light was focused now on stalactites made from the "straws" at the top of the cave.

All she could do was shrug. While Cedric was from Adrun, a mythical land sealed off from all contact with Earth, she had only recently woken from a thousand-year rest, which made her one of the most ancient and powerful vampires to ever live. But it also made modern things like straws an enigma to both of them. She only had a cell phone because the Coven Rehnquist vampires insisted.

The group moved deeper into the cavern. It wasn't a large, expansive system, or so the mortals around them thought. The flier that'd been shoved into Neala's hand suggested stepping into the cave was like entering another world. These humans had no idea how close they were to the truth.

Izell insisted that this cave held a secret so old that most fae had forgotten it. She was going to take them through a back door to Faerie, a land only open to traffic between worlds twice a year. They had a pressing need to get there and retrieve the last five pieces to a set of artifacts called the Fell Keys; otherwise, by the time the bridge between Earth and Faerie opened again, an invasion from Hell would cross over as well. There were only a couple months left to stop this catastrophe.

While Neala had a healthy dislike for magic, she found herself far too versed in it compared to the average vampire. She'd borne witness to the event that'd started their scramble for the Keys in the first place. Two giant orbs of magic tethered a veil of magic that separated Earth from the endless strife of Heaven and Hell warring for control over human souls. One of them, called the Dark Eye, was recently destroyed, and because of that, the veil weakened with every passing day.

Repairing the Dark Eye required all the Keys and a spell cast by one of the first fae to ever live, and thus a miracle. For one reason or another, Izell had picked Neala to be part of the team to make it happen.

She was more concerned over some of Izell's other picks. Neala was here to serve as a bodyguard, or "Blade" as the fae called those who were most adept in physical prowess. Her adopted son, Keegan, had gifted her with his sword for the task. In his youth, he'd named the steel short sword Faebane and burned fae runes upon it so it blazed with magical fire with the correct hand strength applied to the handle. He and his sister,

Sorsha, couldn't return to Faerie with the duties they'd assumed on Earth, so the sword's weight on her hip was a comfort and reminder of them.

With her role so well-defined, she puzzled over those of the rest of her companions.

There were two other Blood Princes here. Closest to her, Sirius, the Dawn, continued to glance around as he simmered with impatience. She tried not to look him in the eye. Truth was, Sirius was becoming more and more unbearable as he failed to adapt to the challenges of modern life. So, why was he coming to Faerie? She figured they needed the extra muscle, of which Sirius had plenty. He was a classic Ancient vampire, impossibly tall and built like a strongman. Red eyes were hooded under a scowl, the color marked with the blood of the creatures that had turned the first men into vampires. The same eyes she and Jaromir, the last Blood Prince present, shared.

She was glad to see Jaromir on his feet. The reason for his presence was more obvious, with his medical kit tucked under an arm. Despite a brush with darkness stealing away his magical Gift, he was still a doctor. She suspected Izell was why the soft-spoken man had shed his sorrow over his lost magic and gotten out of bed for this mission. For that, she had to give the fae grudging respect.

Two more women rounded out their group. There was a second fae with an irritated resting face, wearing a bandolier of daggers strapped over supple leather armor. She was an assassin from another time and the only Unseelie Neala had ever met. While most looked at Ash and saw a youthful human woman, Neala often peeled away layers of glamor for her eyes alone to catch a glimpse of the fae who'd captured her son's heart.

Ash was a fire fae of some kind, with slate gray skin and wings aflame just like her gaze, which reflected two pits of red fire with no visible pupil. Her white hair was tied in a tight braid and tossed over her shoulder like an afterthought. As an Unseelie, Ash could not tell the truth, and as a mute, Neala could only communicate mentally. Add in the supernatural threat they faced, and neither had tried very hard to get to know the other. Neala was determined to change that.

In the fire fae's shadow stood Cossette, a true mystery. Who brought a child on a dangerous mission? Of all Izell's invitations, to take Cossette was the one Neala understood the least. No matter that this particular child had experienced over nine hundred years of life. She was one of the eldest vampires to survive the tumultuousness of vampire politics and inter-coven strife.

"He got the years wrong." Izell scowled toward the guide, amending some detail Neala hadn't heard. "What a terrible time," she added under her breath.

Now that Neala was paying attention, she heard Izell grumbling corrections to minor facts the man got wrong. *"It is hard to do better at history than someone who's lived it,"* she remarked mentally to just Izell. With how much control she had over her psychic powers, she could speak privately to one person or project her voice into the heads of everyone around her.

"They could at least try to get it right," Izell muttered back.

Cedric glanced over. His smile hadn't dimmed, as if he hadn't heard a word Izell said. "Isn't this great?" he asked quietly. "I'm learning so much!"

The fae turned her ire his way and snapped, "Don't get too comfortable. Our stop is coming up."

Neala had a general idea of what to do when their "stop" arrived. Izell would make it look like their group was still on the tour with a set of illusions while they actually went a different way. They approached a bridge that covered a drop in the stone. The guide helpfully pointed out that they were walking over what was once an underground river.

Izell stopped before her feet could touch the wooden bridge. She barely cast a look over her shoulder before she leapt into the former riverbed. Neala knelt down for the first toeholds and climbed after her. She was thankful excavation and time had worn new outcroppings for her to place her feet. Otherwise, it was a good forty-foot plunge in the dark before it evened out into a more reasonable slope.

"Aren't you going to fly down?" she asked, raising a brow when Cedric started climbing downward next to her.

He fluttered his wings, usually hidden within the folds of an old-fashioned cloak. They were dark like his hair, lit with a sparkle here and there to show his astral fae side. But now that she glanced over them, she realized they were probably too small to be useful. "I like getting my hands dirty sometimes," he said with a wink.

Though she rolled her eyes, she couldn't help a little smile. He had no way of knowing how her heart fluttered with such a simple gesture. She was still trying to understand it, the tug of attraction she felt for him.

The moment ended too soon, with her feet hitting solid ground. Izell gestured for them to follow her impatiently, and Neala realized her assumption about the cave evening out was wrong, as around a bend, they came to a new plunge as the path narrowed.

The fae summoned an orb of light so they could see the full extent of what lay before them. Pointed stones lined the bottom of the drop like a bed of spikes. Neala had to wonder if the points were natural or a trap set by a clever fae waiting for someone to bumble in the dark. Smooth rock teased them on the other side of the expanse several yards away, looking how she would expect a river-created tunnel should.

"Is anyone here second-guessing their desire to accompany me to Faerie?" Izell asked. Without her glamor, she was a study in gold, from the sparkling stars that covered her skin to the scales that marked her arms from the elbow down. She was a shifter as well as a fae and wore her oddities proudly.

No one spoke up for a long moment, and she nodded in approval. "You all must stay in Faerie with me until your task is complete. You know what's at stake."

A grim murmur rose from Neala's throat. She knew. They were staring down the end of the world if they could not retrieve the remaining Fell Keys.

"Good. You shall be rewarded," Izell continued. As far as

Neala understood, everyone here was offered a boon if they could see the mission through.

For her, it was deeply personal. She sought to complete a potion that would give her a fresh voice. A *new* voice. Medicine and magic had failed her, but she held a potion that promised to replace her damaged vocal cords with something completely new. It was only missing one ingredient—a siren's tear.

Izell could've told her she was going to Faerie to be the bearded woman at a circus side-show. Neala would've gone if it meant she could speak once more.

"I've been this way recently and disabled the traps," the fae said. "We should probably be safe."

"Probably?" Cedric echoed with more than a touch of nerves.

Izell smiled wide enough to reveal the eight sharp canines that betrayed her shifter nature. "You can always trust me."

Chapter 2
Cedric

To avoid falling to a spiky death, Izell summoned wind to buoy those who couldn't fly. Cedric pretended he was flying for real as the magic hit his halfling wings. Instinct took over, and they fluttered all the way across until his boots scuffed the ground on the other side.

Probably safe, he repeated to himself.

Adventuring wasn't his thing. Sure, he knew all the songs about brave warriors heading into battle to face unsurmountable odds and had invented a few of his own. That didn't mean that he personally wished to do the same. Much as he wanted to save the world and find Fell Keys and not watch demons rain hellfire from the sky...he'd been invited to Faerie for a different reason.

Izell had promised him something priceless beyond the portal to Faerie. She'd help reconnect him with his family. His fae family. The only thing he knew of them was that they'd been performers like him. Trained men and women with voices like a choir of otherworldly birds and instruments just like his.

He felt the case of his lute bounce against his back as they continued to descend into the earth. There were no cool, limestone formations now, just solid rock everywhere he looked. He rubbed his palms on his tunic and focused on the prize.

His family. Fae who could teach him all the secrets of his grandfather's lute. Cedric had lost his fae father before he said his first words, so all the instruction he received in using the enchanted instrument was through Izell, his patron. Her singing may be as terrible as a cat's screech and her claws too sharp to pluck a lute, but her knowledge of the magic in the instrument made up for all that.

"Humans have many myths about us," she said to him over her shoulder. They walked single file now, the tallest amongst them ducking as the cave narrowed on all sides.

"Oh?"

Cedric tried not to pick apart her words too much, but he couldn't help it. Words were his job; words made ladies swoon and men part with their coin. So, when she said "us," he parsed it out. He was part human, part fae, and all shifter. That meant Izell meant either the fae or shifter "us," and he felt his curiosity rising as she let the words hang in the air.

"They say many things about fae. What I always found curious was how close they are to defining the entrance to Faerie. Underground, underwater." Her summoned light flickered as she gestured and floated it ahead of them.

He fingered the strap of his lute's case nervously. "We're going underwater?"

Izell stopped, holding out a hand to catch him before he stepped on her tail. She wrapped it around her waist as she shuffled to the side so the group could see a dead end of fallen rock before them.

"This is one of few intact back doors into Faerie," she said. He noticed she hadn't answered about the water, so they must be finding out where this underground river went. "Last chance to turn back."

"No one's gone this far just to be a coward now," spoke Sirius's low, gruff voice.

The longer they stalled, the more Cedric could feel the tremors in his body all the way to his pointed ears. He did trust Izell; he just didn't trust her *probably*. Because she was Seelie, she couldn't lie, so she could only offer a less-than-perfect chance of success. What tricks and traps lay beyond the natural barrier?

"Very well, then. Let's open this door." She began casting

with fae magic, her hands flashing through complicated, multi-step gestures. The rocks jiggled and clacked like oversized marbles as they heaved and stuck to the ceiling, revealing a fork in the path.

Izell pivoted and went for the trail on the left. "Less swimming. For you, Cedric."

He mumbled in gratitude, picking up the sound of dripping water somewhere down the path.

"Of course, I didn't go this way last time. Keep your wits about you."

He didn't have much time to sputter before a firm hand closed around his shoulder and pulled him back. A yelp escaped his lips, but it was just Neala, positioning herself in front of him. Their eyes met for a moment as she raised a brow.

All the moisture left his mouth. A good thing so he didn't say what was on his mind in that split second. *My, she's smoldering today.*

He'd discovered quickly that most women didn't appreciate the uncommon descriptors that popped to mind first. The very first one he'd thought when face-to-face with Neala was "large," and he'd expected her to break his spine when he accidentally blurted it out. But he hadn't meant it poorly. She *was* large and battle-scarred, much bigger than him since she was well over six feet tall, with a cap of orange-red hair trimmed around her chin line. That put her about as tall as a fae man, strong with muscle. Her presence filled a room even without a voice. Larger than life.

Now, in the midst of danger, her vampire-red eyes smoldered. She burned without fire. She was repressed power, ready for any threat.

His heart kicked into double time. "Are you to protect me today, madam?"

"Can't have anything harming your pretty face," she responded in his head.

"As long as you agree that it's pretty." He dropped his voice to a whisper as he heard its echo.

Someone behind them hissed for silence, and Cedric sighed.

When was there a better time to flirt than on the precipice of unknown danger?

Izell put a finger to her lips as she slowed to a creep. The path widened into a cavern, this time without helpful ropes and a well-worn path. Instead of stalactites shaped like straws—say, he'd never gotten a straight answer about what those were—Izell pointed upward to show the hulking silhouettes of a bat colony. *Not cute, little bats*, he realized with a gulp.

Person-sized bats.

"Most are asleep. Those only dozing will smell us, so we must move quickly," Izell instructed in their heads as she picked her way over mounds of unnamable things that Cedric didn't look at too closely. The stench was enough for him.

He swung his lute around so he was holding the case securely to his chest. No accidental noises here. Izell led them toward an opening on the far side of the cavern, another tight squeeze by the looks of it. Cedric was within ten paces when he heard it. The *crack* of someone's foot smashing into a rock and sending it skipping across the ground.

Leathery wings rustled, and the first bat woke with a sound reminiscent of a screech.

Then multiple voices took it up. *"Screeeeeee!"*

"Oh gods, oh no! I'm too young to die!" He bolted on a shot of adrenaline as the bats descended like a living carpet.

Izell's magic flashed golden yellow above him, and he didn't turn around until he was past her. Her brow was creased in concentration as she held a barrier of magic between them and the bats—except it didn't move, so the massive creatures were already clawing around it.

Ash turned to scoop up Cossette. Her fiery wings flared, sparking an inferno to life behind her. Bats shrieked and veered at the last moment to avoid incineration as the Unseelie crossed to Izell's barrier. "Don't kill!" Izell called to her. The other fae's face creased with displeasure, but she let her flames fade as she dashed the last yards to safety.

As soon as they were safely in the tunnel, Izell cast a new

barrier to seal the opening. Bats thudded inches away, and Cedric edged backward, his chest heaving with exertion.

"I should have mentioned that we have to come in peace. Nothing here dies by our hands," Izell said, turning and dusting a hand on her pants. The other held a bat half the size of its elders. With its wings pinned, it squirmed in futility.

"A wise thing not to tell a group of trained fighters," Ash muttered sarcastically. Cedric prided himself on understanding backward Unseelie speak, but it wouldn't take a genius to see her irritation.

"Let us continue," Izell said, turning to walk as if Ash hadn't said a thing.

Cedric exchanged a glance with Neala, gesturing to the older fae's profile. "What's with the bat?"

Neala didn't even bother with mental speak. She shrugged and sheathed her sword, heading after Izell.

He sighed as the path ahead had even him ducking. He was short for someone with a fae heritage, a few inches south of six feet, which was on the low end for the fae men he knew. "Do you think she's going to train it to be her personal guardian?" He couldn't just let Izell carry a giant bat child and not wonder about it.

"Maybe it's dinner," Neala answered.

"Ew."

Someone shushed him again. He had the sneaking suspicion it was Sirius and resigned himself to a quiet journey as the path sloped further downward. Water was trickling somewhere, unseen.

"Can someone tell me why those bats were so big?" he whispered within a minute. "Do they eat people or something?"

If his ears didn't deceive him, he picked up the sound of screeching even from here. He had a bad feeling this wasn't the only way those bats got around. Izell's bat was crying out too, sure to give their location away.

"Don't look up," Neala warned. Of course, he did right away, spotting something far too large with far too many legs scuttling away from the light of Izell's magical lamp.

So, big bats ate big bugs...which ate people? Made complete sense! He was feeling practically green by the time their group came to a stop again, this time over a fall with no discernable bottom. The tunnel ended at a ledge large enough for them to line up and observe a giant cloud of bats circling above.

"Stay here," Izell said before diving off the side. The baby bat screamed its lungs out, the echoes reaching the rest of its kind, which dove after her.

Cedric bit his fingernails as the cavern plunged into complete darkness when Izell's magical lamp went out. He wondered which song he should sing at her funeral. Would it be a testament to her power, or a detailed recounting of how she so valiantly averted danger from them? Granted, the rest of them had to survive first...

His mental list of appropriate songs drifted right out of his head as something happened below. Aquamarine light drifted up from the bottom of a lake, illuminating the outline of bat wings as they flooded upward—and away—from Cedric and the rest of the group. He saw a wider slit in the cavern wall where even a giant creature could fly. Bringing up the rear was a bat half the size of the rest, and its squeaky calls sounded a lot like scolding before it was gone.

Izell, unmarred, flew on starry wings to hover a few feet before them. "You look like you've seen a ghost." For some reason, he knew she was talking to him.

"Well, yeah! Maybe a little warning next time?" he protested.

She scoffed. "Here's your warning. You're about to jump into the water below, one at a time. No flying, no magic. Lyana, the guardian of this place, will help you swim to the other side."

Faerie, he thought.

"Before she lets you go, you have to let her look at your heart's intentions. Else you drown," she added, drawing a startled gasp out of more than one throat. "Oh, what are you worried about? You've got a good reason to go to Faerie!"

"I sure want to be drowned today," Ash snipped.

"So, who's first?" Izell put on a cheerful smile that made her look like a shark in the low light.

Before anyone could answer her, Cossette took a leap off the ledge. Cedric craned his head over the side with a gasp, noting the little splash when she hit the water far below. "The water will dim as the guardian dips into Faerie," Izell narrated as the cave went dark once more. "Next person can go when it brightens."

One by one, everyone jumped until it was Neala and Cedric remaining. There weren't complaints, not when the future-seeing Cossette went first without even a hint of hesitation. He fretted with his lute case, making sure it was sealed. Not like he was sure he could make this jump in the first place. This really tested his limits. What was the guardian looking for with his "heart's intentions"? There was a lot crammed in that little muscle, so much baggage from over the years.

The water brightened again, signaling that Jaromir was safely in Faerie. Well, hopefully safely. He looked up at Neala. Now was his chance to say something dashing and really impress her.

"Want to go next?" he asked instead.

Her gaze skimmed his face. *"Go. You will lose your nerve otherwise."*

He took a hard swallow. "It's perfectly fine if you want to go, though. Ladies first and all."

"Don't make me push you."

He held up his hands. "All right. You've twisted my arm. I will go. But should I die tonight..." He lined up his toes on the edge and looked back at her. "...know that I will die happy that your face was the last I saw."

Neala bit her lip as she struggled to maintain a straight face. *"Farewell, brave soul."*

He waved and took the plunge. Cold wind caressed his fluttering wings as he fell, and fell. How far down was this lake anyway? He worried for what bones he'd break upon impact when he finally smacked into solid water. It sure wasn't pleasant, shocking the air straight from his lungs. His lute case drifted from his shoulders, spiraling into the bright water.

Bubbles escaped his mouth as he reached for it. A face emerged below him, the strap in its serrated teeth. It placed it in his grip with care.

The guardian, he thought, his lungs already warbling for air as it placed itself below him. He held on to a fin as it swam with a quick dart of its body, taking him deeper into the lake. He saw a circular disk of bright light at the bottom, and that's what the guardian swam them through.

His stomach lurched as if he'd gone through a portal—and he must have, because the next thing he knew, the water was warm, and he could clearly see the guardian's serpentine body as it coiled around him.

It turned and looked him in the face. Those were dragon eyes. He'd seen them a thousand times when Izell grew irritated with him, slitted like a cat's but more expressive than any lizard's. Its body twisted gracefully through the water, twenty feet of bright scales and fins like white gossamer. Even as he wiggled uselessly, his body beginning to burn without a breath, he could acknowledge that this creature was beautiful.

"Thank you." The voice was distinctly feminine in his head. She canted her teal-scaled head. *"You may pass, Cedric Apple-white. I hope you find what you are looking for."*

She let him go, and he breached the crystal-clear water of Faerie with a hard gasp. By the time he slicked the hair out of his eyes and turned to thank her as well, she was gone.

Chapter 3
Neala

THE WATER DRAGON HELPED NEALA CROSS INTO FAERIE next. She admired the sunset lighting the horizon before every muscle in her body threatened to lock up in fear. The sun. It made the water tropical-warm and caressed the pale skin of her arms as she swam toward the shore.

When she was much younger, she'd adopted a pair of astral fae and raised them on Earth. Their dark, starry skin was just as susceptible to sunlight as any vampire's. Since vampirism originated from a fae curse, she'd simply assumed that all fae were photosensitive. However, Keegan and Sorsha, her now-adult children, had warned her in advance of many things about their homeland. Most importantly, that the sunlight was different here. Less intense. Considering that she wasn't boiling alive in the water, she knew it was true.

As real as the other things they'd said, she was sure. Magic lay heavy over this land, and many creatures here would take advantage of a vampire, no matter how strong she was. There was a reason Keegan had given her his sword to take on the journey.

It was hard to think of her former-teenage children as full adults. Not only that, but venerated elders, as time passed differently in Faerie. Her babies were a mind-boggling three thousand years old or so, experiencing three years here for every year that passed on Earth. They had families and lives she was still trying to piece together, as tight-lipped as they'd been after reuniting with her.

The time difference also meant the team here was given the gift of more time, as their two months extended to six at the most. They all wanted to get the task done as soon as possible, to close up any chance of demons coming to Earth at all. Izell had, in no uncertain terms, warned them all that Faerie presented its own challenges and that they would be hard-pressed to get all the remaining Fell Keys and the wording of the spell to use them within six months.

Unlike the world she'd just left behind, Faerie sported the most ancient of eldritch and unknowable creatures. Despite her wariness of that fact, she wished she could live in a place that looked like this. The water was a pure teal, and her group was gathering around a fire pit on a white-sand beach to dry out. She set her bags close to it to do the same. When Izell started enchanting their things with a waterproofing spell, she should've assumed they would all go for a dunk. The fae should've gone a step farther and waterproofed *them* too.

"I live to see your face once more," Cedric said. He sat cross-legged on a towel, smiling brightly at her, his dark hair slicked to his head and his white teeth standing out from his bronzed skin. It seemed he couldn't be without his instrument in his hands for long, as he plucked a simple melody on his lute.

His tunic had been a bright shade of blue before getting soaked. He seemed to like loud, attention-grabbing garb in shades that complimented the brown of his complexion. Unlike a full astral fae, he only sparkled here and there on his exposed arms, with most of his stars clustered over his cheeks like freckles and dusted into his eyes to make them brighter. Neala thought he often looked attentive and interested with how his eyes were lit. She appreciated that he'd inherited a mostly human face, his cheekbones and jawline not as diamond-cut as a pure fae's. However, he did have pointed ears sticking out from the wet waves of his hair.

Now that she knew something of the magic in the lute, she recognized how the upbeat number he played was causing her to smile as well. *"So you have."* She seated herself next to him, the two of them crowding the length of cloth. Cedric's next note was off-key before he caught his fingers and continued a smoother melody.

Her gaze went to the sea, where she expected Izell to emerge at any moment. Yet when the front of her clothes dried and her scalp itched with lingering salt, there was still no sign of their leader.

"It is like Izell to be this late," Ash said, deliberately speaking the opposite of what she meant. She accepted an armload of driftwood from Sirius, feeding it into their fire with a frown.

"Is she okay?" Jaromir directed this question to Cossette, who had her little hands out to appreciate the fresh blast of heat as the fire leapt to new life.

The seer's brow creased. Hopefully, she took the question seriously. The fire reflected in her albino-red eyes as she stared into it. "I don't know," she answered. "She doesn't want anyone to see her right now."

Neala frowned. What was that supposed to mean?

"She blocked you from seeing her somehow?" Jaromir knelt down by her side.

"Uh-huh."

"Can you see her in the future still?" he asked.

"Yes! So, she must be okay."

"But not when she'll be coming to join us," he pressed.

Bless his patience, Neala thought as Cossette considered. "She'll come to join us. I just don't know when," she said finally.

"We might as well make camp," Sirius grumbled, retrieving one of the bags he'd brought. He'd carried most of their camping supplies, all modern amenities that Neala would've killed to have a thousand years ago. Spacious, lightweight tents, soft bedrolls, even pressed food bars for the non-vampires amongst them.

They moved to more solid ground inland, the beach slanting up to sparse grass as far as Neala's night vision could see. The absence of the constant press of mortals was strange—they were the only people here.

Despite the fatigue tugging at her shoulders, she wasn't ready to sleep when the night had just begun. It seemed she wasn't alone, as after they'd set up their tents and Sirius went further inland with Ash to find true firewood, they gathered around a new pit and Neala asked the question that was weighing on her mind. *"What did Izell promise you to get you to come along on this trip?"*

Cedric glanced up from his lute. He let there be silence for only a couple seconds before speaking up. "I'll go first. I'm here for my family...my fae family." He flipped the instrument over, finger skimming over an intricate carved symbol of a tree branch studded with blooming flowers. "This is from a hawthorn tree; I think it's a family symbol. I wouldn't know, though. My dad died when I was young, and my grandfather owned this lute. Izell talks about there being other bards with instruments like mine, traveling performers and one big family. I hope we can find them."

"I hope you can too," Jaromir said, flashing a warm smile.

"What do you mean, instruments like yours?" Neala asked.

He played a few quick notes that made her heart speed to double time. "The enchantment on my lute is old craftsmanship. In Adrun, Izell was the only Sorceress fae around, and she was unable to replicate it. She said it was rare even in Faerie, so having one is a sign of being...in a special circle, I guess."

And now, he wanted to find that special circle he should be a part of. She nodded in understanding.

"I came here to get my Gift back." Jaromir spoke up next, looking down at his hands. The same hands that had healed a thousand injuries, mending them by speeding up a vampire's natural healing capabilities into overdrive with a magical ability simply called the Gift. The man most relied on for his steadiness, Jaromir had become a mess overnight when he'd unwittingly sacrificed his magic. It didn't surprise Neala that he was going straight for it now.

"How about you?" Cossette turned to Neala.

She sighed and dug through her bags before producing a finely lacquered wooden box. Within, on a bed of velvet, rested a glass bottle with a thick stopper. On first glance, she'd thought it was a fancy perfume bottle that was missing a mister. But no, it was something much more precious. *"I came to find a siren's tear because this is a potion that will give me a new voice."*

Jaromir, who'd tried countless medical remedies for her broken vocal cords, frowned at the little glass. "Are you sure that will work?"

"It's not going to mend my old voice. It's going to give a new one. A fine distinction."

His face was still creased with concern. "Anything is worth a try."

"If it doesn't work, I have lost little. But if I don't drink it, I will forever wonder if it would work or not."

She glanced up to where Ash and Sirius were returning with firewood. He arranged the branches and rough-chopped wood, and Ash set the structure alight with a wave of her wrist.

"We were just talking about what we came to Faerie for." Cossette spoke with a child's brightness. She repeated some of what Cedric, Neala, and Jaromir had said before her enthusiasm waned and she put on a more serious expression. "Izell is teaching me how to overcome my handicap. Since she gave up her future sight, she needs me to use mine."

"Gave it up?" Ash echoed.

"Uh-huh! To a scaly guy named the Trader."

Ash's slate-gray skin practically tinged green. "You don't say."

"What's wrong with that?" Jaromir asked.

Ash flicked embers into the fire with little clicks of her fingernails. "The Trader is of upstanding moral character. He only takes what you ask him to take. And he tries to offer something of more value than what you trade for."

Sirius scowled next to her as he pieced together her Unseelie backwards-speak. "So, a con artist?"

"Izell was not desperate to go to the Trader," she answered.

Silence descended around their little campfire. What did it say about their leader, that she was willing to trade away such a powerful part of her magic? Neala wondered what Izell had taken in return for it.

"Anyway, what did you come here for?" Cossette turned to

Sirius and Ash with a smile, like she hadn't dropped such a shock on them.

"It's private," Sirius muttered.

Ash scrubbed at her face. "I'm at my least helpful with Unseelie. Izell didn't see us needing Unseelie assistance."

Sirius sighed. "Great. More Unseelie speak."

"Most Unseelie will speak backward to you like I am, as if you were a child," Ash said sharply.

"I know, and I hate it," he snapped back.

"It's not her fault," Jaromir interjected, seeing the way the two of them were staring daggers. It was a dangerous thing for Sirius in particular, with how dominant his inner beast seemed, as a shapeshifting vampire.

"Why do Unseelie speak only lies anyway?" Cossette interjected.

Ash breathed a sigh, looking to Cedric. "There's a song for that!" he exclaimed, his fingers deftly transitioning to a slower, rhythmic tune. Neala sat back to listen, closing her eyes as his words shaped the story in verse. It was the tale of King Oberon, the first fae ruler, back when there were no Seelie or Unseelie. Just fae of the four elements: fire, water, wind, and earth. They were creatures of balance and harmony, bringing it to their land and also to Earth where they could freely come and go.

Faerie was once approached by envoys of a never-ending conflict between angels and demons, which fae apparently thought was a struggle of hubris. They still spread their teachings amongst the fae, with some preferring the purity and right-eousness of the angels and others believing in the might and promises of the demons. Oberon was heartbroken to watch his people fight along the same lines as their new allies.

He saw the destruction the fighting caused not only in Faerie but also on Earth in the early times of humanity. The balance was irreversibly tipped, careening Faerie toward destruction unless he acted in the defense of his land.

He created a spell he called his crowning glory—a spell so powerful it would take his very life to cast. After gathering two massive orbs of dragon-forged glass, he sacrificed a willing archangel and an unwilling greater demon to create the Eyes of Worlds, casting a dome of protection over Faerie and a veil over Earth that neither angel nor demon could penetrate.

But he included a clause in his crowning glory that closed fae off from reaching Earth except under certain circumstances. In his displeasure, he cursed the entirety of Faerie along the battle lines they'd drawn. Angel-sworn became Seelie, and demon allies became Unseelie. Thus, they and their descendants would know the sins of their ancestors by their slippery tongues.

"That seems extreme," Sirius said once the song was finished.

Ash sighed. "We didn't bring it upon ourselves. Except...it is fair now, generations later." Neala knew what she meant, that after such time, it seemed cruel to continue punishing Unseelie for their ancestors taking the side of demon kind. And, in another way, for Seelie to still have to tell only the truth. It was a double-sided curse; it just seemed one side had it easier.

"*Is there a way to fix this curse?*" Neala asked.

Cedric answered as Ash's lip curled. "Legends say that Oberon's favor can lift it and reunite the fae people."

"*But he's dead.*"

"Well...yeah, that's kind of a problem," he admitted.

"Faerie will never be reunited, and that's the truth," Ash said, pulling a rag from her belt and plugging her nose as she winced. Only telling the real truth would cause her such instant pain, and it was maybe the third time Neala had heard her speak so directly.

"*Well then. That's a depressing way to end the evening,*" she remarked, turning to Cedric. "*Do you have any happier tales of this land to share?*"

His face lit up. His lute filled the space between them all, his smooth voice conjuring stories of clever characters and nimble-fingered thieves.

One could learn a lot about a people from the stories they prized, Neala reflected. She went to bed thinking that not once did Cedric sing of a brave swordsman saving his maiden. That, perhaps, was all human. If fae valued wits and cunning more, it was nothing she was unused to from her stint politicking in another time.

Chapter 4
Cedric

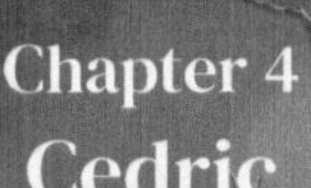

CEDRIC WOKE TO A METALLIC SOUND. HE SAT UP IN HIS tent, unzipping the flap wide enough to give himself a peephole. Stirring up a new fire was Izell, hovering a pan over it with a touch of magic.

Sirius and Neala were already out of their tents, weapons in hand. "Think a little game fowl is going to kill you?" the fae scoffed, holding up a brace of quail-like animals.

The animal spirit inside Cedric gave a little shiver, and he shut his tent back up. He didn't flaunt his shifter nature like Izell did, but he, too, carried the soul of another and could shift into it if he liked. He was a lesser shifter, with a lyrebird for a companion. He liked to think they were friends, but like most shifters with a small spirit bond, he rarely heard from it other than a flash of instincts here and there.

His lyrebird side didn't like it when small birds were on the menu. So, he decided to make a distraction. He tousled his hair and grabbed his lute, striding out in an undershirt and soft sleeping pants. "Oh, hello, Izell! Where did you go?" he announced upon seeing her.

"Looking for you pack of twits," she grumbled.

He picked a lighter tune to play, trying to draw out her less prickly side. "Surely we weren't so hard to find? We all landed in the same place."

Some of the tension left her shoulders as he played on. Much as she brushed off his enchanted music most days, sometimes, she seemed to embrace it. "I also had to pay our dues to Lyana," she said. "Very lonely woman. We had tea in her lair and chatted."

"Underwater?" he asked.

At the same time, Sirius said incredulously, "Tea?"

Izell's scowl reappeared. "Her lair is above water. And she's a shifter. Do you even know...of course not." She turned to Ash, who was just emerging from her tent with a yawn. "Do you at least know of *mort loci*?"

Ash froze with her hand over her mouth. She nodded. "You aren't one."

Cedric's fingers slowed on his strings. "Those are human words," Izell explained. "It means, roughly said, 'death speaker.' *Mort loci* are considered cursed by those Faerie-born. By their definition... all shifters are cursed."

"Because we talk to our spirits?" he asked, brow furrowing.

"No. It's because we're considered possessed. We have a second soul inside us. It would do you good not to show off your shifter side here," she warned. He just wished he'd heard about this earlier. Would his *family* think he was cursed too?

"That guardian was a traditional *mort loci*. She was possessed by a water dragon not willing to die yet. Instead of being executed, she was assigned as a guardian and can't return to polite society unless there is a dire emergency. So...I had tea with her. It was the least I could do." She shrugged. "Oh, and I broke the spells over her so she can go free."

He sputtered as she casually returned to plucking her catch. "Wait, what? Isn't she important?" he asked.

"It's been centuries since anyone wanted to pass through her portal. I doubt anyone remembered she was there," she said, a tightness to her face betraying some private reaction. "It's better to be free. She can go to Adrun, where we are all *mort loci*."

"*What will you do, though?*" Neala asked, gesturing to Izell's whole self. "*If being a shifter is a banishable offense.*"

She glanced down at herself, her tail twitching behind her. Then, it disappeared. Her scales melted off, and her skin lost its golden luster, replaced by the pitch black of an astral fae's night sky visage. "What do you mean? Do I look like a *mort loci?*" she said smoothly.

Neala frowned, her face the perfect presentation of unimpressed. *"I see through your illusion."*

"And some will. My dragon hates it, but I can retract his features as well," she said. "I won't be discovered."

Neala shook her head, glancing to Sirius. *"I wonder what else we will learn now that we are committed."*

"I hope our ally hasn't been keeping any more key information from us," he agreed pointedly.

Izell held up a finger. "One more thing."

Neala let out a sound close to a garbled groan. Her vocal cords pinched somewhere in the noise, drawing a flurry of coughs to follow.

"It's a good thing this time." Izell drew one of her bags into her lap and fished out a piece of paper, which she offered to the burly woman. "For you... and Cedric."

He inched over for a closer look at it as Neala turned it one way and then completely upside down. The ink was moving on the page, blurring his vision the longer he looked at it.

"So generous," Neala deadpanned.

"I know. I had to trade one of my keepsakes for it." Izell tapped the top, where it read "Shifting Wood" in bold script. "I'm sending you two here. There are friends you need to meet."

He spotted the symbol before her finger slid over it. A hawthorn flower in the middle of the page. It rested at the heart of the inky maze like a marker for secret treasure. At seemingly random were several x's on the map like indicators. "The fae you seek, Cedric," she said as he gaped at the simple symbol so similar to the one on his lute. "And the closest alchemy lab with a stock of siren's tears. Two birds with one stone."

"So, when do we leave?" Neala asked. Her usually impassive expression betrayed a hint of excitement.

Meanwhile, Cedric felt like he was going to shake out of his skin. "Right now? Are we leaving right now?"

"You two are leaving when you're good and ready," Izell said. "To return once your training is finished in a few weeks."

His brow furrowed. "What...?"

"*Explain,*" Neala demanded.

"I think it's pretty straightforward." The fae shrugged as she had a seat, prodding at the fire. "You will learn to speak again. More than that. To *sing.*" Her gaze flashed to Cedric. "And you will undoubtedly want to know everything your lute can do. Take some time for it, but don't take too much."

He could practically feel the reluctance coming off of Neala. He put a hand on her stiff shoulder. "Isn't this what we want anyway?" he murmured.

"*You brought me here to be your bodyguard. Your Blade,*" Neala said to her instead.

"I did. And you still are. The best thing you can do to protect me is to make contact with the fine folk that will heal your voice. Just avoid the spots with the x's and try not to kill anything within the wood." Izell, for once, flashed a reassuring smile. "Don't forget that I used to see the future and, in doing so, saw that this is best for us all. Besides...it will give Sirius something to do besides brood."

He turned a red-hot look her way. "Watch your tongue," he growled.

"We're going to get along great without you," Izell said, letting her lips curl upward until she was showing her fangs.

Cedric chuckled nervously. He thought the two of them were about as unified as oil and water. Hopefully, they would figure it out, because he wasn't going to let this chance go. Even if he had to go alone. He hoped Neala would fix the stubborn set of her mouth and agree, too.

"*Then...I suppose it best we go,*" she said reluctantly, to his relief.

"Let's discuss the details over a meal," Izell suggested. She cooked that brace of birds as Cedric studiously looked away, instead observing the faces of those waiting to eat.

Concern was the expression of the day. He saw it on Jaromir's face as he consulted with Neala and Izell, trying to mend something there. Ash leaned back and watched the clouds scroll by, lost in her own thoughts. Even Cossette, usually the carefree one, stared off into space with a frown.

He picked a tune for the occasion, singing of a man who conquered adversity. It was a new song, one he'd composed himself for the new Dragon of Adrun, King Adrius. A man everyone here knew, so he didn't sing his name, waiting with anticipation in his belly for someone to recognize the deeds of their friend.

The best part of the song, though, was the hope it brought. While Sirius was the one who sang the chorus off-key as he caught on, the smiles it brought were priceless. This was how Cedric wanted them to remember parting ways with him and Neala. That there was still hope amidst their worries.

He accepted his bowl of broth and meat once he'd finished and felt the magic of his music lingering in the air. How much more powerful could it be with proper training?

The corner of Izell's mouth lifted with amusement. "Now that we've had our musical interlude. The Shifting Wood is named literally. It is a place of old magic. I can only make you a portal to its outskirts, but from there, you must navigate the maze."

Neala raised a brow. *"What bards would choose such a place to live?"*

"Who said Cedric's people are *just* bards?"

"They're not?" Cedric asked immediately. "What else are they?"

"Find them and see." Izell flashed him a wink. "Oh, and you will need this as well." She pushed a coin into his hand. On one face was a cluster of white hawthorn flowers. He ran his thumb over the image before flipping the coin over and reading the words written in fae script to himself.

"Trust in the process." He would. He knew Izell had the best of intentions for them, even if she didn't want to provide every detail. "Here, this is meant for you," he said to Neala, passing the coin over.

Chapter 5
Neala

"*Trust in the process, my ass,*" Neala muttered the moment the portal closed behind her and Cedric. While the rest of their group would be heading to the Seelie capital, she was going hiking. It didn't sit well with her that she didn't know who they were meeting and why they were secreted in the Shifting Wood.

The woods themselves were a sight, though. It was like a painter had spilled their autumn palette, saturating every leaf with deep oranges and reds, even the carpet of fallen ones stirred by a cool breeze. Too beautiful for the place Izell had warned them of—where creatures lurked in wait of a hapless traveler.

"Good thing there's two of us," Cedric had said. She envied the confidence.

He was now inspecting their map, pointing out a red dot that'd appeared on its outskirts. "I think that's us!"

"*Let's test it.*" They walked past the first tree, and the dot shifted with them. Something completely necessary, she thought. Otherwise, they wouldn't know where to turn even with a clear bird's eye view of the woods.

She offered to hold the map as he started playing his lute with one hand. It seemed the man couldn't stand more than a few seconds of silence at a time.

"What's wrong?" he asked within twenty paces.

She was still tracing possible pathways to the center of the wood. *"Hmm?"*

"You're going to get your voice back! Why are you unhappy?" His cheer was palpable, both from his smile and his music.

When she realized he was using his lute to try and change her mood, she scowled at him. *"Keep your music out of my emotions."*

"It's going to be a long trip if you don't talk about it," he sang.

"I'll break that damn lute over your head."

"It's unbreakable! You'll just..." he flinched as she bared her fangs. "...break my head. Sorry."

The music stopped. He hummed the same tune instead.

"This way." She focused on the map and the right path. It seemed they would not be heading in a straight line—who knew how long this would take? After a while, she snuck a glance at Cedric, who was starting to whistle random smatters of birdsong. As a lyrebird shifter, he'd already proven he could mimic almost any sound.

She envied his carefree cheer so much more than his confidence. Of late, she carried too much baggage from the past. Maybe she did need his music to balance some of that. *"I appreciated your song,"* she said.

"About King Adrius?" He lit up immediately. "Queen Nyah asked me to write it. I'm still trying to get it perfect for her."

"She would love it. Is that how you know of his struggles as well?"

"Yeah. They told me about what they went through." He rubbed an imaginary chill from his arms.

"Adrius was a troubled man without her," she remarked. Just how she feared she was now that she remembered every detail of her deceased husband and what he'd been for her. She couldn't get him back no matter what miracle occurred.

Little as she knew him, Cedric was supposed to be the same for her. A lifemate. She had no way of understanding why, when she looked at his cheerful face, her breath came short. Neala had had her one-and-only already, and no one was supposed to compare. Not that she would tell him before she had a hold of herself.

But a glimmer of concern was in his eyes. "What's on your mind?" His quiet tone was more effective than any upbeat song meant to make her happy for a fleeting minute.

It was just the two of them here. She felt she could trust him with a hint of her troubles. *"I worry this potion will not work."*

He tilted his head. "I mean, that's reasonable. It's a big thing. But that potion has Queen Nyah and Izell's magics in it right? How could it go wrong?"

"If only you knew how many potions with Nyah's magic I've tasted." She sighed, shaking her head. *"None of her treatments worked. Nor Jaromir's. Nor anyone else's. I thought this potion sounded promising. It offers a* new *voice rather than fixing up my obviously faulty first one. But the closer we get to finishing it and me drinking it..."*

"The more you worry about it not working," he supplied. "That's completely understandable."

"Is it?"

"It sounds like you've been burned by everyone's fresh new ideas. So, when confronted with another one, you don't believe in it," he said.

She nodded emphatically.

"I guess all we can do is see if this one works. Because Izell seems to think it will," he said, plucking a single note on his lute. It sounded a lot like *hope* to her ears.

"You are right, of course," she said. That was really all she could do anyway, to wait and see. She turned a curious look his way. *"Can you lie?"*

His song about King Oberon had opened up many questions about him as a half-fae, and she wondered if he was subject to all the same rules as his pureblooded kin. "Oh, yes," he said. "I enjoy the occasional white lie. Just a smidge of lying. Nothing too bad."

"Mmhmm. Still trouble, chicken." She'd first met him when he was shapeshifted into a lyrebird and running from a group of angry and drunk fae men. In the darkness of Adrun, he'd seemed like a talking chicken to her. Now, the nickname made him blush with star shine, so she kept using it.

"I never said I wasn't." His eyelids fell to half mast, slanting her a coy look.

She might've seen how far he would take his casual flirting, but a branch snapped under his feet. He flipped over within a blink, dangling by the ankle from a snare trap. His lute fell from his shoulders with a discordant complaint. "Help!" he yelped.

His squirming set the trap to swinging. She bit her lip to keep from laughing, but a snort escaped. "Are you really having a giggle at my expense?" he exclaimed, his little wings fluttering as he crossed his arms. The annoyed sight of him didn't help her composure.

"We should've been paying more attention," she said, scrubbing her face and looking for the counterweight to the trap. She found it and severed it with a quick swipe of her sword, sending him toppling to the ground.

He groaned as he picked himself up, dusting his instrument off first. "I'm all right. Thanks for asking," he grumped.

She wet her thumb and cleaned a streak of dirt off his cheek. *"Glad to hear it. That trap was built for a person, not an animal."* While he didn't flinch from her touch, his gaze flashed to hers, and her heart fluttered. He had such expressive eyes, bright and inquisitive. Untouched from the darkness that swirled within her own. Clearing his throat, he glanced away first with a sparkle lingering on his cheeks.

They consulted the map, where their path was starting to veer toward the entrance as the topography shifted. She traced a new way with her fingertip before leading him into the trees, this time with her attention fixed on the ground. "Does that mean there's something out here that wants to catch us?" he whispered.

"Obviously."

"And eat us?" he added with an audible gulp.

She rolled her eyes. *"Who knows what security your family employs to keep their secret hiding place safe."*

"I don't think a bunch of musicians would really...need a secret hiding place," he admitted, plucking a few notes on his lute. They sounded picked at random, the melody as confused as he must be at the thought.

"They're obviously not just musicians. We will learn their secret soon," she offered.

Cedric was quiet as they picked their way around a pile of leaves to the side of a new path. It was strange to have a moment of stillness. She'd already grown used to his music being like the glue between conversations, laying the foundation for her most recent memories. But she didn't have to ask what was wrong; he told her the moment they stopped to inspect the map again.

"I just hope I fit in with them, you know?" he said. The two of them watched as the path ahead became a bridge over a peaceful river that wasn't there a moment ago. She rubbed her eyes and took a second look. She didn't know how any sane person could stand living in a place like this when, without a map, one would be hopelessly lost within thirty minutes or less. She glanced toward the sheet of parchment and realized they were approaching one of the black-inked x's.

Her brow furrowed. *"Something tells me that won't be a problem,"* she said, distracted. He seemed like he would adapt. Plus, this was his kin he was going to see. They'd take one look at his instrument and know he was one of them.

"It's not easy," he said with a sigh. He stopped halfway over the bridge and leaned over. The soft afternoon sunlight reflected their images back from the water. Here and there were the scales of silvery fish as they flitted by. "I think part of my success as a performer in Adrun is because of how different I look from most of the fae."

"Not your beautiful voice?" she said.

"I never really fit in with them. And I kind of don't expect to fit in here, either...wait, you like my voice?" She saw a flash of his white teeth in his reflection.

"I do, actually. You really feel that different, though?" She wouldn't have guessed. As an outsider, he seemed like a celebrity as a talented musician. He was as much Adrun as all the full-blooded fae she'd met, as they shared the same strange, shapeshifter ways.

Part of her worried that the fae here would actually see him as even more of an outsider—not because of his half-human side, but because he was apparently a *mort loci*. He would have to work hard to keep that a secret.

And chattery Cedric didn't seem all that good at keeping secrets.

The river water rippled, and a hideous face emerged from under the bridge. "Why does my food talk so much?" it rumbled from bulbous lips.

Cedric fell back with a cry of alarm. Neala reached for her sword before remembering she wasn't supposed to kill anything that resided in this wood. She decided to do the next best thing, pushing her companion along. *"Run!"* And so they did, stopping a few yards away when nothing gave chase. The creature watched them as the woods shifted again, leaving it behind.

Chapter 6
Cedric

"When do you think we should stop for the night?" he asked, watching the sky. The evening light was low amongst the tree branches, casting a warm glow over the multicolored trees. They hadn't seen any more traps or signs of life. But he couldn't shake the feeling of being watched, and his ears perked every time a strange animal or creature called to one another.

He was nervous about stopping. They'd made good progress through the forest once they figured out the pattern of shifting. The proper path was a spiraling one, and attempting to cut corners was punished by dead ends and frustration. "Do you think we *should* stop?" he asked before Neala could finish considering his first question. "What if the woods are smart enough to put us back to the beginning while we sleep?"

"There's only one way to tell. I would rather keep our wits sharp and take a rest." She patted his shoulder. *"I'm a light sleeper. It should be safe."*

"What a coincidence! So am I," he said. When she seemed amused, he chalked that up as a victory. "I will make the fire if you set up the tents?" The last time he'd tried, he'd ended up tangled in the synthetic fabric. User-friendly to whom? Definitely not him.

"Fine." She was laughing again, probably at the same memory.

He'd spent more than his fair share of nights in the woods, mostly in his first years performing. In that time, he'd realized how much women liked a man who could sing. Even if they already had a man. Eventually, he learned who was safe, but first, he gained the skills to survive out where he couldn't be found for a while.

So, he knew what to gather and padded it with multicolored leaves for kindling. He fanned the nascent flame with his little wings, coaxing it to life. With the setting sun rolled in a serious chill promising another cold night. They'd be glad to have this fire shortly, even if it gave away their location to any of the creatures Izell promised were in the woods. Watching them. Hooting in the night.

He lifted his gaze and panned the area. If anything, he bet Neala's presence scared off anything brave enough to approach them. Even sitting across from him on a fallen log, Neala was formidable with the obvious strength in the lines of her body.

She was his type, he thought. He liked a strong woman. If she was hard to impress, all the better. It made any affection from her all the sweeter.

Affection? he asked himself. Was he really thinking that way of someone he'd basically just met?

"*Nice night,*" she said, taking him out of his thoughts.

"Nice night...for a song?" he offered. His fingers were busy plucking a mindless melody.

She propped her chin on a fist. "*Judging by this journey, every time is a good time for a song.*"

"Too true, my lady," he winked.

"*Sing me a love song,*" she suggested. She squared her shoulders like she was expecting something more unpleasant.

A bad experience with a lover, he guessed. He ran through a handful of songs that came to mind. Most of his repertoire related to love, so he always thought of them more by the occasion. Love songs could be sappy or tragic, crass or romantic.

She didn't want romantic, he thought. The hollows under her eyes were more pronounced by firelight. It looked like she'd sigh sadly to hear of someone else falling head-over-heels in love with another.

So, he went for something lighter, hoping it would lift her spirits. "It'd been a long time for Lady Rena...if you know what I mean," he sang, finishing the verse with a wink. Neala's brows rose, but she leaned in to listen.

He strummed his lute slowly. "She donned her best furs and knocked back a drink... for luck." He took a deep breath at the pause as he placed his fingers in the right place.

He launched into the song at double the pace, belting out the chorus. "And out on the town, she went searching for fun! With her assets piled high and her hair undone. Heads turned for a mile—man, they liked her style. She won't go home 'til she's done!"

When amusement filled her eyes, he knew he'd picked the right song. He narrated Lady Rena's wild night until she got laid at the end of the song, finishing the tale with a bowing flourish from his seat. He soaked in her quiet laughter, the husky whisper of it that trailed behind the last fading notes of his lute.

"*Bravo. Just not what I expected.*" She gave him a smattering of applause in the night. Her keen gaze lifted from him to their surroundings. "*Perhaps we should be quieter...just in case.*"

When she relaxed, so did he. No threats yet. "No more songs?" He could deal with that for an evening.

"*No, but thank you. I needed that,*" she said. Her tone hushed to a thoughtful undertone. "*What is love like for a fae? Do you have lifemates as well?*"

He leaned back, plucking a soft tune to match the topic. "Fae do, yes. The old, old fae call them heartsongs sometimes. Shifters have lifemates. It's a fine distinction."

She tilted her head, her lips moving to the term. Heartsong. "*How so?*"

"Well, every fae has a heart's song. It's their own personal thing, right? A fae's perfect match has a heart's song that harmonizes. The idea is that they make better music together." He put on a playful swoon. As a musician, he thought it was incredibly romantic. But as someone who thought of perfect matches as lifemates, the difference between a heart's song, the literal tune, and a heartsong, another word for a lifemate, used to confuse him.

"*But fae that happen to be shifters don't have this?*" she asked.

He snapped his fingers. "Ah, they have two things. Something I understand vampires have too, the ability to know their perfect mate at first glance. Right?" She pressed her lips together and nodded. "They know at first glance, and then later, if they sing their heart's songs, they harmonize. By comparison, full fae don't know each other on sight, only by their melodies." As someone stuck between shifter, fae, and human, he wondered if he would know his match on sight. He'd dreamed of her being someone like Neala—strong, proud, and unashamed of it.

"*How convenient,*" she remarked. "*So, how does a fae learn their heart's song, then?*"

He searched for how to explain it, given how his mind produced plenty of new melodies with enough inspiration. "It just forms over time when you're old enough to want companionship. You start humming something you've never heard before. It's yours, your own unique melody."

"*I assume that it's very personal.*"

Lifting a shoulder, he said, "It can be. I wouldn't know. I throw it out there in some of my songs." Secretly hoping a lady would come back with something similar. "Want to hear it?"

"*You don't mind?*" She shifted forward to the edge of her seat, as if expecting this to be his best performance of the night.

He grinned and picked at a new melody on his lute, more than eager to show off. It was a melody with lyrics as carefree as he was. Punctuated by the clicks and whistles of his lyrebird and the harmony of his lute, it was him in a song.

Neala, he realized, was moved to tears. And that's when the song ended and he nursed a hollow, twisting feeling in his chest. He massaged where it hurt right under his collarbone.

It felt like someone else should've been singing with him. Some phantom knowledge of that other voice haunted his ears.

By the time he glanced up, Neala's expression was schooled and her face was dry. Maybe he'd imagined a more impassioned reaction. *"That was quite lovely. Your future mate is a lucky woman."*

He cleared his throat, the lingering pain in his chest robbing him of any clever words. "I think I'll take my bow here. Good night."

They camped on either side of the fire, and at first, Cedric watched the shadows as strange sounds echoed around them. He grunted and moved out of his bedroll, deciding to shift into his lyrebird form. It was small and low to the ground, perfect to sneak into a bush and take a closer look at their surroundings.

Even though he couldn't see anything, he knew something or someone was making noise on purpose. He stretched out his feathery neck and mimicked some of the sounds he'd heard from his brief time on Earth. Trains screaming by. Video game *pew pews*. A car horn honking.

Silence.

"Was that really necessary?" Neala sighed as he returned to camp and snuggled into his bedroll as a bird.

"Completely and utterly necessary," he answered, muffled from the fabric. He slept like a baby, secure in the idea that he'd scared something off without needing any violence.

THEIR SECOND DAY OF TRAVEL WAS QUIETER. THOUGH A night's rest had chased away the feeling lingering over him in the wake of his performance, he couldn't shake the memory. It'd never happened before, not for the hundreds of times he'd woven in the melody in a cheeky search for a beloved.

He played his lute, and Neala introspected. This was, perhaps, their version of companionable silence.

Out of nowhere, she hissed and snatched his wrist. He followed where her finger pointed, seeing a face in the leaves above them. It snatched away a split second later.

"Do you think that was a fae, or...?" he whispered.

"Unclear." She drew her sword and stood taller. This was her element, he thought. Danger and adventure were her middle

names, not his. He took a step behind her and played a tune for bravery and strength.

She shot a look over her shoulder. *"What are you doing?"*

"Encouraging you!" he said brightly.

They rounded a bend in the path, coming to a clearing. In the center was a bright pink blanket. A tiny hand lifted from one of the folds. Cedric dropped his music with a gasp. "A baby!"

Neala's arm blocked him from a forward rush. *"It's a trap."* She gestured to the leaves between them and the child, revealing a bear trap two paces away and a trip wire a step from the baby.

Shadows emerged from the tree line, forming a semi-circle of muscle between them and the path. They had faces like goats, with the same wide pupils and muzzles topped with a diamond-shaped nose. Three of the four sported foot-long pairs of horns, while the fourth had stubs and a smaller, feminine figure. She had petite hooves and held a sling, while the three males wielded spears and were proudly naked except for scraps of loincloths.

"I must warn you! You face Neala, great and Ancient vampiress from Earth!" he announced. "Turn back now before you do something you regret."

Neala shoved him so a spear just nicked his cheek as it sailed by. "You'll regret that!" he yelped.

With a roar, she leapt forward and smacked the side of her blade against one of the goat-men's heads. He dropped like a sack of bricks, landing with a *thud* that could shake the ground. The female started whirling her sling. Neala was busy with the two goat-men left. The one who'd tossed his spear grabbed her by the elbow, while the other needled her from a safe distance with the tip of his weapon.

Cedric tiptoed around all the traps and picked up the baby. The goat-lady turned her attention on him as her nostrils flared. "It's not a good idea to just leave your kid out in the open, ma'am," he said. The blanket fell aside to reveal a little furry face. The child giggled happily and reached for him.

He realized the two males fighting Neala had frozen, staring at him too. *"Be careful,"* Neala said, now holding back one of the goat-men as he strained toward Cedric.

"Here, this is yours, right?" he asked the goat-lady, holding the bundle out to her. She shoved her sling back into her loincloth and met him halfway, wiggling a finger at her cooing child.

Her doe-brown eyes met his. "You pass," she said, enunciating carefully.

Neala sheathed her sword, watching the two males lean over their fallen comrade. *"I remembered Izell didn't want us to kill anything,"* she said to Cedric privately.

"We watch you long time," the female continued. "Loud male. Ignore danger."

"Are you the most dangerous things in this wood?" he asked.

She tilted her head back and barked a laugh. "No. We just groundkeepers." She waved behind her, and the path moved by ninety degrees. He saw a hint of gray stone through the screen of the trees.

About to ask if that was where his family lived, he held his tongue when he saw someone else walking toward them. It was another fae, a full-blooded fae, with a dark robe over hot, yellow-orange skin and wings like flames tamed into a butterfly-shaped pattern. He was bald, which was unfortunate because his face was long as a horse's.

"Welcome. You've made it at last," he said, sweeping an arm out behind him.

Chapter 7
Neala

THE GOAT CREATURES MELDED BACK INTO THE FOREST, leaving Neala and Cedric to follow the fiery fae. Cedric practically vibrated next to her, his head on a swivel. They were circling around the back of a large structure built with smooth blocks of gray stone. The texture and gleam of the masonry reminded her of the white-stone castle she'd once called home in Nyixa. While she'd admired the stone then, she wondered now if it was a common building material in Faerie.

"*You have a lot of security for a group of bards,*" she said to the fae leading them.

He uttered a quiet scoff, but his voice was cultured and polite when he replied. "I see you've been sent here blind. But someone did, in fact, send you, with your map."

"And coin!" Cedric interjected.

Their escort paused when Neala produced it and placed it in his palm. He turned it over in his fingers, his thin eyebrows forming a straight line as his face scrunched up. "The nobility sent you?" he asked. Like all full-blooded fae, his eyes were one blank sheet of color and magic, yet it felt like he stared at her intently for an answer.

"*Izell Firebrand did.*"

He sucked in a breath, flipping the coin back to her as if burned. "I haven't heard that name in centuries," he muttered, turning in a flurry of robes. "You must speak with the Master right away."

She and Cedric exchanged a glance. It was impossible to look at him and not remember the haunting tune that'd come out of his throat last night. His *heart's song*. To hear it made her feel like he was offering a lifemate bond—something she'd felt before but only in the height of passion with her first husband. Declining it had hurt, and she wondered if Cedric was unaware of their connection. She had no intentions of foisting a surprise bond upon him until she understood their circumstances better.

She broke eye contact first and rushed after their escort. They soon got their first glimpse of this secretive location's grand entrance. It loomed over them, with two expansive wings to either side that created a half-moon-shaped garden. Another male goat person was tending to a shrub cut into the shape of a graceful fae figure.

They rushed by too quickly for her to take in more than a fountain and artfully placed patches of flowers along a walkway paved with carved stones. Each bore a spindly rune.

Outside of the circle of the manor's influence were fields where grain waved golden in the breeze and paddocks held grazing animals. More of these goat-like people tended to their needs in the distance.

The manor itself was at least three stories high, with half a tier of gold-inlaid steps to scale. Beside the doors was a dragon made with blue-purple metal, its glaring eyes pure diamond. It was seven feet high and engraved with such realism in each scale and detail that Neala could've mistaken it for a real dragon.

"This way," their escort said before she could stare at it for too long.

She admired the finery of the building inside, as lavish as any mansion. Their steps slowed to a more reverent pace, allowing her more than a glimpse of the entry foyer. The chandelier was made of gemstones and thousands of tiny balls of glowing magic, sending refractions of colored light everywhere. They entered through a narrow hall. Past another door was what she expected, an open space marked with an even grander chandelier, as if this building had changed hands at one point and the new owner wanted to one-up the last.

There were no obvious stairs, not that a race with wings needed help accessing the top levels. But she felt that immediately relegated her and Cedric to the same status as the groundskeepers.

Neala was used to displays of riches by this point, but she realized Cedric wasn't as he planted his feet and stared up at the lighting. A whole biome of fluttering birds and gilded insects, all made of magical energy, cavorted amongst the crystalline branches of the structure above them. It screamed *expensive* down to every finely wrought detail.

"The Master is this way. His office resides in the North Wing," their escort prompted. The fae visibly simmered as the seconds trickled by, curls of smoke and heat mirage dancing over his head.

"We can take it all in soon," she said, projecting her mental voice to just Cedric. She didn't add the rest of the statement she'd been thinking. They could linger...if this Master figure didn't force them to leave. It all seemed to depend on the reputation Izell left behind.

Cedric gave his head a shake. "Right. I just...my family lives here?" he whispered to her. They followed their escort further into the building, passing rooms that Neala glimpsed through narrow windows. Several looked like classrooms, while others were filled with piles of boxes. One had a set of music stands and tiered seating.

His family, indeed. Those stands proved to her that someone was making music here, despite all hints to the contrary. *"This isn't simply a living space."* It seemed more like a self-sufficient compound to her.

"Yeah. It's like... a school." He waved to one of the empty rooms before they took a turn down another corridor. To one side, a massive, empty hall sat, its velvet seats soft and inviting. It looked like the kind of place to watch a performance in.

To the other side were more doors, this time with no windows. Most were shut. Their escort led them to the end of the hall, knocking once and bursting into the very last room. "Master, may I have a word?" he exclaimed.

Neala peered inside over the fae's shoulder. There was an office inside, with a man hunched over a set of paperwork on a lacquered desk. The "Master" was an astral fae, something that took away some of the tension in her shoulders. She was used to astral fae. His skin was so black it shone blue in the light of a single lamp, the room otherwise shaded with thick drapes over the window.

"A few words have already been spoken, Jerrod, have they not?" the other fae sighed, sitting up straighter in his chair.

"Our guests are here. Ones sent by Lady Izell." Their escort turned back to Neala abruptly. "Give me the coin."

When she did, he passed it to the Master, who beckoned with one gloved hand. "Come in. Have a seat. It looks like he ran you straight here."

Cedric swallowed audibly and followed when she led the way inside. There were two seats across from the table. Ridge-backed and lacking cushioning, they were the kind of chair to offer for a questioning.

Coin in hand, the Master turned to their escort. "You may go, Jerrod."

"But, sir—"

"That's an order."

Simmering again, Jerrod saluted with a fist over his heart. The door clapped behind him with more force than necessary.

The other fae inspected the writing on the coin, smirking. "Trust in the process. She would choose this one," he said to himself. He glanced up, tilting his head with a thoughtful frown. "How dreadfully rude we've been. I am Sondus, Lord of the Shifting Wood. That fine solar fae was someone new to my service."

"He didn't seem to know what to do with us," Neala remarked.

"As to be expected." Sondus shrugged, flipping Izell's coin through his gloved fingers. He was classically handsome, with strong, fae-sharp cheekbones and a clean-shaven face. His hair was cropped at a few inches and stark white. Curiously, he didn't glimmer with stars like most of his kind.

"*I am Neala Firetree, vampire nobility.*" Something told her to avoid mentioning "Fell Hunter" when talking to an astral fae, the group nearly devastated by the Fell curse.

"And I'm Cedric Applewhite!" He played a high note on his lute, immediately drawing the attention of the other fae.

Sondus stood abruptly, striding to the bookcase behind his desk. It was overburdened with massive tomes, many of which had papers sticking out from stray notes. "Like a page out of history." He pulled two books and flipped through the first one. Placing it before Neala, he resumed his seat.

Rendered in black ink was a shaded version of her face. Unlike with the coin, the script in this book flowed and changed before her eyes, becoming a language she could easily read. It was... a biography of her?

She snatched the book up. There was no mistaking it; there was her name: Prince Neala, the Wraith. She frowned at the official, stuffy title she tried to shed at any opportunity, especially as a woman irritated by a male label.

"*How do you have this?*" she demanded, skimming the information under her name. It was shockingly accurate. She flipped the page, coming face-to-face with a drawing of Prince Qin, the Ascended, the coward who'd fled after betraying her and her friends. There were more biographies after his.

A short one for Nyah, which listed her as deceased. She thumbed backward, realizing all of them were labeled the same way. Her date of death was the exact same for Lucia, Adrius, Sirius, and the rest. To fae historians, they'd died long ago.

But past those entries were ones that tore at her heart. Long-forgotten faces, men and women just as powerful and dedicated as her, who hadn't survived the war with the Fell. She tore her gaze away to Sondus, who watched her with idle patience.

"It's like I said, Lady Neala. You are a part of fae history. We are very lucky to have our ways of recording it," he answered.

She flipped the book closed. The title glimmered up at her in gold foil: *An Accounting of the Fell Wars.*

"And you recognized me instantly."

"I am something of a history buff. It's an honor to meet you in the flesh, but imagine my surprise to learn you are not, in fact, deceased." Sondus held up Izell's coin. "Sent here by another living legend and accompanied by a bard using what appears on sight to be one of the missing instruments of the *drasonii*."

It felt like the translation magic between them had faltered for a moment. "The what?" Cedric asked.

"The dragon-blessed," Sondus said, waving dismissively. "What brings such a storied pair to my doorstep?"

Cedric spoke while Neala rooted around her bags for her potion box. "You see, I'm coming because of the instrument. It's part of my family line. I'm here...for my family. Are they here?"

"May I see your lute?" Sondus asked in turn. He took the instrument by its neck and inspected its underside. Flipping through the other book he'd taken down, he eventually made a sound of triumph while, at the same time, Neala found what she was looking for amongst her things and straightened.

Sondus lifted the book, showing an illustration of a flowering tree branch. It matched the marking on the lute. "Many *drasonii* instruments were lost when the Fell attacked. Your ancestor must've been banished to the Fell Lands with it in hand." His gaze flashed. "How did you acquire it?"

"It's one of a kind," he said. "In Adrun—what you know as the Fell Lands—I am the only one with an enchanted instrument. I, um, I'm from there."

The fae sat back, scrubbing at his face. "Indeed? That must be quite the tale. Rather an impossibility, in fact."

Neala nudged Cedric under the table, recognizing a leading statement when she heard one and knowing her bard friend would rush to fill in the gap of knowledge without her look of warning. He kept silent until Sondus sighed and closed his book of illustrations.

"So, you are here for family, Mister Applewhite." Cedric leaned in as Sondus took a few experimental plucks on the lute. "I know of an Applewhite, but not that he had a family," the fae said.

Cedric's smile faded to an uncertain grimace. He waited as Sondus traced the symbol on the lute before passing it back and continuing, "But what a man he was. The first Lord of the Shifting Wood."

"Did you know him?" he asked in a small voice.

"I know the public side of his story. Bendrick Applewhite, one of the original *drasonii*. Mastermind behind the Shifting Wood and the headquarters in which we now sit. Accomplished bard, a true lover of music. And..." He met their gazes in turn. "... Founder of the Unseen Council, the most expansive network of spies in Faerie."

Chapter 8
Neala

Spies, Neala thought in annoyance. All this mystery to be delivered to a spymaster. No wonder Sondus was so knowledgeable. And now holding them here, undoubtedly to glean more intelligence.

"My grandfather was a spy?" Cedric asked. His whole bearing was conflicted. Excitement danced in his tone, while disappointment curved in his shoulders. Neala gave him a reassuring pat. It had to be overwhelming to learn this all at once.

"He was *the* spy. And what remains of the *drasonii* follow his legacy. Performing, entertaining...and listening. Perhaps a history lesson is in order," Sondus offered, gaining a nod from them both.

"The *drasonii* were a full orchestra, once upon a time. Their instruments were given a blessing of perfection by all four fae gods, now seen in the unique marking upon each." Cedric eyed the marking on the back of his lute with new appreciation.

Neala remembered that the fae worshipped four dragons, each representing one of the elements: fire, wind, earth, and water. So, dragon-blessed reflected this orchestra well.

"They performed for the gods and our highest nobility with music pure and inspiring. After the Fell attacked... a section of the orchestra was lost, and the gods refuse to bless new instruments. Those who hold one of the originals have a truly priceless artifact. Most also serve the Unseen Council to this day," Sondus said.

"So, you gave them a new purpose."

"Not me. Master Bendrick was succeeded by a different fae, a Lady of the Shifting Wood. When she retired, she passed the mantle, and eventually, it landed on my shoulders." Sondus gave a languid shrug. "Many things have changed since the Council was first created. We serve the whole of Faerie now, the Seelie King and the Unseelie Queen."

Neala raised a brow. *"Isn't that counter-intuitive? To feed information to both sides?"*

"Izell has told you nothing of Faerie?" he asked plainly.

"Next to nothing," she agreed with a sigh.

"We serve them because they are on the same side. The Seelie King and the Unseelie Queen wedded long ago to put Faerie to peace. It's been the Unseen Council's job to keep it that way," Sondus said. He steepled his fingers as he turned to Neala and gestured with a jerk of his chin. "What's in the box?"

She looked down at the dark, polished wood, now sporting scuffs at the edges from rubbing against other items in her bag. Its contents were precious. Trepidation seized her wrist before she could move to open it and show him the incomplete potion within.

The fae had already told them far too much. Spies didn't just come out and admit their jobs and so much extra information, not without wanting something in exchange. The moment she asked for a siren's tear, she would open herself up for bargaining.

Yet she'd come this far with the knowledge that siren's tears were here. Her voice was on the line. She opened the box, showing him the fancy stoppered glass within. *"It's an incomplete second song potion. I've come here to ask for a siren's tear."*

Sondus picked up the potion bottle with care, inspecting its contents. "I won't lie and say I recognize it," he said slowly, savoring each word as it gave him longer to think. Pure calculation danced over his face as the seconds trickled by. "We do have a lab here, and a number of rare ingredients. A second song potion, though..."

He stood again after replacing the potion in its velvet. Turning back to his books, he retrieved another thick tome to thumb through quickly. "Second song, second song..." he muttered to himself. Eventually, he found the right page and skimmed it with a fingernail. "You are certain this was made correctly?"

"*Absolutely.*" There was no chance of a mistake when Nyah was involved.

His gaze flashed up to her. "But are you aware of the side effects?"

She cursed to herself because of course there were side effects. *And guess who didn't tell me about them?* she thought bitterly.

Taking in her expression, he returned to reading this entry in his book. "This is a powerful potion. It will give you a voice with perfect pitch and emulates the godly blessing on a *drasonii's* instrument. But in exchange, you may only keep it if you perform for another every day."

Dread coiled in her gut, cold and grasping. "*Another like one other person?*"

"One other person. The wording suggests they have to enjoy the performance as well." He muffled what sounded suspiciously like a chuckle. "Else you lose the voice, and your first one, forever."

Her current voice was a joke anyway. Unless he meant... "*Mental and physical?*"

Seelie fae weren't able to lie. So, when his finger moved down the page and his expression tightened, she believed the answer he gave wholeheartedly. "Yes. Failing to fulfill the second song's requirements will render you permanently mute."

The potion box shut with a clap. She winced, her palm resting overtop of it. "*I...must consider this,*" she said, feeling both men's gazes on her.

Sondus closed his book. "Very well. If you decide you would like that siren's tear, we can provide it. But first, I would ask for your assistance."

Cedric exchanged a glance with her. His eagerness tempered

her sudden exhaustion. Here it came, the moment the spymaster would wring information from them to match his own agenda. *"What is it?"* she grumbled.

"You are both outsiders to Faerie. And judging by your lack of knowledge...fresh arrivals," he began. "I want to offer a deal of mutual interest and a regret that your son and daughter are not here to vouch for me, one of their old school friends."

Her brows rose. *"They told you of me?"*

"Eventually, yes. Their words are immortalized as a part of fae understanding of your history and life. You're quite the hero to a small subsect of nerdy historians." There was a twinkle in his eye. "But I don't believe many will recognize you now. Add in your powers over illusion, and you could practically be a ghost."

Her lips thinned. *"I am a warrior, not a spy,"* she scoffed.

"Of course. But you can be both. I would just ask that you listen for me..."

"And in exchange?"

"Izell Firebrand does not rise from the dead for no purpose. Why is she here in Faerie? And why did she bring you both specifically? Perhaps my knowledge can be of assistance," he offered.

She'd only just begun to consider when Cedric blurted out, "The Fell Keys! We need the rest of them!"

Neala practically hissed at him. He flashed her a sheepish look while Sondus rubbed his forehead.

"The Fell Keys," he said to himself. "So, we are all in the middle of the same problem."

"Pardon?"

He sighed heavily. "Were you there when the Dark Eye was destroyed?"

"Unfortunately."

The Dark Eye had shattered right in front of her, its glass surface rippling with huge cracks. She'd witnessed Jazrach, a greater demon of corruption, escaping from his prison at last. It'd merely been the beginning of her problems, with both the demon and Lucia targeting her with their evil magics.

"The very fabric of Faerie society was decided the night the

Eyes of Worlds were created. Not only did King Oberon seal the differences between Seelie and Unseelie, he cut us off from the outside world. A barrier of magic rests over Faerie, limiting our contact with the elves and other forsaken creatures that share our borders," Sondus explained. "That barrier thins."

"The veil between Heaven, Hell, and Earth does as well. That is truly why we are here."

"What would Izell want with the Keys?" he asked himself, sucking on the inside of his cheek. Thoughts darted across his face with the tick of a muscle or the tightening of his jaw. His tells were as fleeting as slick fish, flicking by rapidly before he took a breath. "You need, as you stated, 'the rest of them.' If you truly wish to unite them all...then she seeks to make a new Dark Eye. Am I right?"

Neala nodded reluctantly. "Ah. We are on the same side of this issue," he stated.

"Truly?" It was harder to be skeptical of him when he spoke plain truths instead of the more convoluted fae speak she was warned to expect.

"Yes. Things are...not well here. The Seelie King amasses his best Sorcerers in the capital to reinforce the Light Eye and dissuade any attempts to destroy it too. There have been efforts to attack it, all from Unseelie individuals."

He shook his head. "Tensions rise between the two factions of fae. We have a momentary reprieve because the Unseelie Queen is currently luring most of her people back to her palace for festivities in honor of her birthday. But I fear that one errant spark will set a new conflict ablaze to tear Faerie in half. Just like the old days."

"Grim tidings," she murmured.

"But honest ones. So, what do you say? Will you help me keep Faerie stable in exchange for knowledge of where to find the Keys you seek?" Oh, he had her there. Cedric stared at her, silently pleading that she take the deal.

Sondus held up a finger. "To sweeten the offer, we will train you both. Neala, your new voice will require immediate intervention and teaching. And Cedric, surely you're bursting at the seams to learn everything your lute can do?"

"And in exchange, you want us to 'listen'?" She punctuated it with air quotes.

"That is all," he said with a nod. "To keep your eyes and ears open. To look under *every* illusion and around every corner. And report back, of course."

She heard the extra emphasis and took a closer look at him. Peeling away his glamor for her eyes only, she realized he was missing one defining feature as it disappeared from his back. *"Where are your wings?"*

"I would say you should ask the witch that cut them free, but she's dead." He shrugged like it was no big thing, but under his glamor, his lips pulled with resentment. "So, do we have a deal?"

When he offered his hand, she shook it despite how her hopes soured in her belly for a new voice she wouldn't take, not when failure would make her permanently mute.

Cedric shook Sondus's hand next with great enthusiasm. She would stay here and eventually "listen" for his sake. When Sondus handed her a list of the five Keys and five locations or names to go along with it, she patted herself on the back for a job well done.

They were one step closer to their goals. But she felt her one hope to speak again was dashed as surely as if sirens went extinct along with their tears.

Chapter 9
Cedric

"Isn't this great?" Cedric asked as he and Neala were escorted toward a back stair they could use to access the upper levels of the manor. They'd have rooms here for the duration of their stay.

Once he mastered what there was to know of his dragon-blessed lute, he was ready to ask for more from Sondus. If his grandfather had been the Master here, Cedric felt it was right to learn if he would be a good fit for the same trade—that of secrets.

"*Hmm?*" Neala stirred out of her thoughts, frowning as they ascended to the third floor guest rooms.

"You're going to get your voice back." He elbowed her, wearing a carefree grin. "And I'm going to be a proper bard. What could be better?"

Some of the brightness left him when he saw her expression. Tired, or maybe even defeated. Of all words he could describe Neala with, *defeated* was the last one he'd thought he'd use.

"*I will not be completing the potion.*" Her boots punctuated the words, finality in every step.

He did a double take. "What?"

"*You heard me. It is too risky.*"

"But it's what you wanted," he protested. "It's all right here for the taking. They have the siren's tears; you have the rest of the potion—"

"Let's continue this conversation in private." She motioned toward the fae woman leading them upstairs. Another fire fae, but bouncy on her feet. She hadn't said a word past "follow me," but her head was tilted toward them. Listening.

Cedric clamped his jaws closed despite all the protests in his head. *Why did it matter so much?* he asked himself. It was Neala's life. She could do whatever she wanted.

"Master Sondus wanted you to know that he's calling a skilled *drasonii* to assess your skill level," their escort said once she showed them to their rooms, which were adjacent to one another. "Will you be ready for it in an hour?"

"Yes, thank you. Looking forward to it! Tell them it'll be the performance of their life." He waved her off, untouched by nerves. He performed all the time! It was his job. That would take him head and shoulders over others who'd auditioned here.

Once she was gone, he turned back to Neala, who was halfway into her new accommodations already. "Your room or mine?" He winked. "Looks like your room."

She rolled her eyes and left the door ajar. Her windows were shrouded by thick drapes, leaving her face half illuminated by fading light. She stayed standing, so he did too despite there being a set of inviting chairs and a couch right behind her.

"Silence," she admitted quietly, *"is my nightmare."*

He tilted his head. Neala, afraid? Another word he wouldn't use to describe her. But he saw the truth in her too-pale features.

"But you're assuming you're going to fail without even trying." He mirrored her hushed, urgent tone.

"You don't understand," she muttered. *"There is no 'try' here. If anything goes wrong, I lose what little voice I have. Forever."*

He glanced at his shoes. What would he do without a voice? He would rather curl up in a corner and die. His whole life was his voice. Playing his lute, no matter how fancy and blessed it was, took second place in the scheme of things.

She continued speaking while those thoughts had his tongue. *"I didn't discover mental speech until after the Fell were defeated. A good fifty years of life with no voice at all. I was valued for my fighting prowess beforehand, but I couldn't be a leader of any kind. Fights move too quickly to stop and read lips and sign language.*

"I still have nightmares of those days. Stuck in my own mind, seeing my comrades fall without being able to utter a word. And then I had a brush with something worse. Modern mortals call it locked-in syndrome, when you're awake and aware but paralyzed in your own body." From her expression, it'd been a more recent experience, but he didn't pry further into something that obviously haunted her.

He wet his lips. All the lyrics he knew, and he had to come up with the right words to comfort her. "Then it's off the table," he said. "If you're afraid, you don't have to do it. You don't have to decide now. But..." His heart gave a nervous flutter. "It would be nice to hear your voice. Your real voice. There's no war to worry about anymore, Neala. And if you're worried about having someone enjoy your singing daily...I promise I will."

The side of her mouth tugged upward. *"Even if I'm terrible at it?"*

"Everyone starts somewhere! You should've heard the awful sounds this lute made while I was learning." He patted the side of his instrument, realizing his fingers were still. The ever-present music in his life had stopped for this conversation.

She breathed a husky laugh. *"You are correct. A decision doesn't have to happen now,"* she said. *"Why don't you prepare for your audition? No use in watching me mope."*

Taking his instrument and placing it aside for the moment, he came over to hug her instead. He laid his head on her shoulder since she was a good head above him. "Hey. It's a serious decision. Do what's best for you," he murmured, trying not to gasp when she crushed him fiercely to her. She held him for comfort, yet he was feeling safe and secure in the circle of her strong arms.

"Thank you for understanding."

He smiled up at her. "What's a friend for?" When they parted, he scooped up his lute by the neck and perched on one of her chairs. It was cushioned and comfortable, yet he found himself wanting one of Sondus's uncomfortable chairs to help his posture.

There was a stylized map of Faerie on the wall before him, and a swirling watercolor hung on the opposite wall. Now that he was paying more attention to his surroundings, the room was sparse but comfortable. Not exactly what he'd expected for guest rooms when walking into a manor that screamed its riches for all to see.

Neala eased herself onto the couch, unlacing her boots while his fingers flew through a warmup. He serenaded her with gentle songs of spring and breathy ballads starring hopeful adventurers. She leaned back and closed her eyes, soaking in the positive feelings he tried to push at her. The hope and the new beginnings.

If anyone needed a new beginning, he thought, it was Neala.

When the knock finally came to summon him, they both breathed a sigh of disappointment. *"Good luck,"* she said, walking him to the door.

"Always lucky." He winked in reply, smiling when he saw the same fae woman waiting for him.

Cedric was in the performance hall what felt like a blink later. He'd caught a glimpse of the velvet chairs earlier, but inside, he realized it was large enough to seat hundreds in curved tiers. Smack dab in the middle of those seats was his audience, a man with the bright green hair of a terran fae. His skin was as dark as the earth, and his robe and cushion-shaped hat were a shade closer to black.

The stage here was wide enough for a full performance, or just him. Without music stands or chairs, it was a lonely expanse of well-worn timbers. He stood on the edge and squinted up at the man who would be assessing him.

He opted to break the silence first. The other man was simply staring at him stonily, his pen flying over the first sheet of a thick stack of paper. "Hello! I'm Cedric."

"I know." The answer bounced down to him.

He shifted awkwardly as a paper was flipped to the side. It

floated there, just like the full stack obediently hung in the air awaiting the grace of his pen.

"Do you want me to start, or...?"

He felt the flash of the fae's attention. "Allow me to introduce myself and convene our session together properly," he said, standing at last. "You are in the presence of Lord Trevan Foxglove, original member of the *drasonii*. May the gods bless your music like they have blessed mine, for you hold one of their treasures."

"A pleasure to meet you—" Cedric began.

"You may bow to honor me as an original," Trevan said overtop him.

Gritting his teeth into a smile when a real one was hard to hold, Cedric performed a courtly bow.

"Good. You should've done that when you walked in." He sat back down, scribbling on his next sheet of paper. "Are you ready to begin?"

"Yes!" No more stuffy formalities, just music. "What would you like me to perform first?"

Trevan's answer floored him, but he did it. He played his scales. And then he sang them.

"Name the different parts of your lute," was his next challenge. He fumbled that one without formal training in what a lute's construction was. Actually, the more they ventured down the rabbit hole of instrument basics and what group of mortals had first produced it, the worse Cedric felt he was doing.

Trevan's pen went at a lightning pace to categorize all of his flubs.

Cedric expected this to be a "play your best song" kind of audition, but apparently, he was wrong. "Do you know *nothing* of your instrument's storied history?" Trevan demanded.

"There wasn't much of that in Adrun," Cedric said defensively. "Shall I play for you now?"

Trevan's lip curled. "Ah yes, Adrun. The Master informed me you are from the Fell Lands."

"I was the best bard there," he said.

Ignoring the scoff that received, Cedric was simply glad when Trevan finally asked him to play his instrument. They went through a rapid clip of classical pieces. Cedric relaxed until his weakness was pulled out and floated toward him.

Sheet music.

"Play it for me," the other fae said with an expectant wave.

The paper remained suspended before him, its lines taunting. He'd never learned from a piece of paper.

How would he even convince Trevan that almost no sheet music had made its way into Adrun before it was sealed off? It wasn't any Fell's priority to bring their music with them. What he knew, he'd either learned on his own or from mimicking another bard.

And this classically trained, blessed-by-the-gods fae was about to judge him for not knowing the squigglies and dots on this page.

Before he opened his mouth, he already knew he'd earn another scoff the moment he tried to explain. He wouldn't get a chance to show what he was best at, those songs he'd made himself and stored up in his mind for the right time to perform.

He met Trevan's hard gaze and placed his fingers on his lute. Counting down in his head, he burst into song. His heart's song, disguised in a melody, squished between the lyrics. It was the song that made women swoon and men sigh, built from losses after passion, of kisses goodbye finished with last glances, like the one he gave his audience as he bowed with both arms out.

Silence. And then the scratching of a pen.

"Dare I say it?" Trevan didn't glance up from his writing. "A disgrace to Bendrick's instrument, to come in here with *half* his talent. The best bard from the hole you came from? Probably because you were the only one."

Cedric took a sharp breath, puffing up like the angry bird inside of him while his eyes stung. "You are dismissed. Get out!" Trevan shouted.

"Miserable bastard," he muttered as he turned, knowing the room's acoustics would carry the words upward. It felt like a needle stick verses a knife wound. Like the next thing out of his mouth would be, "I'm telling...someone...about your cruelty!" But he didn't know anyone here.

He took his leave and followed his nose toward the smell of something savory. Maybe he could have a meal and leave this place. It'd make Neala happy to return to their friends, he thought.

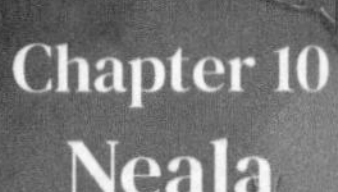

Chapter 10
Neala

Neala decided not to sit around and wait for Cedric. His private performance had lifted her spirits some. It wasn't like she had a bounce to her step, but she no longer felt like she was weighed down on all limbs.

She laced her boots back up and went out in search of the alchemy lab that was here somewhere. She'd seen most of one wing, which was dedicated to music, storage, and education from her quick peek. So, after descending the staircase, she tried the other wing.

The manor was too quiet. How many people lived and worked here? If this Unseen Council was a spy network like she knew it, there would be masterminds here in safety, pulling the strings. It couldn't all fall onto the shoulders of Sondus. He was, if anything, the public face that reported back to his king and queen.

She thought of Sondus and the careful way he'd been sitting under his glamor. His back straight, not touching his chair. Was the lack of wings a constant source of pain?

"Excuse me!"

She startled, realizing a fae in a casual tunic and breeches was stopped at the end of the hall, observing her with hands on hips.

The fae seemed young, with doll-like features too delicate for her face. She was also light blue, with wings soft and puffy like two butterfly-shaped clouds. Her furrowed brows made her seem like a toy frozen in a fit of pique. "Who are you?" she demanded.

"*A guest,*" she answered crisply.

The fae girl wrinkled her nose. "But you're human."

Neala bared her teeth in an exaggerated grin. "*An easy mistake to make. Do you know where I can find the lab?*"

"Oh!" She clasped her hands and took a step back the moment she saw Neala's fangs. "It's, um, that way." She nodded to one side and shuffled away.

The hall dead-ended with two thick, wooden doors to either side. The fae held one open as she slipped within, so Neala caught the silvery shine of several mirrors before the opening was shut in her face. Grumbling, she tried the other door and froze with her feet halfway inside.

It was a place straight from another time. Neala's time. High ceilings and soot-coated vents were the first things she noticed, past several stations of different shaped flasks, tubes, and potion bottles. Some were bubbling above enchanted fires. Others lay dormant, corked with gem-colored liquids within.

There was a fae for each station, and they were all staring at her. An assistant fumbled a tube, spilling purple liquid that hissed on the ground. "This is a restricted area," said the one Seelie in the room, a man as blue as the other fae she'd just encountered. The others were sickly green-skinned, and she'd been warned that an unhealthy-toned fae was Unseelie.

The Seelie man lifted his goggles as he turned from his station. They were all wearing leather smocks, thick gloves, and goggles for their work. As cloying smoke started to sting Neala's eyes, she realized why.

"*I needed to speak with an expert. Perhaps I can borrow a minute of your time?*" she asked. She drew her potion from her pocket, watching the skepticism melt away from his features.

"*Can you tell me more about this? It's a second song potion.*" He wasn't the only one who jumped into motion. He went to take it and inspect it in the enchanted light hovering overhead. The clumsy assistant dashed from the room.

"Look at the color on this one!" he crowed, immediately

drawing the attention of another alchemist. The other man came forward, hands clasped.

"Have you seen anything like it?" the Unseelie asked. Neala supposed questions weren't technically telling a truth or a lie.

"Incredibly rare. I would love to see an ingredient list." They both turned to her expectantly, but she could only shrug.

"It was a gift. It's only missing a siren's tear. I was hoping you could tell me more about it."

Soon, all five alchemists were clustered together, passing it back and forth. One pulled out a dropper for a tiny sample and placed it on a dish, which he whisked to the nearest station to study.

They muttered about rarity and puzzled over its orange color until the assistant returned with a hefty tome from the back room. Their enthusiasm was palpable, and her lips lifted to see them treating it with such care and awe.

"That's why! Essence of saffron," said the Seelie fae as he read over the book's entry on the second song potion. He read out the rest of the ingredients, and she wished he hadn't when he started mentioning phlegm. Her nose wrinkled.

He pulled a stool for her and shooed away all but the assistant, who was young enough not to have the same gaseous wisps for wings as the rest of the green Unseelie in the room. The Seelie, she learned, was Vann, the head alchemist of this lab.

"So, what did you want to know?" Vann asked.

She'd come here hoping that he'd made thousands of these potions in his lifetime, that plenty of fae lived with the side effects. But from the reaction of his whole lab, she was now unsure he had the answers that she sought. *"I have no voice,"* she began, taking a deep breath. *"I'm not a singer or a performer. But apparently, I need to become one, else the new voice provided by the potion will be robbed from me..."*

He consulted the page, humming. "Right. That is a necessity for the magic to continue working."

"Are there any other side effects? Any other rules I would need to follow to keep it?"

Eyeing her expression, he turned the book around. "Here.

This is our most trusted resource on potions and has never been wrong on other obscure tonics." The letters on the page rearranged themselves as he spoke, turning into something Neala could read. So, she did, picking it up and holding it close to her face, as if any words would consider escaping.

What Sondus had mentioned was right there on the page. She had to "bring joy to the heart of" at least one person per day with her voice, or it would be gone forever at the start of the next day. The magic in her vocal cords would start to burn if she came close to not fulfilling this requirement. Presumably, it would get worse until the voice was gone.

"For what it's worth, the requirement doesn't seem that difficult?" Vann ventured as she flipped the page, reading a description of a fae performer who'd taken this same potion.

She felt a touch of heat in her cheeks. *"The problem is, I've never sung before."*

"Ah." There was a touch of gentle understanding to his tone. "Do you think it will be that challenging?"

"I don't know."

There it was, out in the open to a stranger. She didn't know how to sing. How would she "bring joy" to anyone on day one, let alone into the long and lonely years of her immortal life?

"I've...never had a voice. It's like asking a blind person to paint a masterpiece, or one of the deaf to describe the sound a piano makes. What is it like?" She put the book down slowly as the words blurred on the page.

Vann stroked his jaw as he considered. "Not that I am much of a singer, lady vampire. But it is not difficult. And the effects of the potion are immediate—you will go from nothing to everything after a short lead time for the magic to enter your vocal cords. Is there a special person in your life, a heartsong perhaps?"

A heartsong? She'd heard that word before. Fae called their lifemates that, so she thought of Cedric and his gorgeous tenor. *"Not in any official way,"* she hedged.

"The only reason why I ask is because effects like this are considered a shared burden. Your heartsong would be able to sing for you if you are ever incapacitated, to fulfill the requirements of the magic." For a moment, her heart soared before she realized there had to be a catch to this.

"Does that mean that, if he does not perform as well, the magic can take his voice?" She was hushed at the thought of robbing a lyrebird shifter of his prized talent.

Vann cracked a smile and placed his palms up in a soothing gesture. "The magic stays in you, but the requirement is shared. The first fae that discovered alchemy tinkered with side effects and decided what was beneficial and thus allowed and replicated..." He motioned to the book. "...And what was thrown out as a dud or written into our much more expansive set of books on what not to combine into a tonic."

She released a tense sigh. *"You're saying this potion was designed to be manageable."*

"Despite what you may have heard, we have standards for our alchemy. So..." He held up a vial no larger than her pinkie. The liquid was clear and glowed from within. "Would you like to complete it?"

"I would, yes." Even though she wouldn't immediately drink it down, there was merit to having it completed and ready.

The assistant retrieved the rest of the alchemists, who all gathered around to watch with her as Vann carefully dropped a single siren's tear into the potion. Moments later, it started to glow just like the vial of tears. It hummed softly, a single melodic tone.

She held it carefully during a round of backslapping and agreed to wait until sundown to join the lab for dinner. It'd help to know where the dining hall was since Cedric still needed to eat. Because she was really doing this. She would drink this potion tomorrow and learn to sing.

It'd make Cedric happy to stay here and study music together, she thought.

Chapter 11
Cedric

He found a café of sorts by following his nose. Seated at a round table off to the side was Neala and six fae men. An immediate pang of jealousy hit. Why hadn't she invited him? He was the one who needed solid food.

Drifting in unnoticed, he trudged along the wall where there was a walkway downward toward the kitchen. "Late night?" asked a gray-skinned fae with flaming wings, the same species of Unseelie as Ash. She was polishing a bar between them. Another woman was cutting slices of meat behind her from a roast.

"You are new?" She tilted her head as she glanced over him, a spark of concern in the set of her brow.

"Yeah, just for today," he said. A chorus of laughter from the full table startled him. "Are you selling food?"

She scoffed. "Selling. Do you like ham and gravy?" He nodded eagerly.

She ventured into the kitchen briefly, coming back with a plate mounded with thick slices of meat alongside mashed potatoes and some sort of colorful vegetable medley that glittered with oil. As he took it, she waved him off with a, "Have a better night."

"I'll try," he muttered.

Trevan's words echoed in his head as the walk to Neala's table seemed to stretch right before his eyes. *A disgrace to Bendrick's instrument, to come in here with half his talent.*

Why had he come here thinking he'd magically find family and acceptance? He had no family here, just a legacy he could never live up to. His grandfather was the man who'd founded all of this. He must've been fae nobility to be a Lord of anything.

Sighing, he mustered himself by the time he reached the table and eyed the space. Neala glanced up at him, her red gaze roving over him in thoughtful analysis. He cleared his throat. "Mind if I join you all?"

"He's with me." She scooted her chair to the side to give him enough room to squeeze another in between her and the only Seelie fae at the table.

He cracked a smile for her sake and set his lute aside as he sat. "I see you've found some friends."

"By accident." She introduced him to Vann and the rest of his team, all alchemists.

"We only have about five dedicated labs on this side of Faerie," Vann confided as Cedric dug into his meal the moment the formalities were finished. "We're all quite lucky to be here."

Cedric made sure his mouth was full, so it was Neala who nodded in agreement and said, *"We are as well. Can you tell us more about the spy side of the manor?"*

Vann laughed. "Strange lot over there. So many faces come and go. I don't know who most of them are."

"How many musicians do you see?" He couldn't help his curiosity, wondering how much talent walked through these doors on a regular basis.

The alchemist considered over a bite of ham. "Same as everyone else. You have to understand most of the network over there are ordinary folk. They come in for training or to lie low for a while, but few stay unless they're working the portal room.

"And before you ask what that is, it's a secret operated by the Unseen Council. Master Sondus will have to explain it to you if you choose to stay."

"We will be staying." He was surprised she'd confirmed that information to this group. It'd essentially told them that the two of them were to be spies as well.

Now wasn't the time to contradict her or mention that he was ready to leave instead. They had a consolation prize in the list of locations for the Fell Keys in Faerie, but neither of them had gotten what they'd really come here for.

As he thought about it, he realized that little list of names threw his whole plan off. Neala had shaken hands on a deal with a fae—and no one could break a deal like that without dire consequences. It felt like the ground was about to swallow him whole. Maybe that would put him out of his misery.

"Is something the matter?" From how the pitch of her voice changed, he realized she'd asked him privately. He shrugged. He wasn't able to answer in kind. Yet another drawback of being half talented.

"Let's talk once you finish your meal, then."

The other fae were stacking their plates at this point, lingering to chit-chat while he was pushing meat around on his plate. His appetite wasn't cooperating, but he forced himself to take a big bite and savor what he could. It was better than making everyone wait for him.

They chatted with Neala like old friends, and when it came time to part ways at last, they wished her luck with her voice. His curiosity lifted as they took the stairs back to their quarters for the evening. "You talked to them about the potion," he guessed. Why else even seek out the alchemy lab?

"Yes. But first, what happened?" She ushered him into her room.

"Well, I'm ready to leave when you are. Turns out I'm not as good as I thought I was." He scuffed his foot in the carpet. "Think you could talk to Sondus tomorrow on altering the terms of your deal so we can get back to what matters?"

Strong fingers took hold of his chin, forcing him to meet her gaze. She was practically striking, he thought. Her red eyes stood out from a fan of thick orange lashes, bright and hot. The woman didn't hide what she was, her scarred warrior's face within kissing range.

"I asked you what happened," she prompted. Her mental voice was gentle as she read his face.

"I choked. Not only did I not impress the guy, I completely

failed all of his tests. He asked me to read *sheet music*, Neala," he burst out. "It's something every proper musician can do, but I can't! Do you know how little of it survived in Adrun? I learned music with my ears and my fingers, and it wasn't enough for him."

"You're basing this off the opinion of one person?" she asked once he stopped to take a breath.

"Yeah! One of the original *drasonii*, a guy who knew my grandfather and how amazing he was." Someone who was important here, he wanted to say.

"But still one person. And clearly wrong." She released his chin, her calloused fingertips brushing a lock of hair from his face. *"Whomever he is, he clearly did not see the joy and passion you play with. Therefore, not a voice you should allow yourself to hear."*

"But—"

She rested her palms on his shoulders. *"If he gives a poor report to Sondus, go play for him and ask for a different opinion."*

He bit his lip. "Do you really think that will change anything? The guy was clearly a master."

"Sondus can choose to believe his ears or a man with a stick up his arse."

He couldn't help it, he laughed. And once it started, his tension melted away in peals. Without even meeting Trevan, Neala had nailed his presence. "He had a problem with me the moment I met him," he said, swiping at the corners of his eyes.

"Not everyone will be happy that you strode in here with a storied instrument and an abundance of talent. But...I thought you had thicker skin than this, chicken." She grinned when the nickname made him splutter.

He felt heat rise to his cheeks again. "Well, I mean, most everyone liked me in Adrun. And if they didn't, I knew why. He just hit my weak spot, that maybe the people in Adrun didn't know what good music sounded like."

She scoffed, giving his shoulders a shake. *"You may have been the only one with an enchanted instrument, but the good people who live there are more intelligent than that. Everyone knows what good music sounds like."*

"Yeah, okay..." He cleared his throat, feeling warm for her defense of him but awkward to have needed it in the first place. "I guess I was being silly. So, we're not leaving?"

"Not quite yet. Unless you really feel the need to." Her hands drifted to his, placing them back on his lute. The lack of music between them was an oddity. He shook his uncertainties and played the first notes to a simple song. Some melodies didn't invoke feelings, so he weaved those in on occasion when he felt he was intruding on others' emotions.

When he glanced up from his instrument, he realized Neala was still quite close. He swallowed on a suddenly dry throat. What if he did lean up and press his lips to hers? He'd kiss the scar that'd torn so close to her mouth, a sign of everything this powerful woman had survived.

Their gazes met, her own intense like fire. Heat gripped his chest as she cupped the back of his neck, pulling him into the very thing he'd been considering. Her lips were soft and full, fitting against his perfectly in a starburst of sensation. He breathed her in for that moment as his mind went blank of everything but her, the woman who'd walked into his life and stolen his breath away.

Neala jerked away. A sting lingered on his lips, and he pressed his fingertips there, expecting to feel a nick from her fangs. But no, it was a sensation that didn't turn to pain. His heart beat at double time in his chest. It'd finally happened. There was something there between them; he wasn't just imagining the tension. Neala was unlike any woman he'd ever met, attractive and magnetic like the charged air before a lightning storm.

She rubbed away a set of goosebumps on her arms. *"There is something I must tell you."* Her eyes danced like she was looking for the right words. While she did, he set aside his lute, standing it up against the wall.

He hugged her, having to smile when it felt like putting his arms around a tree trunk of solid muscle. She sighed aloud and rested her chin atop his head. *"Cedric, you're my lifemate."*

Shock permeated him. He recoiled enough to look her in the eye. "I am? I mean, we are?"

"I don't know how it happened. I've had one before, but he's

since passed. That's how I know what it feels like." She flashed a nervous smile. *"Haven't you felt the attraction too?"*

Now that he thought about it, his mind's eye lingered on the moment he'd sung his heart's song for her. How he'd felt hollow afterward. Had the magic in him been expecting some response from her? A bond to be formed between them, a special moment when their songs synced up?

His heart twisted painfully. Their songs would never do that, though. She had no voice with which to sing. Maybe that's why he hadn't known her as his on sight. Or it could've been his half-nature getting in the way again? Either way, she'd put the pieces together for him.

She was still waiting for him to say something, though. He sought to wipe her anxious expression away as quickly as it came. "I have noticed it. I never expected...but this is amazing. We were born in different *worlds*, Neala. And somehow, we've still found each other. Did you ever expect a miracle when you protected a little lyrebird from three drunkards?"

"Can't say I ever expected another man to come into my life." Her eyes glimmered with hope in the low light. *"But now I have a reason to strive for a different future. Tomorrow, I'm going on a new journey, once I drink this."*

She drew a potion bottle from her pocket. It glowed with a soft radiance from within. Recognizing the orange color, he gasped. She was going to drink it after all!

"Will you come on this journey with me?" she asked. He heard what went unsaid. Would he see if they worked together? If there was a "we" between the two of them.

His heart answered for him. "I would love to."

Chapter 12
Neala

Early the next morning, she and Cedric were summoned by Sondus. She thought it less an invitation when delivered by a young fae who simply said, "The Master requests your presence for breakfast."

She hadn't gotten much sleep, spending much of the night tipping the second song potion and watching its glowing liquid slosh from one side to the other. The stopper was heavy, solid glass. Not a single drop escaped.

Her mind was preoccupied in the meantime with thoughts of Cedric. She'd witnessed a few moments when he wasn't his joyous self and had only wanted to comfort him. There was no way she could keep the secret of the way fate leaned on her to consider him as a mate. But...he'd been so shocked to find out. Maybe she was the only one who was truly attracted here, and the does-he or does-he-not debate kept her up, recycling every word between them.

"Do you think he wants to talk to me about the audition?" Cedric sighed on their way down. His fingers were still on his lute, tapping the wood nervously.

"I wouldn't be surprised. You know what you have to do afterward." She clapped him on the shoulder, then caught his arm as he nearly pitched forward. Sending him the express route down

the stairs wasn't a good way to start a potential something between them.

"Y-yeah. That's why I'm taking this." He laughed nervously at that near-miss and plucked a single note on the lute. It sang a sweet tone of relief.

"Do you ever not have it on you, though?" Though she teased, she couldn't think of any moments he wasn't holding it unless he was hiding in his lyrebird form. *"Do you sleep with it in your arms?"*

"What?" he spluttered. "No! That would scuff the finish."

"And you know this because..."

"Look, I didn't want it to get stolen or something."

She laughed aloud, a hoarse sigh of sound. Soon, she could laugh for real, not just in her head. Her mental laugh had never sounded quite right to her.

"I'm more surprised you haven't given it a name," she remarked, taking in the smell of warm sausage and sighing to herself. She felt the prick of her fangs on her lower lip, the first sign she needed to feed a darker hunger.

"It doesn't need one," he mumbled, sounding distracted.

There were far more fae here than yesterday, filling the tables closest to the wall. They were like a multicolored flock of birds, so unlike humans who came in a few earthy shades. She took her gaze away from them so she could not be too dazzled, instead looking around for Sondus.

His dark hand lifted from a booth in a nook close to the kitchen. Before him was a stack of paper. Cedric locked up beside her. "He's reading about me. I know it!"

Sondus gestured for them to get breakfast first, which they did. Neala ate sparsely of sausage and a single egg she asked for out of sheer curiosity. It was sunny side up, except the yolk was twice the size she'd expect and red. Cedric asked for toast, just toast. The Unseelie woman behind the counter frowned at him before handing over a tower of toast and a dish of butter. "How can you play if you don't eat?" she reasoned, gesturing toward his lute.

"You're going to help me with this, right?" he asked on the way to the booth.

She had to smile as he eyed the stack with trepidation. *"No."*

She slid into the booth opposite of Sondus first, leaving Cedric to place his lute to the side and slip in next to her. He was obviously sweating what was on that report as Sondus placed a hand over the writing to hide it from a discerning eye.

"Good morning." The spymaster flashed them both a smile. "How was your rest?"

"Eventful," she remarked. Full of at least one event she couldn't stop thinking about, at any rate.

Cedric had taken a big bite from one of his toast slices, so he just gave a thumbs up.

"I see you've found chef Gara's sense of humor." Sondus gestured to the toast. "This just means she likes you. Something to balance out Lord Trevan Foxglove's outrage that you would dare play him a folk song." His thumb skimmed the stack, flipping the corners of several pages.

Cedric's chewing halted. He swallowed in one painful lump and coughed until he managed a sip of water. "I know it looks bad, but I'm willing to play for you so you—" he stopped abruptly when Sondus shoved the report off the table.

"This was a formality anyway. Lord Foxglove has already left the manor," he replied.

"So..." Cedric elongated the word as it drifted between them.

"I've invited a mentor for you both, a *drasonii* I think will understand you better. She's a master vocal coach and plays one of the three enchanted violins that remain intact." Sondus smiled as he glanced over Cedric's head and waved. "In fact, here she is now."

He stood and bowed politely, holding his arm out for a fae woman to slide into the booth with them. Neala did a double take. She was a stately figure in a thin dress patterned with red roses. But she was also unlike any other fae in the room. Her skin was a shade of lavender more suited for flowers, and her wings were like the night sky without a hint of stars. The almond-shaped eyes that appraised them both were a shade of darker purple, glowing from within.

"Aren't you a lovely pair?" Sharpened canines flashed when she smiled, though her tone was warm.

Neala inclined her head to her as Sondus led introductions. "This is Lady Iridia Sesile. A mentor who took a leave of absence from the Artica Symphony to train you both. Iridia, this is Neala Firetree, one of the lost Blood Princes. And Cedric Applewhite. Yes, of *that* Applewhite family."

The Unseelie woman clapped her hands twice in delight. "We are to have an interesting time together," she said.

Immediately, Neala wondered if the opposite meant they were to be bored to tears, or that "interesting" may mean multiple things, of which one was the untruth so it could pass through her lips. Unseelie speak gave her a headache.

"Hi." Cedric's lips tugged into a nervous smile. "Want some toast?" He passed her the plate, and she took a moment to butter a piece primly.

"Sondus tells me you have the original Applewhite lute?" she asked.

"Yes, it's right here," he said proudly, lifting it by the neck.

"Why isn't it in a case while you eat?"

A hint of color dotted his cheeks. "I thought I would be playing."

"Certain collectors have paid what, millions of marks, for an enchanted instrument?" she asked Sondus.

"Sorry, I'll put it away," he rushed to say.

She laughed and put up a hand. "Quickly, of course. I don't want to hear you play it once you finish your loaf of bread."

He tore into another slice to take the attention off of him. Her purple gaze seemed to flash to Neala, who said, *"You will be training me as well, I presume. Once I drink this."* She placed the second song potion on the table, where it glowed enticingly.

"And isn't it an honor for me to train someone straight from our history?" Since she posed it as a question, Neala took it as truth. What an interesting loophole Unseelie fae here in Faerie had. She hadn't heard Ash phrase her speech this way.

Unless, of course, a lie was also phrased as a question. The sword cut both ways. *"Is it?"* she asked, toying with the stopper on the potion.

"Depends on if you drink that or not," Iridia remarked.

Neala huffed. That wasn't much of an answer. But Cedric turned toward her as she set the stopper aside and lifted the bottle to her nose. Her nose wrinkled at the pungent kick. It was every bit as unappetizing as she expected now that she knew the ingredients.

She glanced to Cedric and toasted him with the potion, knocking it back before she could second-guess the decision a moment more.

At first, her belly gave a roll as the liquid mixed with the watery egg she'd eaten. Pressure built in her throat. Warmth sank into her lungs, like she was sitting too close to a fire. She coughed into her fist.

"Is it working?" Cedric asked, watching intently.

She shrugged, waiting out a surge of discomfort. The potion wasn't causing her pain, but she couldn't help massaging her neck to work out the strange tingling within. Something was changing, tinkering with her inner workings until she felt tension release in her throat. She could breathe more easily.

Wetting her lips, she felt three sets of eyes watching her. She waited until the tingling passed, until she was doubly sure it wasn't coming back. Sweet air caressed her mouth, and she let it back out in a clear, loud sigh.

Just that sound had her wanting to recoil. *Just say something,* she told herself. *Try it.*

"Hello, Cedric." The words sounded like they came from a stranger. They were from her lips, smooth and womanly, as befitted her stature.

Cedric's eyes rounded in awe. He hugged her around the middle with a wordless cry. "Your voice! Did you hear that?" he asked the other two. "The potion worked!"

She laughed and put an arm around him, feeling effervescent as she continued to hear herself. "Do you know how long I've waited for this moment?" she asked, just to get used to the idea of being heard when she spoke.

"Far too long," Sondus offered, watching her with a hint of the joy she and Cedric were taking in the moment.

"I can't wait until—" She cut herself off there abruptly, because most of the friends and family she wanted to talk to were far from this place. There was a journey of learning to embark on first. She had to maintain this voice. "How long do you think it will take to teach us both?"

Some of her sudden impatience must've shown, as Sondus and Iridia exchanged a glance. "It's not like I'm still growing and learning even now," the Unseelie said.

"That is mastery, though. These two seek to learn quickly and move on to more important tasks." Sondus stroked his chin. "A month? That will give me time to assist you in understanding our culture as well, rather than having you rely on one fae."

She thought of Izell, so tight-lipped about what was ahead. A month was too long. "Two weeks," she said.

Cedric made a sound of protest. "We train every day," she added. "Sunup to sundown if that's what it takes. I don't need to be an expert anyway." She only needed to learn how to sing, and that would take care of itself. Cedric was the one who had a better chance of learning advanced techniques.

Iridia rubbed her palms together. "A fan of a challenge, aren't you?"

She grinned. "It's the Blood Prince in me."

Sondus nodded in apparent approval. "Then we'll split you up for today. Neala, you need vocal training first. And I'll start working with you, Cedric. Let's see how proud your grandfather would be."

He went rigid next to her. "I'll make you both proud!" he blurted.

Chapter 13
Cedric

His chest still felt warm and fluttery from the sound of Neala's voice. It was perfect for her and a missing link for him. He liked his big, strong ladies, but they needed to have a good voice as part of the complete package. She had the kind of voice that could whisper to him in the dead of night. He could write songs about it...

"Here we are." Sondus jarred him from his daydreaming as he unlocked one of the classrooms and gestured him inside. There were enough desks for twenty people, so he sat himself front and center while Sondus departed for a few minutes and came back with a dusty book.

"History?" Cedric asked, putting aside his wonderings about what Neala's singing would be like.

He cracked the book, realizing what it was for as he beheld a family tree and flipped to another random page. Biographies. *Boring*, he thought.

"We don't have time to memorize everything, but it's necessary for any operative to recognize the events that shaped our world." Sondus gave a vague wave. "This place you came from..."

"Adrun," he supplied.

Sondus drew a chair. "Tell me about it."

Despite the stuffy old book in front of him, Cedric spent what felt like a blink but must've been several hours explaining Adrun as best as he could. It was a difficult task when he had to sidestep talking about shifters and their magic. He didn't want to seem like a possessed man to the spymaster.

Instead, he talked about Queen Nyah and how their world was eternally dark, shrouded by a huge dome of magic. They revered their druids, who created the weather and nurtured life where there logically could never be any. Adrun had thrived on the ashes left behind from the Fell.

"So, Izell really did save the survivors," he said, tilting his head. "You haven't mentioned one thing, though. I was there when Izell decided to head into the Fell Lands. She'd managed to heal herself of the Fell curse through a bond with her deceased familiar, the dragon Queldian, and became one of the first willing *mort loci*." Sondus recited these facts as if he was a living textbook. Maybe he was, Cedric thought, starting to feel himself sweat.

"So convinced that this was the way to go about eradicating Fell forever, she coaxed a host of departed familiars to follow her into the Fell Lands. Did nothing come of that?" His gaze seemed to pierce right through Cedric.

He waited a few beats and swallowed his nerves. "Um, no, not that I know of."

"For what it's worth...I wouldn't care if you are a *mort loci*, since it means you are not Fell and here to eat the rest of me."

Though Sondus's words were almost flippant, Cedric recoiled anyway. "A-are you talking about your wings?" he asked quietly. Unlike Neala, he wasn't able to see under the glamor hiding Sondus's disability.

He nodded. "A group of Unseelie caught me trying to pass as a different kind of fae. Things were different back then. Astral fae were blamed for the Fell curse, and many of us were punished unjustly. Lady Izell more than most. She told us she would be back and stronger than we could imagine someday—and now, she has returned, according to you and Neala." He got lost in his own head, staring somewhere in the distance before finally shrugging. "It is interesting to know that you can lie, Cedric. That's the human in you. An advantage here in Faerie."

Cedric felt a warm wash of shame. There it was again, his half side coming into play. And Sondus had seen right through him. He cleared his throat and decided to at least clear the air. "We call that day Spirit's Fall," he said quietly, well aware he'd gotten the spymaster's complete attention. "It was the day the Fell curse died in Adrun. We love our spirits. There's no *mort loci*, no shame in being a shifter. Do the fae really judge folk like us?"

"Many will," he said bluntly. "Though they've never seen a Fell outside of a textbook and cannot understand the lengths your people went to avoid becoming one. I am glad you told me. And... I hope you know what you've shared will be kept in confidence."

Cedric breathed a sigh of relief. "I also hope you will tell me more about Adrun sometime," Sondus continued, gesturing to the book in front of him. "Allow me to teach you of Faerie."

After a scare like that, he embraced more mundane knowledge of the history of this world. Once they got into it, there were more scandals and adultery than any one person should know about those who rule the vast territory of Faerie.

He'd also learned that there were four regions to the Seelie side, corresponding with the seasons: winter, summer, autumn, and spring. The Seelie royalty and the wealthiest of the nobility moved to special cities of each region to celebrate the seasons as they came.

"Of course, the King is currently residing in the Summer Court so he and his forces can remain close to the Light Eye and protect it. Many traditionalists say it's bad luck, but so is being visited by demons." Sondus concluded their lesson for the day with a weary sigh.

Cedric had been a bystander for one demon attacking Adrun's army. He shuddered at the thought of encountering more in any significant numbers. "No kidding."

Sondus reclaimed the book and nodded to him. "Great job today. Your homework is two simple tasks. Go listen to Neala sing. And then teach her the names of every species of greater fae. You do know them, right?"

He hadn't heard much past "listen to Neala" because that's exactly what he wanted to do. Stuffy old history could barely hold his mind back from wandering toward her, wondering how she was doing.

"Right, yes, thank you," he blurted, out the door quickly.

Halfway to the stairs, Neala's voice entered his head. The old one, which sounded a little bit like his own thoughts. *"Are you finished for the evening?"*

"Yes," he tried to project back.

A long, awkward pause followed. *"Meet me on the roof. There's an extra set of stairs at the end of our hall,"* she finally said.

Walking faster, he climbed up to the third level, where their rooms were. The hall ended with another door which indeed had a set of stairs as well as a bevy of cleaning equipment. Evening air filtered down from a hole in the ceiling. As he climbed up through it, he realized it was a hatch already thrown open for him.

Neala helped haul him up onto the flat roof. She'd set out a cushion of towels from the supplies they'd brought with them, along with a meal that smelled straight from the kitchens. A hearty tomato-based soup, bread, and a slice of pie still steaming. "Is this for us?" he asked, having a seat when his belly rumbled in approval.

"I wanted a moment alone with you. Hope you don't mind a picnic," she said, sitting cross-legged across from him. "It's such a good view."

He nodded in agreement, taking his eyes off of her with effort. Oh, it *was* a good view. The sun backlit the Shifting Wood as it sank slowly into the horizon, gilding even the most stubborn green leaves. "I could sit here all evening." He shared a smile with her.

He took one of the soup bowls and a normal serving of bread to enjoy with it. The thought hit him seconds later as she did the same. This was a date. She'd gone out of her way to figure out how to get up here with dinner and invite him. Aww. The lady had a secret sweet side.

"How was your training?" he asked.

She laughed to herself. "Dry. I am a long way from having my singing affect emotions. Yours?"

He considered babbling about how Sondus had plucked a secret from him as easily as peeling a banana. *Later*, he thought.

"Good, I suppose. I learned about Unseelie royal family scandals."

"A fate I'm sure I'll share tomorrow. We are to switch off until Sondus has something better to do than tutoring," she said, waving dismissively.

"Let's forget about that for now." He had his homework anyway. Listen to Neala. "What do you think of finding a goat-man and getting a tour of the gardens tomorrow?" They could see into the courtyard from here, a riot of special blooms and intricate walkways.

"Sounds like a nice break. And what shall we do the day after?" she asked.

"I can almost guarantee there are secret passageways in this place. Let's find them." He smiled at the mental image of her rooting around in search of secret switches.

She sat back on her hands to watch the sunset. "Sounds like we have a few dates. Something to enjoy before we return to reality all too soon." There were still Fell Keys to find, but Cedric wanted to enjoy this bubble of peace they'd found together.

First, they need to address something that weighed at his thoughts, though. "Yeah. Could I, um, ask you about something?" The butterflies in his stomach fluttered harder with pointed wingtips. She glanced over at him and gestured for him to go on. "Last night, you mentioned something about knowing what a life-mate feels like. Because you've already had one. How is that possible?"

What he meant was: *how do you know you're not mistaken?*

She breathed a long sigh. "I'm not quite sure how it happened. But I've met another vampire who found a second mate after his first passed away. He's very happy with his new woman. Perhaps what we know of lifemates is wrong...or incomplete." Her lip quirked to its scarred side. "Maybe we will never know everything of lifemates and how fate guides us to them."

Well, he couldn't argue with that. But he still fidgeted. "What was he like?" he asked quietly. "Your mate, I mean."

She raised a finger. "Former mate. He was a good man and a powerful warrior, back in a time where being a talented fighter could get you a job anywhere." Her gaze grew distant, and she shook her head, sending her red hair around her in waves. "He turned on me in a way lifemates should never do, through Lucia's meddling. He left me for her."

"*That* Lucia?" he asked, jaw dropping.

Her expression shuttered. "Yes. So, excuse me if I don't want to talk about him."

"Perfectly understandable. Let's throw the whole memory away." He mimicked balling up the air and tossing it over his shoulder.

The ghost of a smile lit her lips.

"In fact, why don't we start fresh?" He suggested. The moment Neala mentioned her former mate, her heavy burdens sagged her shoulders. "Let the outside world be for two weeks. You're a new person now, with a new voice. Why not start over, here and now?"

"I wish it were that simple." She considered the darkness closing in overtop them now that the sun was no more than a faraway sliver. "I will try, how about that? You deserve my best efforts."

"And you deserve to be happy."

That's all he really wanted, to see her truly content with the life she chose to lead. She wasn't yet. Maybe together, they could get there.

She cleared her throat. "I learned a song for you." Without warning, she serenaded him with the incoming night, her voice husky and warm as she sang a simple verse.

"Again, again," he coaxed, catching on and plucking his lute. They discovered together that the first song she'd learned was one of perseverance and second chances as his instrument set the melody.

Chapter 14
Neala

Day one of her new start still began with Lady Iridia, who ran her through the basics again and taught her a new song. In the afternoon, she traded off with Cedric so they could both have time with their music coach. Neala felt the daylight hours trickling away sitting across from Sondus in a classroom desk that barely fit her. They discussed the spy network when she steadfastly refused to talk about Izell.

She kept a straight face, realizing quickly that the spymaster was probing for information past the basics. He wanted to know how her group had crossed over to Faerie and the details of Izell's plans.

"She doesn't tell me such things," Neala finally said. "Sometimes, I don't think even she knows."

There was a glimmer of disappointment in his eyes. "How troublesome. Well, there's something I should show you." He strode to the door, holding it open for her. She'd wondered what he would pull out since she refused to waste time studying history like he'd pushed on Cedric.

"I can tell you are eager to be about your business," he said, staying a step ahead of her as he led her away. "So, let me show you how we will be communicating once you leave the Shifting Wood. We agreed you will assist the Unseen Council with

matters pertaining to Faerie's stability in exchange for the knowledge you're receiving here."

She frowned at the back of his head. "We did. But that is not
specific." What exactly did assistance entail?

"I don't intend to ask you for much, Lady Neala. Let's see
how the political climate fares before you step out into my world.
Some things change quickly."

While she could see the wisdom of that, she wondered
exactly what he was gearing up to ask her for. It had to be in line
with Izell's plans—which she was no longer privy to.

"In the meantime, did Cedric teach you about greater fae last
night?" he asked.

"No?" They were a little distracted up on that roof, talking
until the stars dotted the sky and Cedric couldn't keep his eyes
open.

Sondus led her under the grand chandelier, its gleaming
facets causing his skin to sparkle under direct light. "Ah, to be
expected. Surely you've noticed Seelie and Unseelie fae are quite
different?" He stopped and held his arms out to bask in the effect.

"My voice was gone, not my eyes," she remarked, raising a
brow when he lingered there. She'd already seen too many fae to
be dazzled by them.

He turned and continued on, unperturbed. They were heading
toward the wing with the lab, where she'd already seen Seelie and
Unseelie working side-by-side. "Well, the species of fae you're used
to are considered greater fae. We're the most human-like. Ten fingers,
ten toes, generally a decent height." He glanced up at her in amusement. "The longer you stay here, the more species of lesser fae you
will meet. Like the satyrs and fauns that tend to the Shifting Wood."

"Oh, that's what they are," she muttered. She hadn't caught
sight of a goat-person since she'd settled in the manor.

"But I bring this up because even the tiniest youngling knows
all eight species of greater fae. There used to be four—fire, earth,
water, and wind—before Oberon's final spell separated us into
Seelie and Unseelie. Care to take a guess what element astral fae
are?" His gaze twinkled playfully.

Humming, she considered the fae she'd met and what elements lingered in their skin and wings. "Water. But what is the connection between stars and water?"

"The heavenly bodies move the tides. Astral fae, like the rest of the Seelie, are named for that bit of angel in them. We have astral, solar, terran, and aether."

"What is 'aether'?" The rest were pretty self-explanatory to her.

"The area high in the sky, of course. They are Seelie wind fae," he said. "Unseelie names are far more unpleasant. Unlike their truth-telling counterparts, they still have hints of magic from their demon benefactors."

He paused at the junction between the doors to the lab and the other room she'd only caught a glimpse of earlier. Turning to the unfamiliar room, he invited her inside with a wave of his hand. It was like walking into a surrealist's dream, with mirrors on all surfaces except the floor. Her image was twisted and echoed into a fragmented army with every step she took inside. Dozens of mini Neala's twisted around, squinting when she did.

Along the center of the room were raised podiums, each with writing tools and crystals as big as her two fists combined. The young lady she'd startled on her first visit to the lab was behind one, with a hand on a crystal, the other taking notes at a furious pace. She froze when she looked up and spotted Neala.

"Welcome to the portal room," Sondus said, climbing up on the raised platform behind the next podium and gesturing for the other fae to continue writing.

As Neala joined him, she realized what the significance of this room truly was. Her reflections faded away from several panels, instead revealing the faces and surroundings of multiple different fae, greater and lesser alike. While she watched, the fae next to her flicked her wrist and cleared one of the panels. She shuffled her papers and pointed to the next panel, which activated with a flash at the corners.

"I see no portals," Neala murmured, aware that a conversation across some considerable distance was going on beside her.

"This room is manned at all hours by operatives that can activate the crystals. We can make portals all across Faerie." He patted the white dome of the crystal on his podium. "Such magic is rare. We're lucky to have access to it."

She shook her head in disbelief. "Lucky. That's a word for it. How does it work on the other end?" She pointed to a fae at random.

"Two-way mirrors. Each of these panels has an activation spell that can be tapped at any distance. You'll be receiving your own mirror before you leave."

"I suppose it's 'lucky' you have access to this kind of magic too?" she asked dryly.

He flashed his teeth. "Now you're understanding."

Once he confirmed that those waiting to report in couldn't hear them, he pointed out Unseelie to continue his lesson in greater fae. The one she was most familiar with, destruction, were Unseelie fire fae that could cause explosions at a whim. She saw her first curse fae, an Unseelie earth fae who had a corpse-like pale pallor and green eyes that rolled with smoke just under the surface.

"You never cross a curse fae," Sondus warned. "And you avoid making deals with them whenever possible. They choose what curse you are afflicted with if you break a pact with them."

She nodded, lips pressed tightly. "Duly noted."

She was familiar with the green-tinged blight fae, as she'd worked with several in the lab. Sondus took a few moments to introduce her to the lesser fae waiting around, including a cloud of glowing lights that were apparently pixies and an obese crea-ture with one cavernous nostril and a bulbous eye, called an ogre.

"So, there's a fourth? An Unseelie water fae?" she prompted, not seeing anyone with purple skin waiting to report in. She thought of Iridia, who must've fallen into this last category.

"Thankfully very rare," he said. "With black wings as dark as their magic. Death fae."

"Death, blight, destruction, and curses. You weren't kidding about their titles." But something else was bothering her more than the pretentious names the Unseelie gave themselves. "Just how large is your organization?"

He clasped his hands behind his back. "Let's just say extensive, Lady Neala. And it's *our* organization. May I remind you that we are all here for the betterment of Faerie?"

"That's a weird way to word it. 'The betterment of Faerie,'" Cedric remarked later that night. They'd had their stroll through the manor's garden and watched the sun set over another day.

"Indeed. Be careful what information you share with him," she warned quietly. Now that she'd sung for Cedric and relieved the pressure that'd tickled her neck, she wanted to get this conversation out of the way.

If she only had the evenings with this man, she wanted to make them count.

"And how was your day?" she asked.

He plucked a new tune, and her heart sped to a blur, her gaze narrowing to pinpoint focus. When her palms began to sweat, she recognized the shot of adrenaline he'd given her.

"I have some new tricks up my sleeve now," he said, changing the song so it slowed her back down. "Unlike some people, Iridia actually thinks I have talent and can handle the more advanced techniques. Like playing with a focus."

He showed her his bracelet, which was a woven cord strung with a heavy bead. "When I'm wearing this, I don't feel my own music's magic. It's like a confidence thing. Now, I can play more dramatic chords without having a heart attack."

She laughed. "You'll just make the rest of us have one instead?"

"Not you! Just people I don't like."

She considered him for a moment. While he'd delivered that with a straight face, the longer she waited, the more he cracked up. She started to do the same until they were laughing together.

Neala held on to the lightness in her heart just like she reached over to hold Cedric's hand.

Chapter 15
Cedric

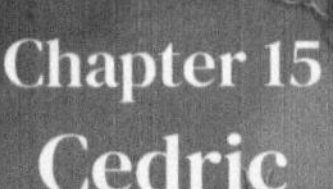

IT WAS THE SHORTEST TWO WEEKS OF HIS LIFE. HIS MOTHER had human logic when it came to time, that it moved faster with enjoyment and slower in the darker times of life. The fae he'd grown up with had the immortal view of it: time was time; minutes were still sixty seconds no matter what.

Cedric agreed with his human side in this case. Unlocking his potential with the enchanted lute was fulfilling and left him with a warm glow inside as he achieved more than he thought possible in the limited time he had with Lady Iridia.

On the other hand, he was about as much of a spy as when he first set foot on Faerie. Sondus was "pulled away" days into their stay, and Cedric had to wonder if it was because he and Neala had agreed to speak more carefully to the spymaster. So, that training was pushed to the side in favor of sharing Iridia with Neala and playing melodies as backdrops for her dusky voice.

Ah, Neala. The first time she'd suddenly turned her lyrics into a bawdy drinking song, he'd turned red trying to contain his laughter. That'd been a week ago. She was...different. No, that wasn't the right word. She was *transformed*.

The dark circles that rimmed her eyes were fading some every night, like she'd finally gotten the sleep she needed. But most of the changes were more subtle. The widening of a smile, the gentle tilt of her head when he spoke to her. Neither of them brought up the past. Without its burdens, she was free to be wild.

To say he liked the new her was like saying he loved singing. Two obvious statements about himself that were as much a part of him as the stars that dotted his cheeks like freckles.

Would the old Neala want to spend her evenings with their hands entwined, talking about everything and nothing? He thought not.

The old Neala never could've sung a heart's song. Each day, he hoped Iridia would help her find and nurture some hidden potential to perform one despite her human-born heritage. He realized it was a selfish wish even as he sought the Unseelie woman out alone on day thirteen. The count of the days weighed heavily in the back of his mind, ticking away until he found himself in Iridia's favorite room.

The practice room was large enough for one person, a chair, and a music stand. The walls were enchanted to bounce sound back, allowing one to hear their playing or singing like a bystander. He crammed himself in with her, forced to stand while she remained seated with her enchanted violin in her lap.

"Are you troubled?" she asked, her lavender gaze reading his face.

"I just don't want to go tomorrow. It seems like I have so much more to learn from you," he said.

Her brow raised. "A man does not wear your expression just to chit-chat, does he?"

One thing he'd learned Iridia didn't do was speak idly. He'd barely gotten a word out of her sideways about her life as an original *drasonii* or what it was like to play music for the fae pantheon of elemental gods. Those were secrets lost to time, or maybe the depths of Sondus's library of a mind.

"Well, no. I was wondering if you've ever seen a lifemate bond between a human and a fae," he admitted.

She stroked her jaw before gesturing to him. "Were your parents not such a pair?"

"I don't know. My mother doesn't speak of my father in the mushy gushy way most people talk about their lifemates." He could only shrug, though. His mother had also moved on, which he understood was fiendishly hard for those who'd lost their one true match. "I'm asking because Neala can see that she and I are lifemates."

Her smile widened, showing her little fangs. "Condolences."

"But I'm not exactly sure how it's going to work and how we might pair up." Once he put his worries into words, it felt like he couldn't stop them from rushing past his lips all at once. "She can sense the connection, but I can't. Because vampires see lifemates, but fae only know through their heart's song, and I guess I'm more fae in that regard. Not to mention I'm somehow her second life-mate, which shouldn't even be possible. I just worry that—"

He stopped when she put her hands up. "No one here's noticed something going on between you two," she said. Well, they hadn't been subtle, he thought, noticing the negative in her words and flipping the statement in his head to make sense of it. "You're not worried about the mechanics. Humans have heart's songs and fae can't offer...how do vampires bond their mates anyway?"

With her asking so bluntly, he figured she really didn't know. Heat pinched his cheeks as he whispered behind a hand, "It's...they have special sex."

"You haven't done that yet?" she deadpanned.

"Not yet! We're only just getting to know each other." He was just glad he hadn't carried his reputation to Faerie with this expedition. A charming smile and a nice voice had earned him many admirers in Adrun. But with Neala, he wanted to do it right, and that meant taking it easy.

"True lifemates find a way to mesh together, no?" She drew up her violin as she spoke, planting it on her shoulder. "Do you remember why I love music more than life, young Cedric?"

"It never lies," he parroted obediently. A concept he'd strug-gled to understand when deciphering her Unseelie speak until she put that enchanted violin on her shoulder and played her first song for him.

It's not that the music itself didn't lie, but his emotions certainly didn't. He'd ended up in tears by the end of her song, understanding the raw emotion of the story the melody conveyed without needing to hear a single word.

Iridia played for him again and wove a new tune. She started with a mournful burst of notes, immediately wrenching his heart. It was an echo of pain, sadness wrapped in a prickly thorn bow ready to rend open loss's hard-to-heal wounds.

She lingered there to weave the beginning of the story. The loss of a lifemate, a tragic ending to an immortal love story. Iridia then changed the song so abruptly he almost missed how the first and second half were similar. Hope stirred anew when she played the same basic notes but lighter, happier.

Same chords, different song. She changed the song three more times just to prove her point. It clicked with him, from one musician to another.

"Aren't there stranger things in this life than meeting a second person whose song harmonizes with yours?" she asked after the last stirrings of music faded from the room. "Perhaps it would not happen often if fae died more frequently. How wonderful life could be, if one was only ever given one chance to be happy."

He pressed his lips together to hold himself in check. Iridia couldn't wave her hands around and divine what the future held for his relationship. But she still stirred some certainty that he could be a vampire's lifemate without hearing her heart's song, if her magic-enhanced voice could ever create one.

"Thank you, I think that's all—"

"Cedric." She halted him with his hand already on the doorknob, ready to give her privacy to practice. "If you don't sing for her, maybe she can accept you then and there. Try it?"

"When she's ready," he promised, raising a hand in farewell. He couldn't help but notice the knowing glint in her eye.

He kept Iridia's wisdom to himself, instead savoring his last sunset with Neala before they were to leave the manor. The next day started too early. The sun hadn't even cracked its eye open when there was an insistent knock at the door.

When he opened it, he expected one of the younger spies that often had to run messages. Instead, Sondus stood there, a shadow in the morning. Cedric would've asked what the occasion was if his jaw wasn't locked into a massive yawn a moment later.

"You and Neala are needed in the portal room," the spymaster said.

Good morning to you too, he thought, grumbling as he shuffled back into his quarters to splash some water in his face and change out of his nightclothes.

When he was presentable, he realized he'd missed the chance to even talk to Sondus, as he was gone and in his place in the hall stood Neala, still scrubbing at her eyes.

"Do you know what this is about?" she asked.

"Nope. But it's important if he got us himself." He followed Neala's lead downstairs since she'd seen the portal room and he hadn't. She explained what it was for mentally so they didn't disturb anyone else on their way by.

The portal room was dim, lit by the crystals in each podium. One was occupied by Sondus, who held his hand over the glowing surface and conversed with the lone figure on the other side of the mirrors. "Lock the door," Sondus said as they entered. Neala did it with a snap of her fingers, her mental powers sliding the bolt without even a glance.

The spymaster gestured over the podium he stood at, muttering a few words of power. The silent conversation that'd been limited to him and the other person suddenly filled the room.

"The little girl suggested that you two aren't finished training." Ash's gruff voice echoed off the walls as she scowled in place of their reflections. Cedric reminded himself that, unlike Iridia, she chose to communicate mostly through saying the opposite of what she meant.

"Neala, Cedric, you know Princess Ashaela, right?" Sondus asked smoothly.

Ash winced, while Neala grew very still, her red eyes blazing. "Princess," she repeated, turning to face Ash's reflection. "I grow to hate surprises."

"Princess of what, exactly?" Cedric spoke on her heels, hoping Ash had some explanation before tempers flared too hard.

"What do you think?" Ash sighed, pinching the bridge of her nose. "Go ahead, Sondus, tell them everything."

"Crown Princess Ashaela Dread, last blood relative to the Unseelie Queen, Her Majesty Kalimea Dread." While he spoke, Ash fixed an angry look somewhere over their heads. For his part, Sondus seemed as pleased as a nobleman presented with a lavish feast.

"A title I so dearly want," Ash said waspishly. "A matter we won't speak on later. Izell doesn't want you to return right away."

Neala glowered. The air practically warped around her with the force of her ire. Cedric edged away from her, rubbing the goosebumps from his arms. "Are you prepared to tell us why?" she demanded.

"There's been a situation." Sondus spoke up for Ash. "Traffic to and from the Unseelie Palace has been shut down for nearly a week. It's the sign of a dead zone—an anti-magic measure. We've been scrambling to figure out what's going on."

"Any luck?" Cedric ventured, swallowing a mouthful of nerves.

"Kalimea may have set it up herself," Ash said. Her fiery eyes widened, trying to impart some silent knowledge.

"We're still waiting on our operatives to find out why and to assist the Queen. This is where I ask you to leave with my blessings and a mission to complete in exchange for the knowledge you've gained here." Sondus held out two round objects to them. They looked suspiciously like a woman's compact, something Cedric didn't want to be caught holding. He opened his, revealing the shine of a mirror.

With a resigned expression, Neala demanded, "What is the mission?"

"Assist the Unseelie Queen. As simple or as complicated as that." Sondus spread his palms. "The longer she holds a dead zone over her palace, the more her subjects will get sick of partying with no magic. And the last thing we need right now are bored Unseelie."

Ash seemed to roll her eyes, judging by the way the flames in them jostled. "We sure did a good job putting all our entertainers in one place."

"It was your sister's decision," Sondus snapped. "While you were off cavorting in mortal lands again."

Cedric wished he'd brought his lute, just to play a calming tune as he felt the temperature in this room rising by the moment. He put his palms up. "Is this still the birthday party you were talking about?" he asked Sondus. "When is her birthday anyway?"

The spymaster took a deep breath and considered. "Three days ago?" He glanced to Ash, who nodded. "With months of parties and entertainment planned."

His discomfort became like a bad meal, leaving an oily, gross feeling to gather in his middle. "Like, after the birthday?"

"Until midwinter. To keep our malcontents occupied until the end of the world so they can't make it worse," the spymaster murmured. "Your mission is to help the Queen keep up the act. Is this something you accept?"

Cedric and Neala exchanged a glance and then an agreeing nod. They didn't have to say a word.

Ash pressed a handkerchief to her nose. "And Neala, a few words of the truth," she said. "Your new voice. It's nice." Her image faded away moments later, the cloth stained with a few dots of scarlet.

Chapter 16
Sirius

Sirius remembered Nyixa's politics like he'd just fallen asleep in the white-stone palace rather than sleeping through the last thousand years. The Seelie court was a stark reminder that while the faces were different, politics never changed.

Everyone had an agenda. Even him.

He acted as Izell's Blade in Neala's absence, meaning he had a front row seat to the frustration. He was by her side as they milled in the jeweled throne room or more private feminine parlors with delicate flower motifs that made him want to retch.

When they weren't pursuing the fruitless task of waiting for an audience with the Seelie King, she was browsing the monolith that was the Library of Faerie. He preferred those days because Izell would cut him loose to explore while she poured over arcane texts with Jaromír by her side instead.

Sirius wondered if she knew the gravity of what she'd offered him to get him here in the first place. Her invitation was a sealed letter and, in her strict script, promised the one thing he wanted most: control over his inner beast.

As he exited the apartment building Izell had rented for their group, fresh air hit his nose and he groaned. His inner beast was awake and as demanding as ever.

Run. Fight. Kill.

His feet were stuck in place as he shut his eyes tightly, waiting for the strongest urges to fade. While the beast was always there, its instincts came and went on a whim. Not *his* whim, but its own. A thousand years had made the manifestation of his shapeshifting magic far stronger than him, as he lacked the millennia of practice in controlling it.

It wanted the one thing he hadn't managed to give it yet: revenge. Since they couldn't fight their ally, the nephilim Gwendolyn, who'd feared Fell Madness so much she'd nearly condemned him and his fellow Ancients to death, the inner beast bayed for Lucia's blood instead.

Too bad for him, Lucia was mostly dead. Rendered to ash and a curl of smoke after becoming a demon. His brother had had the honor of dealing the blow, leaving Sirius to wrangle his jealous beast and plan. Demons not killed by angels or angelic weapons always regenerated, though the where and when and how were elusive.

Frustration cramped his gut. The beast wanted a good fight if Lucia wasn't available. Fighting was all he was good for.

Fight! Fight! His inner beast practically salivated.

He wrenched his eyes open, fists curled and trembling as he took a few steps into the city. *No fighting today. We have something more important to do,* he told it.

Izell still had the pull to get them a sleeping place within walking distance of Summer Palace, where an overflow of simpering nobility milled about. He already hated the sight of the place, with its terraced floors and grand orchards that supplied free fruit to inhabitants year-round. Unfortunately, that meant they attracted a species of lesser fae called "puckish woodwols," whom he also already despised.

"Smile, mister!" exclaimed one from a tree bearing blush fruit with a bittersweet aroma like grapefruit. He stopped and forced a more pleasant expression, trying to spot the woodwol since it was like a fruit come to life, the same color and general round shape but with dexterous little limbs that could tuck to the side as a disguise.

He already knew from experience that a woodwol would

throw rotten fruit if you didn't do as it asked. Sometimes they did it anyway. Thankfully, he spotted this one and caught the fruit it threw—which was firm and ready to eat.

"Thanks," he grunted, walking away quickly. His red gaze scanned the branches above him for any more of the creatures as he took a bite of the fruit. His beast wanted to reject it, not liking that it tasted fruit instead of bloody meat, but Sirius enjoyed the flavor and forced himself to swallow. He'd grown used to even the small things being a struggle.

An orange woodwol scampered by. He dodged a bomb of rotten orange as it burst where he'd been standing and muttered uncharitably. Any appearances he made at court were in one of two outfits: either his armor, polished and buffed to a silvery sheen, or what he was wearing now, the single suit he'd packed since he'd foolishly assumed he wouldn't be making social calls.

He was about to head back to court on his own. He was tired of waiting. If the Seelie King wouldn't see Izell, then he'd see Sirius, and one of those interactions was bound to be less pleasant.

He mounted the sweeping staircase with singular intent, already picking up on the hum of voices past the wide-open palace doors. *Some immortals have nothing to do*, he thought, marching past fantastical lady fae wearing dresses of living flames or sparkling gowns that clung to their curves and changed patterns as they gestured and laughed. There was a buzzing behind his ears, a sense of excitement that hadn't been there yesterday when he and Izell had milled about with the others, asking questions and simply waiting.

Sirius perked his hearing, one of the only things he thought his inner beast was good for. Conversation drifted over him as if he were standing right next to the gossip.

"There he is again, the angry vampire."

"...Archfae Firebrand's pet. Did you know he growled at Mikata?"

"Who brings a human instead of a proper Blade to court?"

Great. That told him nothing except that these bored chin-wags saw him as a new oddity to ridicule. He let their words filter through as he headed for the throne room, hoping to find that the stuffy old fae king had resumed his seat. Judging by how many fae milled about, he knew it was futile.

The Seelie King believed in holding court and listening to all his subjects. But with him locked behind a solid wall of security and magic as he spent all his time with the Light Eye, nobody was listening to the people anymore. Sirius was uncomfortable with the idea, knowing from experience since his brother was a king. Subjects that felt unheard quickly became *furious*.

"...says he's an angel." Sirius stopped short when he heard that from a male fae with delicate wings who stood with his arms around two women.

One of those ladies scoffed. "Angels aren't around anymore."

"I don't know; this one was different."

Sirius marched up to the trio, who startled into silence. The male eyed him warily, pulling his women in closer. "Where is the angel?" Sirius demanded. If there really was one, he could bargain for an angelic weapon. All the better to kill Lucia with.

The fae pointed him to a parlor he hadn't been to yet, a sun room occupying a good section of the second floor. Sirius felt a little foolish when he went all the way there just to be confronted with a closed and locked door. Even to his advanced hearing, there was no conversation inside. After trying the handle with more aggression than it deserved, he turned away with a frustrated growl.

A lock clicked as he started to walk away. In the doorway was a confused fae wearing the gold-and-green livery of a palace servant. Hushed voices flowed out the open door, proof of some sort of silencing spell. "Can I help you sir?" the servant asked.

"Is there an angel in there?" Sirius asked.

"Yes, but—" the servant spluttered when Sirius pushed past him. "This is a private meeting! Sir!"

Five sets of eyes raised as Sirius glanced around the room looking for the angel. The sunroom was three times the space of a normal parlor, with floor-to-ceiling windows and even some on the ceiling for good measure. Since there was only one man there who could be human, Sirius fixated on him.

The man in question was seated in the middle of a loveseat as to take up some of each cushion. He seemed at home with sunlight bathing his well-tanned skin, his simple white robe glowing. He smiled over at Sirius as if about to greet an old friend.

Meanwhile, four fae were seated around him and looked ready to flay the skin from Sirius's back for his interruption. The hair on his neck raised in warning of the supernatural power rising from them. It felt as humid as when Lucia was flexing her power, multiplied by at least three.

"State your business," said one of the men, an aether fae with a glowing white ball of an occultarus circling his shoulders and fluffy wings. The occultarus was a warning that this man was a Sorcerer, a fae capable of wielding all schools of fae magic. His wings were wider than those of any aether fae Sirius had met, with a peculiar roll of clouds running through his flat gaze.

"This is a private meeting," agreed the solar fae seated primly on a cushion. She had a rich dress in reds and golds, to match the shine dripping from her ears and fingers. Another occultarus rested by her hand, bobbing patiently as it waited to unleash spells more focused and deadly than she could cast on her own.

Sirius squared his shoulders. "I'm here to speak with the angel."

"Make your own meeting, then," the aether fae scoffed.

Smiling and silent throughout this exchange, the angel finally raised a hand. "No need to be so hostile, friends. I know this man." He turned merry brown eyes toward Sirius. "You're Adrius's brother! You must be Sirius. I'd recognize you anywhere."

The fae exchanged a glance while he stood and went up to Sirius for a handshake. "You know my brother?" Sirius asked in undertone.

"Why, I'm his guardian angel!" It had to be Soren, then. Adrius had shared tale of visiting a man with a garden island in the sky the few times he'd recently visited Heaven. Soren had a smile for everyone and a way about him that had even Zerenth, Adrius's recalcitrant dragon, acting warm and polite. He was the kind of man Sirius never expected to meet, yet here he was in the heart of Faerie.

Soren grinned as he leveraged the handshake to pull Sirius over to where he'd been sitting, making room for them both. "How's he doing? Are he and Zerenth getting along? Actually, better question, are you two getting along? I've heard so much about you!"

He cleared his throat, wondering which lucky stars to thank. It wouldn't be so hard to convince this angel to give him a weapon if he already knew and liked Adrius. "He wed Nyah again and was crowned King of Adrun," Sirius said, feeling a flush of pride for his brother. After so much suffering and loss, Adrius had finally gotten everything he'd strived for. "And I would say he gets along with both Zerenth and me most of the time."

Soren threw his head back and laughed. "Oh, most of the time! Better than nothing."

"I'd say it's a big improvement," he said, feeling some of the tension leave his shoulders. The Sorcerers in the room were no longer menacing him either, so his inner beast relaxed.

"Well, Sirius, have you been introduced to the Committee of Archfae? We were having a lovely meeting before you came trying to tear the door off," he said cheerfully. "Everyone, this is Prince Sirius, the..." His gaze flickered minutely.

"Dawn," Sirius whispered.

"Prince Sirius, the Dawn. One of the original Fell Hunters."

He felt the change in the room, hostility sheathing its claws now that he was revealed as a sort of nobility as well.

"Sirius, this is..." Soren gestured to the aether fae, who was named Anderos, meaning, with title, he was Aether Archfae Anderos. *Unfortunate,* he thought with a flare of amusement.

The only lady fae in the room was Solar Archfae Risaria, and then there were two terran fae, one the Archfae Onyx and the other more curious. He had pupils, just the hint of an animal-like slit in the center swimming in the middle of a sea of forest green. He was dressed in plain leather, his long, evergreen hair woven with beads, autumnal leaves, and a few white feathers. This man was practically a commoner in the midst of the finery of the Archfae. Something about him was sharp and wild in a palace full of soft nobles.

"...and last but certainly not least, Archdruid Theron, sitting in for his mate, Astral Archfae Sorsha, in her absence."

Sirius took a moment, clutching at the loveseat cushion beneath him. He knew so little of Neala's adopted kin other than that they were now quite ancient themselves, with lives of their own outside of helping the vampires with their problems. They didn't talk about what they'd left behind in Faerie nearly enough. Where was Neala when he needed her? Where were *Sorsha* and Ash, who would already know this man? He breathed out his tension and forced his best polite tone from his throat. "It is a pleasure to meet you all. Especially you, Archdruid Theron. Your mate has been key for us on Earth to thwart a Sorceress-turned-demon."

Theron's expression tightened. "The same one who broke the balance?" He jerked his chin toward Soren.

"That's the one," the angel sighed. "Sirius, you would've been bored sitting here. I was telling them what she did to break the Dark Eye and become a demon."

"What *did* she do to become a demon?" he asked. His inner beast was ready to hone its claws on this knowledge.

Soren's smile finally faded. "She died, dear man. The problem at hand isn't that...It's that she came back. Hell broke one of our cardinal rules: no resurrection. However, since the rules also dictate that if there is one demon released from Hell, there's also an angel returned from Heaven...here I am!" He spread his arms.

"You're going to hunt what's left of Lucia." He licked his lips, savoring the taste of those words.

"Gabriel has that well under control. I'm here to speak with the good people of Faerie instead," he said. "The Archfae and I were discussing a potential audience with the Seelie King."

Sirius wanted to scoff and say *good luck*, but maybe this was his gateway to also getting an audience with the man. Izell insisted that the Seelie King owed her a favor, and that favor would come in the surrendering of one of the missing Fell Keys.

"He's not seeing anyone at present," the aether fae, Anderos, cut in. "Not even us. He's meditating at the base of the Light Eye and is not to be disturbed under any circumstances."

"The Light Eye's magic is powered by the sacrifice of an archangel. You can let myself—another angel—help him. Then I will get my permissions and be on my way," Soren said.

"Our king's orders were crystal clear. This is a matter of Faerie's utmost security. Now, if you wanted to fly into Unseelie lands, there's no law against it..."

"As an angel, I must be invited into Unseelie lands." Soren bared his palms in a helpless shrug. "It is part of the treaty between our peoples. But you know I am here to speak with Queen Kalimea, not to bother your king. Yet apparently, she is unreachable?"

"We're still waiting for our people to report on why she's placed a magical dead zone over her palace and the surrounding area," Anderos sighed.

"We are too reliant on magic and will need some time," Theron cut in. "But we can and will send word to the Unseelie Queen that you wish to meet with her and need an invitation."

Risaria had her gaze fixed on Theron. "I think it's time we retired to discuss this matter in private rather than make promises we cannot fulfill, Archdruid."

"My apologies," he gritted out. "I thought you called me to convene the Committee of Archfae so we could be helpful to our people."

She turned a bright smile toward the two human-born in the room. The expression didn't quite reach her eyes. "Gentlemen, we will be in touch. If you would excuse us?"

"Of course," Sirius said, glad to have some time alone with Soren as the two of them were shown the door.

"What peculiar people the fae are. I look forward to meeting more," Soren remarked, keeping pace with him as he found the stairs down to the first floor. "You came looking for me for a reason, though."

"Can I have use of your weapon? Just like Adrius killed Jazrach with an angel's sword, I would like to do the same with

Lucia," he said in an undertone as they passed a gaggle of giggling ladies.

Soren didn't answer until they were outside the palace and Sirius's gaze was back to the trees for signs of any woodwols. "That's a problematic request. I'm not a fighter and brought no weapons for that task."

His inner beast didn't like that answer. *Useless,* it snarled. He was suddenly ready to take a bite of the angel.

"I am a man of peace," Soren continued, placing a calming hand on his shoulder. "Here to make allies for the fight ahead. In short, I'm here to get you an army rather than to be another fighter. Put away your fangs, my new friend. There are no demons here anyway."

"Lucia's a curl of smoke. She could be anywhere she pleases," he grumbled.

Soren tilted his head. "And how do you think you'd mortally wound a curl of smoke? I imagine you have more to concern your-self right now."

"Like with what?" he snapped.

The angel's eyes twinkled. "Don't worry, I'll help you. Where are you staying? I just landed here myself." He chuckled at his own joke, and Sirius couldn't help but think his brother would too, if he were here.

Chapter 17
Neala

By the time the sun rose, Neala and Cedric were packed, fed breakfast, and punted through a portal to an unfamiliar place. The cobblestones and hawking merchants reminded her distinctly of big cities back in her time, before she'd slept through mortals inventing technology and other crazy things. Yet no city she remembered had elk and unicorns serving as beasts of burden, nor any magical demonstrations to sell the latest and greatest novelty spell.

"Welcome back." Ash waited a few feet away, looking more at home in her skin wearing thick leather armor and her bandolier of daggers without anyone sparing her and her flaming wings a second glance.

Neala bowed. "Princess Ashaela," she said formally, still irritated that she'd been living and working alongside true royalty unknowingly.

The fae's cheeks lit dark gray as she inspected the sky. She muttered uncharitably about Sondus. "I can explain," she sighed, rubbing her nose.

Lute music rolled over them both as Cedric played a calming melody. "But first, where are we?" he asked.

Neala could spot an obvious royal structure in the distance, mounted atop a high hill. What made her breath catch was the barest hint of a magical implement peeking around its tiered floors. It was the curve of a massive occultarus, its glass surface a golden-white and sparkling in the sun. *The Light Eye,* she thought. She'd lived in close proximity to its black counterpart, the Dark Eye, and wondered if the two were anything alike. The Dark Eye had been an unnerving monolith, always full of mocking shadows and a silent, watching presence. So, surely its opposite was a beacon of warmth.

"Some call this place Summerhail," Ash said, turning in a swish of her cloak. "Certainly not home to the ancient Summer King before fae kind was consolidated into one people and then split into Seelie and Unseelie."

"How long ago was that?" Cedric asked as he and Neala flanked her.

"Not before humans or anything." Her ever-present sarcasm twisted the meaning around.

"Oh, *old* fae. So now, the royal family moves between locations in honor of some tradition few people remember?" he guessed.

"Something like that."

Neala couldn't stand it anymore once they were on a quieter stretch of street. "Does this make Keegan Crown Prince of the Unseelie?" She hadn't pressed about her children's relationships. They'd parted ways when Keegan and Sorsha were still teenagers, and now, they were seemingly well-respected elders with how time passed differently for fae. But ever since she'd caught Keegan and Ash kissing, she burned to know if she had more family than she expected.

With a sigh, Ash dug into a pouch at her belt and withdrew a cluster of flowers like tiny buttercups. "For redirecting pain," she said, eating them whole and wiping at the single drop of blood that'd leaked from her nose from telling a truth. Cedric shot a puzzled glance over at Neala, who shrugged.

"Very few Unseelie can tell the truth ever. The fact that I can is a well-guarded secret I expect you both to keep," Ash said once she swallowed and pulled a face at the flavor of the flowers.

"That's fair." Cedric sounded as confused as Neala felt that they were learning this now.

"Keegan is Crown Prince of the Seelie Throne, actually, an arrangement both of us dodge," Ash continued. They slowed as she started to limp. "My sister married King Orin for political reasons. They've been married for three thousand years and, somewhere along the line, had to admit they'd never produce an heir together. Seelie and Unseelie can't have children, you see. The magics in us clash."

"So, you're next in line...and don't want to be." Which seemed like an understatement to her, as Ash had taken pains to avoid talking about her station.

"It is unnatural," she said plainly. "Fae royalty doesn't work that way. Up until Orin and Kalimea, every royal couple produced four children—one of each element. Seelie inherit by eldest sibling, usually the solar child. Unseelie have a merry war, and the last sibling standing is the new ruler. Until Kalimea." Her expression grew tight with repressed emotion. "She and I have broken many laws together, but to date, the biggest one is that she refused to put me to death. Instead, she put a tiara on my head just in case something ever happens to her."

Neala scratched her head, a simple motion Ash responded to. "I know I seem ungrateful. It is more complicated than I can explain...just know I pay Kali back every day by eliminating threats for her. Kali will rule Faerie forever as far as I'm concerned."

That seemed terribly unlikely, but Neala didn't say so. She saw something new in Ash, a fondness in an expression otherwise pinched by pain. "So, that's what you, Keegan, and Sorsha do in your free time?" she asked instead.

"Before the Dark Eye exploded, yes," she said dryly. "Keegan's been dying to tell you everything, but you vampires are always together, gossiping. The Unseen Council and its sister organization are supposed to be a secret, not something to chatter about."

"I suppose the next thing you're going to say is the sister organization is why Sondus seems to dislike you," Neala ventured.

Ash scoffed, the irritation returning to her sharp gestures. "He thinks we're in a competition. I lead a much smaller network of assassins started by my egg donor. His people listen, mine act. He's jealous."

Cedric paused his playing with a confused tangle of notes. "Um. Egg donor?"

She rolled her eyes, stopping short at a cluster of two-story buildings. "I guess I've spent too much time in the mortal world. Imagine a woman who gives birth to you and then hands you off to your sister. She's your egg donor," she remarked. "Here's where we've been staying."

The rooms were townhouse style, Neala quickly learned as Ash lead them into one and collapsed into a chair, elevating one of her legs onto a table with a pain-filled grunt. Apparently, they all spent time in Izell's rooms, which had the largest sitting area, before splitting up to rest for the night.

Cossette came over with towel-wrapped ice and a tray of sandwich squares. "I saw that you might need these," she said, surprisingly solemn. She applied the ice to the Unseelie's thigh while Ash devoured the platter of food.

"Where is everyone?" Neala asked while Cedric looked on in concern.

The little Ancient glanced up and cocked her head in deep thought. "Izell is at the library kissing Jaromir."

Ash spluttered an undignified laugh for someone who was supposed to be a princess, showering crumbs over her tray.

"And Sirius should be stomping in any moment with an angel," Cossette finished. She beamed. "Did I do good? Was that an adult response?"

Ash was turning vaguely purple as she tried to contain her laughter further. Cedric flashed a thumbs up in her stead. "Nailed it!"

The door opened in a quick whip seconds later, with a wild-eyed Sirius preceding a completely normal-looking human man. Neala still jumped to her feet, hand instinctively going for her belt even though she'd long packed away her weapon during her stay in the Shifting Wood.

"Good day, friends," the man said, smiling warmly.

"You're back," Sirius practically grumbled in Neala's direction. She inclined her head instead of saying anything, and he moved on like he always did out of habit. "Damn it, where is Izell? We need to talk."

Ash stifled herself for a moment to reply. "Kissing Jaromir, apparently!"

If anything, the Blood Prince's expression hooded further. "I knew she was wasting time," he muttered. "This is Soren. An ambassador, not a fighter." He stomped back out of the building with a growl in his throat.

"What an utter bucket of sunshine," Ash said dryly.

"Actually, madam, that's correct. I can be." Soren summoned a ball of light between his palms, which he molded like putty until it was vaguely bucket shaped. He earned a chuckle she hid by finishing off her meal.

Only minutes later, the door slammed open again. Sirius had a hawk perched on his fist. His scowl was gone, at least.

Soren made his light disappear and greeted him with a hearty, "Welcome back!" Sirius muttered uncharitably and tossed the hawk, who shapeshifted smoothly in midair, away from him.

When Sirius shifted, his massive animal form shredded clothing and left him naked on the transformation back into a man. The few rare vampire shapeshifters she'd met had the same problem. But the fae man who appeared before them obviously didn't, his whole self covered in modest brown leather.

"Theron?" Ash blurted.

"Ash?"

"What are you doing here?" they asked at the same time.

"Being a terrible Archfae. You?"

"Being a terrible Unseelie," she grumbled.

He took a closer look at her and tisked. "You know what that shit does to you."

"Ladies and gentlemen, meet the illustrious Archdruid Theron Shadestone, who refers to one of the six great healing herbs thusly." She stuck her nose in the air.

He held up his hand. "Now that we're on the subject, it *is* the worst, most pointless addition to the healing compendium. It doesn't get rid of pain or offer any comfort. It just redistributes the pain you take to cover your entire body within six hours of use." He prowled over to stand behind her chair, laying his palms on her shoulders.

"I'm fine," she grumbled.

"Don't start lying now. You must have five more hours before it all hits." His hands glowed faintly. After that exchange, Neala hoped he was channeling some healing magic through her. "Soren, by the way, I really did mean that we would get word to the Unseelie Queen for you. I'll fly a message to her myself if I have to."

Ash chewed on her lip thoughtfully. "What did you want to tell her?"

Soren perked up and explained the rules he was bound by. To go on Unseelie lands, he had to be invited by the ruler herself. It was hard to make allies if he couldn't talk to them.

"Why Unseelie specifically? Plenty of fae to make allies of over here," Neala asked. She smiled to herself when Sirius did a double take, staring at her from across the room.

"Certainly!" Soren said cheerfully. "But only Unseelie can visit Earth when midwinter comes and with it, the demonic hordes of Hell."

Silence passed between all of them for an extended moment as his words sank in. "Isn't the Unseelie Queen keeping her people distracted so they miss the date?" Neala asked. She couldn't really see how they would make good allies in that case when some, if not many, would fight to help the demons.

"Maybe so. But it's worth a discussion." Soren lifted his shoulder, his expression reading that it wouldn't be a big deal either way. Not like lives and hopes were in the balance depending on what he had to say.

Ash sat up, clearing her throat. "I wanted to discuss this with Izell present, but you all should know...I intend to go into Unseelie lands personally and see what is causing my sister trouble."

"Mind carrying a message to her?" Soren asked.

"Of course."

Cossette raised her hand as if they were in a schoolhouse. Soren smiled and gestured to her, likely mistaking her for a real child. "Most of us should go," she said, turning solemn, albino-red eyes toward Neala. "Especially you. You will change everything."

Chapter 18
Cedric

"What is that supposed to mean?" Neala asked in a hush.

Cossette lifted her shoulders with a sweet smile, clasping her hands under her chin. "I've seen you in the future! Isn't that cool?"

Next to him, Neala flexed her hands and breathed a frustrated sigh. Cedric played a subtle song with peaceful waves in the melody, hoping it would help her find some patience with the girl Ancient.

Cossette's attention shifted to Cedric. "She dies when the music stops," she told him solemnly.

His fingers slipped, missing a note with a discordant *twang* that drew more than one wince around the room. "Who does?" he asked. He could feel his heart beating all the way up to his ears.

"Who does what?" The little girl in her was back, smiling but...empty. It made the hair on his nape stand on end every time the transition happened. No one would explain why Cossette was Cossette to him, so he had to assume what terrors she'd been through to end up fractured into two uneven halves.

Ash held up a hand when he reached for the girl, ready to shake the answer out of her regardless. He needed more information than a vague warning!

"Don't," the Unseelie ordered. "Let Izell ask."

"I hope she comes back soon," Cossette said, punctuating the words with a giggle as she wandered from the room.

"Izell has been working with her," Ash told them in a hush.

Neala nodded in approval. She snaked an arm around Cedric, her gaze fixed on the doorway the girl had slipped through. Though she didn't seem worried, her eyes darted with rapid thoughts under a puckered brow. "So, in the last two weeks, what's happened?" she asked.

"Nothing," Sirius snarled.

She turned, as unamused as a granite statue. "Stop it." They stared each other down like a pair of wild animals. A growl rose in the other vampire's throat. "Korin isn't here to soothe your temper tantrums. Do I need to beat this one out of you instead?"

For a split second, Cedric thought Sirius would actually lunge for her, as his expression promised murder. Instead, the Blood Prince drew himself up from a threatening crouch and whirled around, storming outside again. Breathing a sigh of relief, Cedric strummed a single note to hang in the air like an audible question mark.

"Be right back," Soren murmured, following after him.

"If he were one of my druids, I'd have him inspected for rage fever," Theron muttered.

"That's just how he comes," Ash told him.

"Tell me more later," he said with a dismissive wave. "What *are* you doing here? You, Sorsha, and Keegan made it to Earth at midsummer when the Dark Eye exploded. Did they come back with you?" His tone held a kernel of hope.

She patted his hand. "Sorry, no. But I have plenty of messages from both of them just in case our paths crossed. To answer your question and loop around to Neala's as well, we're here for the Fell Keys. Izell intends to create a new Dark Eye before midwinter by using them. But we've had little luck with our endeavors. The Seelie King has a Fell Key somewhere in his safe-keeping, but he's not seeing anyone."

Theron rubbed his forehead. "You're telling me. I got called to fill Sorsha's spot so the Committee of Archfae can hear the people in his stead."

Neala nudged Cedric as they spoke, gesturing to them as they spoke intently. He shrugged. He was learning things but certainly felt like he was a fly on the wall.

"Izell is trying to find information in the Library of Faerie," Ash continued. "But apparently is also using it as a rendezvous with the last man I'd imagine her to take interest in."

Theron snickered. "Why's that?"

"Well, he's a vampire."

Neala cleared her throat, drawing their attention back to her. "Gods above," Ash blurted in a singularly un-Ash-like manner. "I'm so sorry. Theron's a good friend...and Sorsha's husband. Theron, this is Neala."

His jaw dropped. "Her mother?" He released Ash's shoulders, bowing formally to Neala and staying there for a prolonged moment.

Neala parted from Cedric, blinking rapidly. "Oh, do get up. My little girl married a giant like you, hmm." When Theron stood straight, they could almost see eye to eye, but Neala had the edge on him.

"Yes, ma'am. We've been together since our school days." He clasped his hands and kept his gaze averted from hers in respect. "Sorsha speaks highly of you."

"As she does of you, though I never got specifics from her except that you both have a family. I intended to meet them eventually, but I didn't expect to run into anyone on this trip," Neala said. This expedition was, after all, supposed to be business over pleasure. Yet here Cedric was, hoping they could have another side journey.

This was what Cedric had come here for. Family. He felt a surge of happiness when he realized she'd found it instead as Theron smiled and started naming children and grandchildren. Fae were not the most fertile species, so Cedric was impressed to hear a handful of names.

"Most of our family lives in Springhall. Maybe you could pay a visit?" Theron suggested brightly. "After you help Ash with whatever half-brained plan she's cooking up now."

"Hey," the Unseelie protested.

"I would love to." Neala was beaming. Another great word for her, Cedric thought. *Beaming.* His nimble fingers flew over the lute strings, weaving this moment into a new tune he played quietly, committing it to memory.

"My only regret is I need to stay here and help the Committee. Their heads would be too far up their rears without me," Theron sighed. "It's one thing to hear your mate complain about the Archfae. It's another to actually work with them."

"There's no one else who could do it instead?" Cedric asked.

The other man shook his head. "No one I would trust. The idea of the Committee hearing the people is mad anyway. Find me a stingier group."

He didn't know what to say, and a vibration at his waist saved him the necessity. "Excuse me," he said, stepping outside as well. There was no sign of Sirius or Soren, so he went around the side of the apartment and lifted the compact from his pocket. He still wasn't happy about his direct line to the Unseen Council being inside of a woman's makeup case, but it made sense as far as compact mirrors went.

The half-circle reflected his face back at him, glowing with a dim blue light. He touched the surface, watching in fascination as the mirror transitioned into someone else's face when the magic activated.

"*Hello, Cedric. Is this a good time?*" Sondus's voice echoed in his head while his lips moved on the other side of the mirror.

"I suppose?"

"*Word has reached us from the Unseelie palace at last.*" Cedric held his breath, knowing the others would devour this information. "*Queen Kalimea suffered an assassination attempt and called for a full lockdown of her city. Our operatives were able to find holes in the defenses to give us the message.*"

"The bad guys could figure that out too," Cedric murmured. What a way to turn a party into chaos.

Sondus nodded, a thoughtful frown pressing his lips thin. "*Have you been in contact with Princess Ashaela? What does she plan to do?*"

"She's going there personally. As are most of us," he said,

thinking of Cossette's words. Most of them had to, else someone important would die.

The spymaster's eyes lit up with stars. *"Then I have a mission for you. Are you ready to serve for the good of Faerie?"*

Cedric only hesitated when he realized how loaded that question was. He was expected to say yes before he knew what the task was. But he had big shoes to fill if he wanted to make it in his grandfather's organization, and here was the first step. "I'm ready," he answered.

"Outstanding. I am coordinating a group of drasonii *to head for the palace under the guise of joining the party. You and your friends will join them. We have the same goal as the Unseelie Queen: to keep her people occupied. That means you all must do everything in your power to help uncover these assassins before too many lose faith in her festivities."*

Cedric worried his bottom lip between his teeth. "If they're in lockdown, wouldn't they already think the party was over?" He knew he wouldn't stick around for that.

There was no hiding the bitterness in Sondus's tone. *"You'd be surprised what atrocities Unseelie can ignore."*

"All right..." Something about that felt strictly personal and off limits, so Cedric didn't probe further. "How are we to know where to meet with your people?"

Now the spymaster smiled in a brilliant flash of white. *"If I know Izell, I know which road she'll send you down. You'll be entering the city through the front gates."*

Cedric didn't doubt that he was right.

Chapter 19
Neala

Theron stayed until evening, sharing tale after tale of her children. Neala ate it all up and still ached to know more of their lives when he had to leave. He was, by far, the most open fae she'd met and even drew Ash into sharing some of her favorite stories as well. It so turned out that Sorsha, Keegan, Ash, and Theron formed a perfect unit in the eyes of the fae. Sorceress, Blade, Spellbreaker, and druid, capable of the most powerful geas, or group spells.

It was a shame he hadn't come across at midsummer like the others. But at least she could speak with him now and make plans to visit the rest of her adopted family before he left for the evening.

The other thing she'd learned weighed on her much more, even when she and Cedric retired to the roof to watch the sunset tinge the world in shades of orange and red. "Keegan and Ash have no children," she said aloud.

She'd interrupted him mid-tune, his brow furrowed with concentration as he wove the melody together and replayed problematic spots. "Yeah?" He spared her a quick glance.

"Seelie and Unseelie cannot have kids."

He shrugged. "Presumably so."

"Which means the royalty of this land will never have heirs," she continued. "Do you understand how unstable that leaves them?"

He finally stopped strumming and looked at her. "They've ruled for nearly three thousand years."

"But the moment either of them die, it will be chaos. And whoever tried to assassinate the Unseelie Queen knows this as well as we do." He'd already shared Sondus's message. Their excuse for coming up here was to intercept Izell and Jaromir the moment they stepped into sight, except Neala had just wanted to continue their little tradition. She enjoyed these moments of stillness and sharing them with Cedric.

Troubled thoughts flashed over his expression. "Good thing we're going there personally." He resumed his playing for a few bars before making a sound of disgust and placing his lute aside. "Can't we talk about something else?"

"Is there something on your mind?" She had to assume his thoughts were like his playing. If he couldn't find the right song to fit the situation, there was some mental block there to overcome.

"Well, yes..." When he met her eye, she knew. It was about their relationship. Her nerves tied up in instant, complicated knots. Was she doing enough to keep him close? She'd barely dated, even before finding her first lifemate. With a face like hers and lack of voice, she'd never assumed to hold a man's attention for long. Would Cedric, who'd never seemed to lack for female admirers in Adrun, decide to cut her loose now?

"I talked to Lady Iridia before we left. About us," he said. She couldn't help her skeptical look. "I know, why would I talk to her when you're right here? She's seen things and is almost as old as Izell, so I thought maybe she'd seen a fae and vampire pairing before."

Some of the tension left her as she realized he wasn't about to call things off between them. "Has she?"

"Well, no..." he shrugged. "But she suggested the theory of how we could bond."

"With your heart's song," she interrupted. "I already know. We almost bonded that night you sang your heart's song to me."

He paused, tilting his head like he raked through his memories for that moment. "That's right. *I* almost bonded myself to *you*. So, I guess I wanted you to know that it's possible. And that... well, she described it in music terms. But it's not unheard of to meet a second person who harmonizes with you."

He began to tug at his nimble fingers as he continued with an anxious laugh. "What am I saying? This is going way too fast. I just didn't want to hold on to the knowledge without sharing it with you."

She pressed his hands between hers before she could echo his nerves. "Then there's something I should tell you, in the spirit of sharing knowledge."

Leaning in, she could count the stars that glittered on the apples of his cheeks like freckles. "I like knowing things." He held his breath as she searched for the best way to phrase it.

Which she was never good at, if her short time in various courts was anything to go by. She opted to tell him straight. "When the alchemists were reviewing the side effects of the second song potion, there was one fact that swayed me into taking it." The moment was clear in her head, when her whole being had swayed to the decision with Cedric's name in mind. "It was that a mate could sing for me and still fulfill the magic of the potion. I would still shoulder the magic and the burden of its requirements, but simply put, a mate could save my voice should I ever have need of it."

He spoke in a hush. "I don't think you'll ever *need* that. Your new voice is beautiful, and you sing so well..."

"But I didn't know it would turn up this way. The only thing I know is that I'd never be able to look at it the right way. Then I look at you. You are a performer. You were practically born with that lute in your hands." Hands she now held, rubbing the calluses built up from years of plucking those strings. "If we end up mates someday and anything ever happens to me, you can save me from silence."

Her swallow was a dry click. Memories pressed in, wanting to be felt anew. The dark silence of her thousand-year rest, when she was aware and frozen for far too much of it. Unable to speak, unable to *scream*. She would rather die than return to a reality where she couldn't be heard.

How could she ever explain this fear to Cedric, who'd never lived a day with that kind of silence?

"It would be an honor to help if you ever needed it—" Neala cut him off for the rest, swallowing the "which I doubt" that he spoke, muffled, against her lips. She had a fistful of his bright shirt, drawing him firmly into her as their mouths pressed and tongues jockeyed to the backdrop of the fading sun.

"Hey!" The sharp tone interrupted them. Cedric drew back with a startled blush, while Neala flashed an irritated look downward.

Izell was on the ground, her glamor up to conceal the way her tail flicked around while she had her hands poised on hips. Jaromir stood by her side, laden with a stack of books up to his chin. "You two want to do that privately?" Izell called up to them.

"Depends. Do you consider doing the same thing in a library private?" Neala called back.

Jaromir's shoulders hitched up, struggling mightily to keep from laughing. "Don't you get smart with me now that you have a voice." Izell sighed, heading into the apartment.

She glanced to Cedric. "She backed down fast."

"Well, yeah," he said, flashing a grin. "She can't lie and say you're wrong!"

"So, you have learned a few things while you were gone," Izell remarked once she heard everything from Neala and Cedric. She smoothed out the piece of paper where Sondus had written the whereabouts of the five remaining Fell Keys. "Hmm. More or less what I expected." They all sat around a table, which was cramped quarters in the small space of the apartment even without Sirius and Soren.

"Do you know the names?" Neala asked. There were three specific names or locations, as well as the Seelie King and Unseelie Queen marked as possessing one of the precious rings.

"I don't know every fae in Faerie. But don't you worry, I know what needs to happen next." Izell folded up the paper crisply and slid it off the table. "But first, we need Sirius."

Neala wasn't the only one rolling her eyes. Ash, who was paler than usual as the pain of telling the truth caught up with her, uttered a scoff. "He's out of control," she said, wincing as she added another prick of discomfort to what was building up.

"Which is precisely why he needs to go with you," Izell said, turning to Cossette. She pinched the girl Ancient's arm, drawing her out of her daydreaming. "When will he return?"

A little pain seemed to do Cossette good, as she immediately put on a serious expression. "Not too long. He's talking with Soren right now." Her gaze flickered, and she covered her mouth to hide a gasp. "I see what's coming," she whispered between her fingers.

"You must be specific. Future sight is more than useless without context—it's dangerous," Izell lectured.

Cossette drew herself up like a chastened child. "Sorry, Miss Izell. I see what's coming for Prince Sirius. I would tell you what it is, but..."

The man in question walked in a moment later, a letter held carefully between his fingers. Gone was his feral anger, leaving a slump to his shoulders as he spotted the meeting happening in the next room. "Lock the door. Unless Soren is coming?" Izell called.

He locked the door, drawing up a chair to wedge between Jaromir and Neala. "Just me," he sighed, placing the letter before him. "And Soren's words for the Unseelie Queen."

"You are leaving. It's time to pack your things," Izell told him. Her claws drummed on the table as she considered the faces around it. "I require Jaromir and Cossette."

Now it was Neala's turn to speak up. "That leaves us without a doctor should we encounter danger."

"I have no magic to heal you," Jaromir said, looking down at his hands. "The Seelie King possesses the Fell Key I need."

"There is more to the healing art than your magic." She could feel her temper rising with her voice. She'd tried to hammer this idea home in his brain ever since he refused to get out of bed upon discovering the absence of his Gift.

He wore his disability around his neck like a yoke. When he turned a pained look her way, she realized that he hadn't shrugged off that burden yet. "The Gift was the only magic I had. I would be less of a burden here, assisting Izell," he said.

Crossing her arms, she was glad of Sirius between them, a solid wall of muscle keeping her from shaking sense into him. "Then you are hiding behind excuses. That is not the Jaromir I know." Though she stared, he refused to glance up from his hands.

"The Jaromir you know just needs a little support. Haven't I given you enough of that? Or need I remind you how many times I've stood by you when you struggled." He still spoke to his fingers, the same ones that'd healed countless wounds and saved even more lives.

"It's not personal," she sighed. "You came along with us as our doctor. Now, you're refusing to fill that role."

"Leave the man alone. He's obviously made up his mind," Sirius said. "If you need it, I'll stich you closed. Maybe I'll put him out of a job."

Izell had her chin propped on a hand. "By all means, keep bickering. But you're leaving at dawn." Ash punctuated the elder fae's words with a nod of her own, worry for her sister etched into every line of her body.

Neala scoffed, taking a moment to elbow Sirius. "I'd trust you to make a needlepoint before you come anywhere near me with a needle and thread." She supposed they would be okay without Jaromir. What could go wrong?

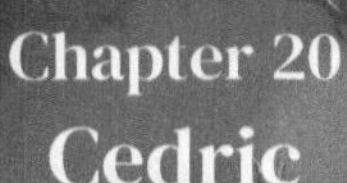

Chapter 20
Cedric

Izell showed them what happened to a portal destined to go to a dead zone in the sheltered back yard of their apartment block. The perfect circle of her portal showed a hint of dark gray stone and glowing rune work before it all shimmered like a heat mirage and the portal itself fractured with spider web cracks. It fell to the ground in fine, powder-like clumps before Izell dispelled it.

"That is why you don't accept a portal from someone you can't trust. You'd be turned to dust, not safely to your destination." Izell brushed portal remnants from her hands. *Point taken,* Cedric thought with a shudder.

They'd rented elks for the journey, further calling on Izell's remaining wealth. Someone had invested her assets instead of taking them, sure that she would return. Cedric wondered who it was, because Izell wasn't telling.

He turned to rub his elk's snout. In it, he saw a cousin to the graceful, dark elk which served as mounts in Adrun. Those had larger racks, each point used to string lanterns or magical light to illuminate the path ahead in the darkness of his homeland. The elk he'd received had a coat of ginger fur reminiscent of Neala's hair, built with a thick barrel chest and the youthful beginnings of a rack still covered in fuzzy velvet.

Its liquid brown eyes still held the intelligence he was used to seeing in these beasts. It lipped his fingers for treats while Izell made portal after portal in front of them, each failing like the first and coating her scaled arms in dust. With each, she muttered a distance. At "one hundred twenty miles," her magic finally held. On the other side showed a dense forest of emerald green and a brick-paved path slicing into the horizon.

"That's a seriously big dead zone," Cedric commented.

"It's not emergency protocol or anything," Ash said with her usual sarcasm. Without whatever herb she'd eaten yesterday, she was back to Unseelie speak.

"Why that many miles? Why not a round hundred?" he asked curiously. He mounted his elk alongside the rest of the group, Neala, Sirius, and Ash. His lute case bounced off his back as he settled in the saddle. For once, he figured it would be unwise to play as they traveled—plus, there would be no magic to make his lute special. He worried the dead zone would render it breakable.

Izell shrugged. "Why not?"

Neala patted her elk's neck. "This thing is no horse. I imagine we will reach our destination in two days."

Izell stepped away from the portal with a grin splitting her face. "Should we tell them?" Cossette asked her, waiting alongside Jaromir to see them off.

"Specifics, dear," the fae said.

"Should we tell them how fast an elk runs?"

"Some things are better discovered." Izell ruffled the girl Ancient's snowy hair, only to be pushed away by a little hand.

"I'm not a little girl," Cossette grumbled. "You're supposed to help me."

"And I will. But first..." She raised a hand in farewell. "Don't dally for too long. It's Kalimea. She's probably fine."

Ash waved to her briefly, clucking to her mount. The elk leapt through the portal so smoothly it looked like its hooves barely graced the ground. One by one, they followed her, with Cedric bringing up the rear and clutching the reins when his own mount skipped along. Now *that* he wasn't used to, seeing as the elks he knew were endurance beasts that could put a horse to shame.

He wondered if the elks they rode would put a horse to shame in a different way. But before they could gallop away, Ash's mount halted as she spoke crossly to a trio of fae on their own elks. The leader of that band flashed something silver in his palm.

"We sure need minstrels," Ash was saying. "If Sondus is going to send men, why send performers?"

Now that Cedric looked more closely, he saw instruments strapped to the saddles of all three newcomers. The leader of the group was a dark-skinned terran fae with a warm smile despite the reception he was receiving. "We're just following orders. You need eyes and ears you can trust." He gestured to his two men, both Unseelie, who quickly nodded in agreement.

"Humph." She turned her scowl toward Cedric, her mental voice piercing into his head. *"I don't task you with keeping an eye on them."*

Since he couldn't respond in kind, he flashed a thumbs up. Ash turned back to the head minstrel. "If you can keep up, which I doubt, you may come."

He bowed in the saddle. "Thank you, Princess. I am..." He drifted off as Ash set her mount's nose to the north and set off at a gallop. The rest of them fumbled to do the same.

Cedric realized he could see the dead zone mere minutes into the hard pace Ash set. The road split a massive tree in two, its insides hollowed out with an arch that was shrouded in darkness, like the entrance to a cave. The moment his elk's hooves cleared that space, they entered a stretch of road shaded by a towering grove and Cedric felt something missing. He rubbed at his chest and took a closer look at his arms. The pinpricks of light from his astral fae side were dull, winking out to leave him nearly as starless as Sondus.

A few yards ahead, Ash leaned over the neck of her mount, her fiery wings leaving behind a comet trail of burning embers. The wind stung Cedric's eyes to watering, so he gave up on the idea of socializing with the new minstrels as they, thankfully, kept up as well as the rest of the group.

Their first break came when Ash stopped to give her elk a drink before a river that spanned as far as a lake. She hopped off her mount to stretch, her back to their newcomers as she spoke quietly with Sirius.

When Cedric went to dismount, his legs spasmed into one big cramp. Muttering a litany of curses, he stumbled as his elk walked out of supporting range, nearly falling until strong hands lifted him back into equilibrium. "Easy now," Neala said. He breathed easier to hear her voice even in this dead zone, unchanged.

Looking up at her, he noticed something else was amiss. Her face was...different. While she walked him through some basic stretches, he kept stealing glances at her to see what it was.

"Neala..."

"Hmm?"

Gods above, he was about to put his foot straight into his mouth asking this. "Have you been hiding some of your...marks?"

She had scars, which he respected. She was a warrior and the strongest woman he knew. His thumb skimmed a scar on her neck that he swore he'd never seen. Recoiling, Neala touched it too.

"I am not too unsightly, am I?" she asked, searching his face.

His heart leapt to his throat. That she would immediately jump to *unsightly* meant she was hyper aware of the scars to hide them. Glancing around, he saw everyone else was distracted in their own conversations. He closed the gap between himself and Neala, leaning up to place a kiss on the single scar she'd never hid. The one that tugged at the side of her mouth.

"Each one's a story," he said. "How did you get this one?"

She rested her fingertips on it, her gaze distant. "A Fell claw grazed me. I wouldn't be here if it'd been even a little more accurate," she said. "It might be ugly, but it reminds me of how lucky I am to be alive."

"Then it's not ugly," he murmured. "What about this one?" A knot on her neck was from an unwanted bite by another vampire. Crossing her throat was the slash of a sword, a fatal strike, except she'd been saved by Jaromir's Gift. His fingertips were dangerously close to dipping below her collar as she spoke, wanting to see every mark and know the full story.

"You're not ugly at all, and neither are your scars. Gods above, Neala. How many times have you cheated death?" He caressed her jaw, not caring anymore if the others saw their moment together.

Her red gaze captured his, soft as shimmering rubies. "You really mean it."

"Why would I lie?" And of course, he could see why she'd expect it. How many people had been disappointed by this strong woman in place of a soft-spoken lady? "I wish more people would look under the surface and see you, the person who faced down Fell, instead of judging you for what it cost."

With a husky laugh, she swept him off his feet, her lips warm and insistent upon his. Their mouths tangled in a surge of electric heat, his toes curling as they dangled off the ground.

He nearly forgot where they were. However, Sirius certainly didn't let it slip his mind for long as the Blood Prince walked by and said, "Get a room, you two."

Neala flashed a gesture after him as she let Cedric slide down her front. He was dizzy for another reason, holding on to her until it passed.

"I saw that," Sirius said over his shoulder.

She did it again for good measure.

<h1 style="text-align:center">Chapter 21
Cedric</h1>

They went one at a time over the bridge, leaving Cedric between Neala and the leader of the minstrels, whom he learned was named Miles Hazelwind, a second generation *drasonii* with a delicate flute that barely seemed to fit in the man's big mitts. They walked their mounts across the bridge until Ash stopped the group halfway through, talking to someone in their way.

"Lord Sondus wanted us to assist in any way we can," Miles said. "I understand that you're not from Faerie originally. There are a lot of quirks to learn. Such as the Bridge Keeper." He jerked his chin forward.

"Let me guess, a minor fae of some sort?" Sirius asked, leaning around Neala.

"If only. She's a ghost. If you don't barter a treasure to her, she pitches you into the river. And as you can see, it is not where you want to be." The water was edged in white foam, rolling in a massive sheet beneath them. As if to prove his point, a full tree passed under the bridge, roots and all.

Miles's deep voice was perfect for the story, Cedric noted. He could tell a fellow storyteller and singer just from their cadence, something the other bard had in abundance.

"Legend says she was an Unseelie maid who would bring the day's washings to the shores of this very river. She dreamed of a

128

better life for herself than washing and hemming. That day came when the lord's son caught a glimpse of her bending over to clean a mess on the floor." He paused for effect, glancing past Cedric, who was his audience of one. He sighed.

"Well, their whirlwind romance led to a proposal. The impropriety was not lost on his family. His mother was said to be the one to inquire about the removal, but of course, when she heard what happened, she fanned herself to keep from fainting. The fair maid was drowned in this very river. Now, her ghost remains, while the settlement she came from is long lost to history. She asks for fine things to dress herself up into the lady she should've become on her wedding day."

"I didn't think fae could be ghosts," Cedric said in a hush.

"It is exceedingly rare. Fae ghosts still have the magic they wielded in life. Most can be soothed to return to their elements, but not the Bridge Keeper. At least not yet." Miles shrugged. Their line moved forward again, but all Cedric saw of the ghost was her fading profile as she held up a glimmering necklace to the sunlight. She was made of cobwebs and the tracery of a pencil around her edges.

Not fancying a dip in the river, he said nothing but felt goosebumps wander up the back of his neck when he turned away from the apparition. He breathed more freely when they were back on solid ground and mounting up for the next stretch of their journey.

Ash preserved their elks by leading them at a more controlled pace. "Anything else we need to know about the road ahead?" Cedric asked Miles as he drew his elk alongside the other fae's.

Considering, he answered, "You are aware we are headed for the Unseelie capital, Ironhold?"

Cedric shook his head. Fae were terribly allergic to the touch of iron, so to hear anything in Faerie named after it was a shock. "Unseelie are contrary in every way," Miles continued. "Just like we travel upon Plunder Road, one of the main trade routes this side of Faerie."

"Should we expect to be plundered?"

"I think it's more suspicious that we haven't seen any other travelers or caravans. Despite the dead zone, Ironhold is still a major consumer of goods." Now that Miles mentioned it, Cedric craned his neck just to view a long expanse of open road as the tree line receded into rolling plains dotted with farms and grazing animals.

"There has to be an explanation. Maybe the dead zone is scaring everyone away? Especially since it's been up for what, a week?" Cedric asked.

"Indeed. Maybe I'm just overreacting." The other fae shrugged. By the time sunset approached, he had his flute out and Cedric his lute, the two of them serenading the great disc as it vanished for the evening. Neala caught the tune and sang.

"Did that satisfy the magic?" he asked her once they were done, their joyous song drifting into the night.

She smiled and nodded. "I'm good for another day."

"What a relief." Maybe she hadn't considered it as hard as he did, but he was still nearly limp with gratitude that her second song potion didn't falter in the dead zone.

Actually, that was the feeling of all his muscles protesting their prolonged journey. It was a relief when Ash finally stopped, her head on a swivel before her shoulders dropped. "How can I rest when my sister needs me?" she sighed even as she dismounted.

"It is better to tackle that tomorrow, when we're fresh," Neala said. She and Sirius drew their group to a hollow surrounded by thick, thorny bushes. They pitched their tents while Cedric watched the minstrels' expressions at the modern fabrics and design of the camping items they'd taken from Earth.

"Seems they're better prepared than us," Miles commented, setting out a bedroll for himself as the two Unseelie did the same.

Cedric set up their fire pit, glad he wasn't the only one to sit by it once Ash lit it with a flap of her wings. Neala lifted him easily to place a towel underneath him. "Hey!" He laughed, settling into her side. All seven of their little group formed a semi-circle around the crackling fire.

Ash remained for a terse drawing of straws for who took

watch first. "We won't be leaving at first light," she said before shutting herself into her tent.

"Something tells me she'd prefer to make this trip without any of us," Sirius remarked. He flicked chips of bark into the fire, the planes of his face sharpening by the contrast of firelight.

"Too bad," Neala said. "The girl said we are important to whatever happens next."

Next to them, Miles perked with obvious interest. "As much warning as she gave, though," Cedric complained.

She kissed the side of his temple. "It was enough."

He wondered if anyone else around the fire could hear his heartbeat as it stuttered in his chest. The gentleness was back in Neala's gaze. Somehow, he'd stripped away the last piece of her armor, because that was absolute trust written on her face.

They whiled away some time around the fire as the night deepened to a purple twilight, its rich tapestry sprinkled with stars like an astral fae's skin. The first thing Miles asked him was, "Who did your audition?"

Cedric's face screwed up immediately as he tried to remember his name. "Some terran fae. Um. Foxglove?"

Miles elbowed the Unseelie bard next to him, both of them bursting out laughing. "Trevan Foxglove! The bane of our apprenticeships."

"Too important for us lowly, second-generation *drasonii*," the other bard agreed.

Cedric relaxed again, glad to hear he wasn't the only person with a problem with Trevan. "We tried to get him assassinated," Miles said, which caused Cedric to sputter in surprise.

"What? How?"

Miles shrugged casually. "Well, the boys and I put all our money together to hire an assassin. Anything but attending yet another one of his daily lectures or to be criticized about daring to change anything about a classical piece written thousands of years ago."

Cedric propped his fist on his hand, fascinated. This couldn't have gone well. Miles continued, "Lord Sondus heard about it, of course. I guess when you start asking newcomers if they're from the assassin's guild, word gets around."

"As it would." Neala chuckled and shook her head.

"So, he decided to promote Trevan from a teaching position. He now manages shows for a few symphonies over in Winter-haven. He gets all the classical music that he wants and is on call for emergency auditions, I guess." Miles punctuated it with a roll of his eyes. "And Lord Sondus added to our pooled marks so we could throw a manor-wide party instead."

"Sounds like everyone won," Cedric said. Well, except for him. He'd gotten to meet the guy as well.

"I'd say so! He didn't die," Miles laughed.

"I have a story for you, too." It was hard not to be distracted by the warm thrum of Neala's voice as she and Sirius recounted one of their many battles together. Cedric knew the others were fellow bards, as all of them ate up the words like the feast they were. Both Blood Princes were walking ballads waiting to be composed.

In a quiet moment, he reached out to stroke Neala's jaw, scar and all. She turned a look on him so hot he nearly melted on the spot. It was the moment he'd been waiting for, the rare bloom of a woman like Neala. And she was about to show that untamed side to him. He barely noticed that they were alone until he heard the zipper of Sirius's tent. The only open eyes around them belonged to one of the Unseelie minstrels who'd drawn first watch.

"Let's get some more privacy," he whispered, drawing her back toward their own tent. In the privacy of the small space, he realized what he'd accepted without question. Neala hadn't pitched a fourth tent for him. And he'd just assumed they would be staying in hers together.

The moment they were in semi-privacy, she had her hands fisted in his tunic, drawing it over his head alongside the foppish hat he'd held for most of their journey when it was in danger of flying off in the breeze.

She pressed kisses over his lean chest, her eyes like red flame in the dark as her tongue explored the hairless dips of his body, courtesy of his fae side. His excitement only grew as more of their clothes were shed in haphazard piles.

She was down to her underclothes when it happened. A sound in the night just louder than the crackle of their campfire. A gurgling cry of agony.

Both of them froze. Neala's gaze whipped to the side just in time for the fire to snuff out with a final hiss.

"Stay here," she whispered, reaching for her sword.

Chapter 22
Neala

Neala's vampire speed had her out of the tent, low to the ground as she sized up what she was up against. The wan light of nighttime was no handicap as her eyes adjusted to make out a grayscale understanding of her surroundings. Coiled up in the middle of their encampment was the largest snake she'd ever seen. Considering she'd been to the pits of the world hunting Fell, that was saying a lot.

Its fangs were a silver flash as she leapt to the side. One grazed the side of her cheek, its hiss caressing her ear in a venomous whisper. She ignited Keegan's sword, Faebane, with a flick of her wrist. Most beasts shied away from fire in her experience, but this one whipped its tail around to trip her.

She cursed to herself as the air left her lungs on impact. It was *smart.*

Rolling out of the way of its next strike, she released a wordless holler as she drew upright. Sirius was a sensitive sleeper; he'd soon join her to take this thing down. In the meantime, she struck in a flaming arc, breaking inky black scales in the snake's midsection.

Ash's form leapt into sight as she thrust twin daggers into the back of the creature's head. Its whole body went limp, head canted to the side with its fangs leaking clear venom like a salivating wolf.

"Thanks," Neala said, giving Faebane a shake. Its flaming surface extinguished, leaving her to see by the light of the fae's wings.

"I've certainly seen snakes like this before," Ash replied with a heavy dose of cynicism.

Neala knelt beside it, drawing back the membrane over one of its eyes, which was a black pit with no sign of a reptilian slit pupil. When Sirius released a string of curses, she said up to him, "You're late."

"I tried to get dressed," he grumbled. "Unlike you."

"Did the Fell ever wait for you to get *dressed?*" she scoffed.

"We were all active at the same time. Night." He frowned up at the heavens. "You have to admit, having a human sleep schedule again is strange."

"Can't you two chit-chat later?" Ash sighed. She pointed out the blood seeping from the snake's mortal wound, a slow drip of darkness.

Neala took a reluctant lungful of the liquid's scent, nearly gagging. "Speaking of Fell," she said.

"Smells just like one," Sirius agreed, his nose wrinkling in distaste.

Ash shook her head slowly in denial. "Does it make sense that it's Fell when there are no Fell?"

"Jazrach was able to corrupt more fae into Fell. It's possible," Sirius said.

"But Jazrach is dead." Neala straightened up as she spoke, shaking her head. "Another demon, maybe." But how could there be a demon in Faerie? She mulled it over as she went to check on the Unseelie who was supposed to be keeping watch.

Faerie, as she understood it, was demon-proof. The same veil that kept demons and angels from entering Earth wove a dome over the land of the fae. Everything she'd seen so far suggested that fae disliked both sides for the way they'd made their mark on fae culture. But they were on Unseelie lands, and each Unseelie still held a kernel of demonic magic.

Maybe it was possible for an Unseelie to foster that seed of magic and become a demon themselves. Troubled by the thought, she spotted the outline of the watchman lying prone on his side. The blood scent hanging over him was ripe. She crouched down, fingertips finding a faint pulse in his neck.

"Is he okay?"

She jumped before realizing the squeaky little voice belonged to Cedric. He emerged from the underbrush as a small bird with a fabulous plume of tail feathers. A *superior* lyrebird, as she recalled. "He's still alive, chicken," she said. "Why don't you shift back? The danger has passed, but something less imposing can still snap you up."

"Well, I was naked anyway..."

Her lips curled in private amusement, though it faded as she carefully turned the Unseelie onto his back. Blood leaked from twin punctures in his side, and with a snake that large, she worried she'd find broken ribs with any prodding. She cursed under her breath—the man was awake, his face purpling as he struggled for breath.

"You're going to be okay," she told him. "We're going to get you help."

In his immobilized state, his gaze was fixed at a point over her shoulder as she arranged his limbs. Her only warning was a bulging of his eyes and a huff.

It happened in a flash. Her limbs jerked and blood blossomed on her shift from two punctures right under her collarbone. Cedric released a bird shriek of alarm, dodging as the second snake snapped at him, its mouth wide enough to make him one bite. The lyrebird continued to scream in horror.

Shouts echoed from the camp. Neala's next breath was wet, and numbness traveled rapidly down her arms. She struggled to stand, her sluggish hand flicking Faebane back to life as she stared down the beast baring its bloodied fangs with a hiss. The venom worked much faster than she expected, and she dropped the sword the next moment, her fingers jerking as they froze.

She was a vampire, but her healing wasn't helping as spots gathered in her eyes from a lack of air. Thankfully, she had something the fallen Unseelie didn't.

Lashing out with her mind, she captured the snake's massive, struggling form and held it off the ground. It snapped at air as it tried in vain to reach her. Decades of speaking with just her mind had honed her psychic abilities so that they continued even as her muscles locked painfully to her bones, even as she tottered and struggled for air.

In a flash of metal, the snake's struggles ended and Sirius's deep voice blurred in her ears. She released the corpse from the hold of her mind. Rough hands grasped her shoulders, holding her steady. He called for Ash, or just for help, because soon, several pairs of hands were carrying her until she was laid out by the rekindled fire. Seconds or hours later, blurs of motion laid someone else out with her.

Someone sat by her side, stroking the hair from her face as others spoke somewhere out of her line of sight.

"...not healing," came Sirius's voice.

"Suck the venom out?" asked the lead minstrel, Miles.

"That's a myth," the Blood Prince snapped.

Why aren't I healing, though? Neala asked herself. Either the dark spots enveloped her vision, or her eyes closed, too heavy as the venom circulated and brought its clenching fire to every fiber of her body.

Ash's voice slipped in on the edge of her hearing. "...move now."

She slipped away to the dulcet tones of Ash and Sirius bickering like old women.

Chapter 23
Cedric

"I'm telling you, it won't be faster to get to Ironhold." Ash stood with her arms crossed.

Sirius was inches from her face, snarling like a wildcat. "There's no *magic* in Ironhold. There's no magic anywhere but back where we came!"

Cedric exchanged a glance with Miles from where he knelt by Neala's side. His heart still pattered in his chest at three times its norm, a side effect of nearly getting eaten while in his timid bird form. The lead minstrel cleared his throat and spoke up over both of them, "I believe we should follow the Princess's judgment while in her lands."

Both of them flinched when Sirius's furious expression panned their way. "I didn't ask for your opinion!"

Ash stuffed a handkerchief under her nose. "When we get there, I can have Kalimea lift the dead zone. Or get an artifact to make a healer immune to the spell's effect. It'll be faster." The cloth came away stained with the sign of her telling the truth.

The horizon was beginning to brighten with the sun peeking over the horizon. Cedric smothered a yawn as the fuming Blood Prince stared her down. Anxiety bloomed in him for a new reason. Neala struggled for air even unconscious, propped on her side as they all cobbled their limited first aid knowledge to keep her and the Unseelie bard alive.

"It gets better as you wait," Ash sneered, ducking backward to miss a right hook from Sirius. "Your anger is *really* helping right now."

"Keep talking, you flaming bitch," Sirius snapped.

Cedric longed for the magic of his lute; even a subtle suggestion of inner peace might be able to curtain Sirius's rage. He didn't dare get in the middle of it as he called out from a safe distance, "She's not taunting you! Remember that she's Unseelie!"

"Oh, I'm not taunting him?" Ash smiled as she dodged another strike, making Sirius look clumsy even though he swung faster than Cedric's eyes could track. "This rage is the problem with you, Sirius, isn't it? No wonder Neala didn't mention beating it out of you." The moment he nearly connected his fist to her jaw, she caught it, her wings flaring brighter.

The next moment, Sirius was on the ground. "It sure doesn't endanger all of us, going off like a loose cannon. Calm yourself. Or I won't do it for you," Ash continued. She planted her boot on his chest, her expression promising much worse if he struggled. In that moment, Cedric realized that Ash really had it in her to be an Unseelie princess.

To his surprise, Sirius broke eye contact first with a chuff of air. He lay there even when Ash took her foot off of him. "You've proven your point," he murmured. "I still think you are wrong."

"A matter of opinion, no?"

He jumped to his feet, ignoring her proffered hand. "Neala is as close as a sister," he muttered over Ash. "If her injuries did not fire up my blood, I would be dead." Brushing past her, he moved to break down his tent, missing how she watched with a softer, more understanding expression.

It was like a spell had broken over all of them, and they launched into motion to assist. Cedric sighed as he folded up the clothes he and Neala had discarded earlier. Full of nerves, he approached Ash and offered her the pile, gesturing to his lady's unconscious form. She took them with a nod, and he noticed Neala was more modestly dressed by the time they were ready to move on.

"I will ride with Daron," Miles said, indicating the fallen bard.

No one stopped Sirius when he placed Neala carefully over his elk's back.

The ride toward Ironhold was slower than yesterday's dash. Ash rode up front, her wings spread to illuminate their immediate area and potentially dissuade any other beasts before the sun rose in full. Cedric held up the rear. His nervous energy went into the reins he held, twisting and rubbing at the slack as his gaze darted toward any errant rustle. A crow's caw had him nearly jumping out of the saddle.

He just felt so helpless, watching Neala's boots sway over the side of Sirius's saddle. The Blood Prince handled his steed like a professional, shifting both of their weights with every twist and turn in the road. Cedric was just...a chicken now, in the less-than-joking sense. He'd distracted her by playing around as a lyrebird rather than helping her fight.

This was his fault. He wasn't able to help her when she needed him most, and now, she had a demonic snake's venom in her bloodstream. What kind of lifemate did that make him?

And what kind of Unseen Council operative was he when he barely looked at the man riding with Miles? He shot a guilty look toward the other pair riding together. The Unseelie bard Daron was even less equipped to handle the venom than Neala with her vampire healing. If said mending would kick in while she was unconscious.

He felt like dead weight tugged along throughout their early morning journey. They only paused for a break at the peak of a hill as Miles's elk started tossing its head and bellowing. "We need a change of beasts," Sirius muttered. "Princess, why aren't there any villages or townships along this road?"

Ash stood with her hands on her hips, gazing into the distance. Following where she looked, Cedric saw the road snake along for countless miles before disappearing into a valley ahead. In the far distance was a heat mirage of dark spires and high walls. *Ironhold,* he hoped.

"There aren't, of course," Ash responded acidly. "A lockdown in Ironhold doesn't mean a lockdown of the immediate area too. Do you see that?" She pointed straight ahead.

Cedric squinted but didn't see anything amiss until she came around and personally pointed it out to everyone. A shimmer of magic in a long line crossing the valley. "A bridge?" he asked, to her nod. "How is it possible to have an illusion in a dead zone?"

"A dead zone isn't a military defense. It doesn't hide civilians and removes easy access to the capital." She scrubbed at her face. "Kalimea has used it before."

"You mean...she hasn't?"

She shot him an annoyed look.

He put his hands up. "Sorry, you're hard to understand sometimes," he mumbled.

With a sigh, she plugged her nose with her handkerchief and said, "She's never used the dead zone before. The fact that it's up suggests to me that an advisor or some other fop placed it up in her stead."

He repeated her words to himself. "So, you think she's been overthrown?"

A flash of horror passed over her expression at the suggestion. "No! I think she's been hurt. An assassination *attempt*, a lockdown, and an ending to her big extended birthday celebration. That's not Kalimea. She wouldn't sign off on any of that unless she had to."

She peeled the delicate fabric from her nose and tossed it aside with a sound of disgust. He felt like he needed to say something. "Ash, hey. I'm sorry...you can't even tell the truth without hurting yourself." His words felt small and lame as her burning eyes narrowed. "It just seems unfair."

A smirk twisted half her face. "Am I your first Unseelie friend?"

"Well...yeah," he admitted.

"Isn't it a shame I'm not a normal Unseelie?" she asked over her shoulder as she went to check on their elks.

What's that supposed to mean? he thought. Drifting over to Neala's side, he knelt down and brushed some of her hair away from her face. Her eyes flashed open.

"Neala? How do you feel?" he asked, hopeful. He soon realized he could hear her sucking in air raggedly. Smile dimming, he watched her with the same sinking feeling as before.

Sirius came around to retrieve Neala for the next stretch of their trip. "We're trading elks to share the burden. You'll be riding that one." He hitched a thumb to the elk Miles and Daron had shared. As if noticing their attention, it jerked its head with an ornery cry.

"Great," he said halfheartedly.

Minutes into them resuming the journey, he knew for a fact that this elk was done with them all. He stroked its neck, murmuring praise. The elk from Adrun were always smarter than they seemed. Maybe this one would be the same way and understand how important it was.

He wasn't tossed from its back, at least. They gained momentum down the steeper slope heading into the valley, losing sight of Ironhold at the bottom. A sigh left his lips. He'd expected the city to be closer, with how Ash had championed it. It truly felt like they were going the longest possible way there.

"Cedric?"

He nearly fell from the saddle, much to the annoyance of his elk, who shot him a dirty look over its shoulder. He apologized while also rubbing goosebumps off of his arms. Neala's sudden voice in his head was more unexpected than anything. Now he just had to reply in kind, with her still paralyzed and riding several lengths away on Sirius's mount.

Mustering up his mental energy, he pushed back the words, *"I hear you."*

Her reply was as timely and smooth as conversation. *"Not for much longer."*

"Stars above. The potion!" he exclaimed in horror. The second song potion, which required one small thing from her to maintain. The same task she couldn't complete while her muscles were locked down and she struggled to breathe.

Her reality sank in with the silence that followed. Even if they reached Ironhold before the end of the day, they still either needed to find a healer with an artifact that allowed them to continue using magic or Ash had to take down the dead zone, which promised to be a political nightmare if it came from anyone other than her sister.

It was a long shot with a toy bow, he thought.

"It'll be okay. We'll get you there," he said, just to realize she wasn't listening. Her mental presence was gone. Unconscious again?

They chased the sun across the sky, their mounts progressively slowing as exhaustion won over endurance. None of them had gotten more than a wink of sleep, and Cedric could feel himself drooping even as his thoughts went wild in his head, bouncing around the confines of it.

What if Neala had more time?

Maybe he wasn't worthless after all, because *he* could provide that time. All the time in the world that she needed to heal while he sang for her. A loophole they'd discussed and he'd brushed off, thinking nothing could silence a vampire of her advanced age.

Neala wouldn't ask for it, he thought. She was too proud, and their relationship was too young. But he decided to make her an offer she couldn't refuse.

Their next stop was at one of the many streams lining the valley's bed. Cedric couldn't tell it was autumn here; the sun scorched down on them without mercy or shade. He splashed his face with lukewarm water, taking more than his fill to smother the nerves in his belly.

He faced his reflection in the stream while the rest of his traveling companions were busy with more important tasks. "Is this what you want?" he asked.

Yes, it was. When they were still near-strangers, she'd turned down the invitation he'd unwittingly extended to her the first time he'd sung his heart's song. Thinking back to that moment brought tinges of disappointment. They'd had two weeks to figure out their relationship, and he'd only tiptoed into it, respecting the woman with heavy shadows in her eyes the moment the word "lifemate" was uttered. Now that he knew her better, he understood she needed someone to push past the discomfort and accept her for who and what she was.

"Do you love her?" he whispered, seeing the truth in his reflection's expression.

He knew what it was like to love music, his life's devotion. But ultimately, it was a one-sided affair, for as much as he heaped time and attention to the craft, he only discovered he wasn't as good at it as he thought he was.

With Neala, he'd had to work out his awe that his perfect woman had appeared out of nowhere and literally saved him from danger. A stranger from a strange world, the only lady he couldn't impress with a song and a smile alone.

But did he *love* her? He couldn't tie himself to another if it wasn't serious.

He sat back on his haunches, considering. He loved sunsets by her side; he enjoyed her wise mind and their deeper conversations. She was strong, passionate, and protective. What was love, really, but an enjoyment of moments together? She'd plucked away his heart with un-Neala-like subtlety, a quiet given as he tried to be a better lifemate than her first.

He'd rehearsed for the job, and now came the interview. A woman like Neala didn't *need* a pretty little man like him often, unless as a cheerleader. That's what this moment was, a need, and he had to be brave enough to step forward and offer himself as her match.

"Admiring yourself?" Sirius asked irritably, stepping in Cedric's stream and interrupting his reflection with ripples.

"Not much to appreciate, I'm afraid." His clothes were a mess, and he was sure he smelled ripe. As far from a charming bard as he could get.

He turned away from the Blood Prince, dodging that temper like his heels were on fire. When he glanced at Neala, her eyes were open again. Butterflies fluttered in his belly in time with his runty wings. "I think it's time for a song!" he announced. A collective groan echoed back at him from all sides.

"Is it time to see if your lute can be set on fire?" Ash asked with faux sweetness.

"N-no," he stammered, but that didn't stop him from

retrieving his instrument and checking its tune. "C'mon, relax. This one's not for you anyway."

He sat himself cross-legged before Neala's prone form and plucked a simple melody. She closed her eyes. *Don't leave me now,* he thought, letting a note hang in the air until she blinked.

False start. Replaying those notes, he acclimated to how it sounded without magic. That wasn't what was important anyway. He let it be a background compliment as he literally sang his heart, weaving his heart's song into lyrics he'd sung hundreds of times but had never meant like this.

A heart's song for his heartsong, a melody for his mate. This time, he felt the offer, bright and musical, like a bridge between them. His world narrowed to her as her mind held his bid, neither accepting nor rejecting.

"Are you sure?" she asked quietly.

"More than anything," he said.

"There's no coming back from this. It will be permanent."

"It would be yours later. Why not now, when you need it most?" He held his breath as she lapsed to silence. If only he could listen in on her thoughts, hear what was holding her back. He still took a guess. "I won't regret it. Not one moment. Fate's already decided that we're lifemates, and I was a goner from the day we met."

The faintest of smiles curled her lips. *"When you were a chicken?"*

"Yeah. I watched you fight later that night, you know? I wasn't just hiding," he admitted. "You were a force of nature. You were *heroic.*" Yet another wonderful word for Neala. "I'm not a hero. That implies sacrifice, and I'm only gaining if you say yes to me right now."

"No regrets."

"None."

Her acceptance of his song was like someone had tied a rope around his midsection and pulled. They entered a new equilibrium, his next one-sided love affair where she was his mate but he was not yet hers. Her everything poured into him—thoughts, feelings—but mostly, it was pain. Bone-deep pain from crown to toes. His next breath was a gasp for air.

Her expression changed to a concerned frown, the most movement she'd had since the snake bite. *"Seems you can take some of my burden."* Followed by a dry chuckle. *"But not too much."*

His sense of her faded to a dull ache. "How are you conscious?" he asked, breathing like he'd just ran for miles.

"Maybe I just like looking at my little bard." She winked.

His smile was fleeting on the heels of this discovery. He coaxed some of her pain onto himself, though she gave a trickle compared to the initial flood. Still, he cursed himself for being a wimp as he staggered to his feet, walking past a solemn Ash to strap his lute back into its proper place.

"Did it work?" the Unseelie asked.

"Right now, it's Cedric Firetree, but it could be Neala Apple-white if I'm lucky." He stuck to humor because he needed her to snort and look away. That way, the sarcastic woman couldn't razz him for the clumsy manner in which he climbed into his mount's saddle.

Chapter 24
Cedric

THEY ARRIVED AT IRONHOLD BY NIGHTFALL. ITS DARK, STONE peaks were still miles away, hidden behind high walls of smoky metal lined with spikes. Cedric wondered if some Unseelie architect had imported real iron as a symbolic gesture of oppression but wasn't willing to run up and touch the walls to see.

Camped out along the shallow ring of earth separating Ironhold from the valley at its back were hundreds of performers. Maybe they'd arrived after the dead zone's magic was placed, just like them. Cedric spotted multicolored tents and bored jugglers practicing their routines close to the city's gates, which were shuttered tightly.

"Are there any healers here?" Sirius bellowed, drawing his elk up short to face the crowd of waiting fae.

Murmurs and motion advanced through the tent city as they waited. A terran fae woman came from one of the larger tents as word spread to her, wiping her hands on a rag as she approached. Her apron was stained and expression tight as she approached. "I'm a healer."

Sirius gestured to Neala. "She and another of our companions were bitten by a huge snake."

"Black eyes or blood on the creature?" the healer asked curtly.

"Yes."

"Bring them."

Miles turned to Cedric as they walked their elks into the encampment. He tugged his ear. It was a simple gesture, but Cedric knew what he was actually saying—listen. The Unseen Council would want to know what was happening.

Cedric managed a nod. The riding felt all the harder after he'd made his bond with Neala, her extra pain massaging into every muscle he had. His neck and back were stiff, his legs hovering on the unpleasant edge of numb. But Neala was able to stay awake and reassure him that his performance had saved her voice for the day. Every moment after that was worth it.

"Has anyone passed you an artifact so you can use magic?" Ash asked.

The healer scoffed. "That would imply that someone in that blasted city cares about us out here." She held the flap of her tent back so they could carry Neala and Doran inside. Cedric held the elks' reins, catching a nose full of pungent herbs as the healer disappeared inside.

Ash glanced to him. "Come with me?" She jerked her chin toward the city.

"The gate is locked," he said.

The flames in her wings flickered brighter. "So? Am I not the Princess?"

"But Neala..." Just the thought of leaving his new mate had his insides tying in knots.

"While she rests, don't you want to do something that will help her recover faster?" she asked. He hovered on the edge of indecision as Sirius's heavy tread preceded him.

The Blood Prince emerged from the healer's tent, dusting his hands off. "We're welcome to camp here for the evening," he told them. "Neala and Doran aren't the only ones suffering from poison or other wounds from strangely large and vicious animals."

Ash's lips tightened to a thin line. She passed Sirius the reins to her elk with a sigh. "The elk don't need resting. Cedric and I will not be going into the city after I speak with the healer."

"We..." Cedric didn't remember agreeing to that. But he did want to help Neala, and if being momentarily parted from her would achieve that, then he would go. He let Sirius guide his mount away. The elk were all exhausted by this point, a state that he mirrored as he followed Ash into the tent.

The healer had a tiny area in the entryway for racks of herbs and potions. Lining the tent were cot after cot, most of them full. Neala and Doran were near the front, as were Miles and the healer as they conversed in hushed voices.

"Here's the Princess now. She will want to hear this too," Miles said, gesturing them over.

The healer eyed Ash with an unimpressed "humph" and said, "Few travelers are getting through Plunder Road without being attacked by magic-twisted wildlife. It started when the Queen closed the gates to Ironhold and locked us all out. The guards have heard our testimony, but the dead zone remains. I'm here to heal wounds caused by circus accidents, not triage in this way."

Ash nodded in understanding. "Can you tell me anything about the attack on my sister?"

"Not much to say. Rumor has it that she was nicked at most." The healer shrugged. "If you ask me, getting her wings tied up over it is causing nothing but grief for the rest of us."

"Unless she wasn't poisoned..." Ash murmured.

"Which is an even worse look. Why shut the rest of us out of our own healing magics to hoard care in the safety of her palace?" The bitterness in the healer's voice triggered a wave of heat from Ash's person, and the combination had Cedric shying back. The Unseelie Princess stomped from the tent. "Typical Unseelie, though. Selfish," the healer said under her breath.

"Cedric, I'll wait here. Why don't you go with her?" Miles suggested, tugging on his ear again. Valuable information to be had, Cedric realized.

He dropped down to place a kiss at Neala's brow. Her eyelids fluttered before landing closed. *"Go. There's nothing to be done here. I'm not going anywhere,"* she told him.

"I'll be back as soon as I can," he promised her anyway before standing with a reluctant nod. He left, finding Ash standing a few yards away, her hands on her hips as she stared up at the city's walls.

"Why are you asking me to come with you?" he blurted.

"Every time I return to Faerie, I don't bring Kalimea a token from my travels." She glanced his way. "I thought maybe you could perform a song for her?"

"Sounds like good diplomacy to me." He rushed to retrieve his lute. Thankfully, their elks were nearby, with Sirius still unsaddling and brushing them down.

By the time he returned to Ash, she was at the city gates, hollering up to a set of guards. "I demand entry to Ironhold!" A statement could be considered neither a truth nor lie, so it was refreshing to hear her speak clearly.

The Unseelie guard who answered her scowled. "I believe the Queen's orders state that no one can enter or leave." And since beliefs could be untrue, Cedric tilted his head. Maybe it *wasn't* the Queen's orders but those of someone else pulling the strings in her absence.

"I believe that I don't care," she responded acridly.

They conferenced quietly up there, leaving Cedric to bounce on the balls of his feet. He had no doubt Ash was about to get what she wanted, proved when the guards let down a rope ladder. Ash started to climb it with ease, while the moment he had good hand and footholds, the guards started hauling the whole ladder up to ensure they were the only two to use it.

For a moment, they stood with the guards atop the wall. "Thanks for nothing," Ash said over her shoulder as she spotted a guard's stair and led him down it. The smell of garbage hit Cedric's nose. He gagged.

"Ah, Ironhold. How I missed you." He glanced up at her face, almost expecting a drip of blood from her truth telling with how honest she sounded. But her nose was dry. She gestured for him to follow as they took a side street away from the main thorough-fare that connected to Plunder Road.

The more space he put between himself and Neala, the fainter their connection grew. He felt the burden of her pain slip from his shoulders and breathed a guilty sigh of relief. If he were to perform for a queen tonight and have any kind of quality, he needed to be as clear-headed as possible.

The hours spent awake and worrying over her swept in to

weigh him down instead. Hopefully, there was a nice bed awaiting them that both he and Neala could collapse on once this was all over.

"What is your sister like?" he asked as they followed a labyrinthine path through this part of the city. He wondered if he would still be coming with her if magic was possible—she could fly over all of this with the magic in her wings, while he couldn't.

Ash held up a finger and led him out into an alleyway. She gestured to a window, and they both peered inside. Unseelie were lined up, receiving generous portions of food. Some broke bread together inside the building. "Kalimea didn't found this quarter," Ash said. "Where the poorest can't come and receive a meal and a warm place to stay." She ushered him onward, impatient now that they could see the shadow of the palace looming over them.

"That's kind of her." Now that Cedric knew what he was looking at, he saw Unseelie benefitting from that generosity every time they caught a glimpse of this road.

"Kalimea personally didn't decimate mansions to make it happen. Those that betrayed her in the old war didn't lose everything, including their riches, to fund this district for decades to come," Ash continued. "Kalimea is...good." She swiped at her nose. "I always thought she was too good."

"For an Unseelie?"

"As a person," she corrected. "You won't see more in the palace."

It wasn't until they were before the gates of the palace that Cedric realized they'd dodged most of the guards patrolling the main streets. He was glad Ash and her clever mind were on his side.

After a brief argument, the guards saluted Ash and let them through the gates. This palace was everything he expected but on a grander scale. They climbed stairs several stories into the air, the pointed towers above still seeming a mile up.

"Where is Queen Kalimea?" Ash asked another fae wearing a servant's smart, black tunic.

"All rumors I've heard point to her resting in her quarters, Your Highness," she responded with a curtsey.

Ash beckoned to him, and they entered a new maze. The fatigue was catching up to him, and he knew he'd be lost if he and Ash parted ways. It didn't miss his notice that the halls became more richly appointed with both art and guards the further in they went. Ash barreled right through a golden door, picking up speed like a charging bull while Cedric stopped with his jaw hanging.

The walls had a texture like black velvet, glimmering in magic light like they were studded with precious gemstones. Marble lined the floor and ceilings. And on that velvet hung portraits as large as him.

"This completely sufferable hall isn't the Gallery of Rulers." Ash had stopped at the end of it, where three stairs and a small banister led to another door painted gold. "Notice anything about them?" She gestured to the portraits, which he took in on the way.

At first, he wasn't sure what she expected him to notice. The monarchs were all painted with severe, royal expressions. Some with spouses and children, some without. It took his tired brain a minute as he stopped and surveyed them a second time. "They're all death fae. The rulers, I mean," he finally said. While the royal consorts were any type of Unseelie, only the purple-hued kind sat upon the throne in portrait after portrait.

Ash nodded. She gestured to the last portrait, where the throne was occupied by a destruction fae, a pretty redhead in a green dress. By her side was a Seelie, a solar fae who broke the norms by smiling. The plaque at the bottom read what he already knew—it was Queen Kalimea and King Orin. He never thought he'd get closer to the royalty of Faerie than viewing this kind of painting.

"There wasn't favoritism or anything," she muttered. "But you see how my sister is different, yes?"

When he saw the worry pulling at her mouth, he stepped up next to her, ready to move on. She shook herself from her thoughts and continued through the next door, revealing a hallway lined in more iridescent velvet and marble. Two guards and a wizened death fae man all turned toward them.

"P-Princess Ashaela!" the old fae gasped.

"Hello, Master Ervin." Unlike the guards, he didn't bow, and it didn't seem like Ash expected him to. "How is my sister?"

"T-taking visitors, I'm afraid." He shuffled before the door the two guards were stationed by, as if to block her by sheer nerves alone.

Ervin clutched his hands when Ash approached and leaned down until they were eye to eye. "Why not?" she demanded.

The guards crossed their weapons behind Ervin's back. "By royal decree, no one is to see Queen Kalimea as she convalesces," one of them said.

Cedric's eyes narrowed. Since the guard was Unseelie, there was a lie there somewhere. Ash apparently thought the same way. "By whose decree?" she asked coolly.

"One of the ministers, perhaps," the guard responded. "Do not make us disobey orders, Your Highness."

"The orders of your Princess overrule whomever issued yours, no?" she said.

He scoffed. "Sure."

Heat licked Cedric's cheeks as Ash's temper blazed. "I *will* see my sister."

"Yes, Princess, you will."

In a blink, the guard's staff was striking the floor where Ash stood. Taking his cue from his fellow, the other guard swiped as Ash dodged again. "G-gentlemen!" Ervin gasped, pressing himself to the wall.

"You'll probably go to the same place as her." The guard grinned, a flash of white in his helmet.

Ash pulled out two daggers, moving with the grace of a dancer as she was beset on either side. She led them away from Cedric, who took the opportunity to grab the front of Ervin's tunic. "Do you have anything that will let me use magic?" he whispered.

The elderly fae produced a slender rod that practically hummed from his sleeves. Cedric felt a jolt when he took it. He ran through all the spell-songs he'd learned as Ash continued fighting, denting armor and nicking any exposed flesh her daggers could find.

"Ah, screw it," he muttered. He held the item from Ervin against the neck of the lute as he swung it with both hands.

Twang!

One of the guards dropped, unconscious, his helmet dented. Ash flashed him an incredulous look before she disarmed the second guard, pinning him to the wall with the point of her blade just under his chin. "Talk," she barked.

He strained against her hold, to little avail. "No one should bow to a Seelie King," he said with strain. "We need old leadership."

Her lip curled in disgust. "You want to go back to the times of Queen Lorelei?"

"Worse than her. More terrible still." He let out a strained laugh. "You'll know her splendor when you're dead."

Their struggle ended when Ash tapped him hard under the jaw, knocking him out next. "Perfectly sane," she mocked, turning her flaming gaze on Ervin. When she made a motion for him to scoot aside, he did immediately. She went into the room and returned with the silken cords used to tie back curtains. "I assume you know what to do?" She gestured toward the two guards, and Cedric took the cords with a nod. "What were you thinking, using your lute that way?"

He held up Ervin's rod. "It's enchanted. And unbreakable," he said as cheerfully as he could muster.

Ash rolled her eyes and plucked the artifact from his hold. "Stay out here for now," she said, jerking her chin toward Ervin. The old man was inching his way toward the exit.

"You got it," he said. He tied the wrists of both men and propped them up far from their fallen weapons.

Once that was done, he sat cross-legged in front of the golden door to discourage Ervin from leaving. "So, um, do you know what they were going on about?"

"M-maybe."

Sighing, Cedric plucked a simple melody on his lute to keep the last of his adrenaline occupied. "Look, if you don't tell me, you'll have to tell Ash. And she's obviously much scarier than I am."

Ervin listened to the music instead, staying mute for so long that Cedric thought he wouldn't reply. When he did, he had his head bowed. "I can't tell you much, all right?"

"Whatever you can say."

"Queen Kalimea was not struck with a poisoned dagger. And the wounds have not festered with demonic taint."

Cedric's fingers faltered. "Demonic?" he echoed.

"I-I may have seen a demon or more in my time," Ervin stammered. With his advanced age, even by fae standards, Cedric wouldn't be surprised if he was old enough to have met King Oberon himself.

"That means you know how to treat the wounds, right?" he asked hopefully.

New fear hunched Ervin's shoulders. "I can say."

He hummed. So, Ervin couldn't talk about it. "Does that mean these guards are in some alliance with a demon or something?"

"I can say."

"Is there a demon?" he demanded.

The old healer gave him a miserable look. He didn't have to say it. He couldn't talk about it.

Ash came storming out of the queen's quarters a minute later, her face pale. "He can't talk about it," Cedric interjected as she grabbed Ervin's collar and hauled him to his feet.

"So, you can't heal her, then?" she snarled.

"I-I-I..."

She released him, and he dropped to his knees, hyperventilating. "There is only one solution, okay?" She surveyed the area and beckoned to Cedric. When they both were in the queen's quarters, she locked the door and began dragging over a plush sofa to barricade it. "Listen closely. You're staying here. I am going to lift the dead zone, but the focus for the spell is in the other side of the palace." She swiped at her nose with an impatient noise.

"But there may be more corrupt guards. Ervin was talking about a demon..." he stammered.

She held up the rod. "Don't underestimate me. Take this." She tossed another object to him, a glass ball about the size of his palm. Gray smoke rolled just underneath the surface. "It may be Kalimea's focus. If you have a song that can wake her up...use the focus to amplify your magic. Otherwise, leave her be." She'd closed the door to the rest of the queen's quarters, which he was thankful for. He had no intentions of interrupting her rest.

"Is she in bad shape?" he whispered.

Ash's grim expression told the story. "Best and worst of luck." The rod vibrated as she started to dissolve, turning into a plume of smoke which leaked through the cracks in the door.

"You too," he said. He muttered a curse as he continued barricading the entrance. If Ash really wanted to bring someone to meet her sister, she should've picked Sirius. At least he knew how to fight.

Chapter 25
Sirius

Sirius was on edge. While that was a constant state of his being, it was even worse with how furious his inner beast was. The dead zone had a curious effect on his magic—he was unable to shift, but his beast was still awake and able to project its feelings.

Something was wrong, more deeply wrong than him being alone in a camp of strangers. Worse than Neala fighting for her life as her supernatural healing refused to kick in. More fore-boding than Ash and Cedric entering the city without him. Not that he thought Ash would invite him after their last encounter.

He had his tent set up, but instead of going inside for a well-deserved rest, he wandered the mega camp right outside Iron-hold's walls. He didn't talk to anyone and gave a dirty look to anyone who asked why he, a "human-born," was here in Faerie.

Not right, his inner beast whispered. But like usual, the bundle of instincts that ruled his life couldn't give him specifics. He hunted for something amiss in the crowd instead. As the night deepened, more and more fae went to sleep to wait out another night. With Plunder Road reportedly unsafe, it was the only haven for this mass of performers.

But *was* it safe? His beast was sure the answer was no. He prowled from one end, where the elks and a handful of horses and mules were stabled in a makeshift overhang against the city wall, to the other, where the newest arrivals were a quartet of singers who greeted him in harmony.

He had to smile at that. "Stay safe," he murmured, standing in the shadows beyond their little campfire. There weren't enough performers to surround the whole city, so they just swarmed this section of the gate. He was about to turn around when he caught a glimmer of light in the valley as it continued around the east of the city.

Keeping to the darkest part of the night, he moved like a shadowy predator, that gleam his intended catch. He peered over the side of the sheer cliff above where he thought he'd seen it, rewarded with the sight of...a portal? *Here?*

Though he couldn't do a partial shift to sharpen his eyesight like a hawk's, he still saw two humanoid figures below ushering shadowy forms through their portal. *They must have some artifact to allow their magic,* he thought, suppressing a growl. He recognized the gait of different animals, but all of them were of exaggerated size.

He couldn't let this continue. The portal was well-placed; even though he knew it was there, he couldn't just scrabble down the rock face and confront them right away. He searched the steep drop for any sign of handholds, coming up with nothing. If he had to take the long way, though, so did the creatures coming to attack them. And he had no doubt that was what was about to happen. The city couldn't be sieged by a group of animals, no matter how large.

But the group locked outside the gates was a different story. He went back to the quartet of singers, urging them out of their bedrolls. "We're about to be attacked," he said in a low voice. "Go wake up the camp." Hopefully, they had a few fighters amongst the group.

Sirius ran into the night alone, striking out in a wide arc to avoid the notice of the two spell casters and their growing army of beasts. A cautious voice told him to lie low, and it sounded a lot like his best friend, Korin. He missed the big guy and his gentle ways—the calm to Sirius's anger.

This is a terrible idea, striking out on your own, he knew Korin would say. Oh well. His best backup was Neala or Ash, and neither woman was available.

He didn't have much cover here anyway, this stretch of land either purposefully barren or illusioned that way. When a telltale hiss sounded from nearby, he knew his time was nearly up. The portal's glow was within sprinting distance, and one of the people next to it was looking out into the night.

Sirius put on a burst of speed, calling on every part of him that was vampire to cross the distance quickly. His sword left its scabbard soundlessly, the hilt in both hands as he leapt and impaled an overgrown mountain lion as it was emerging from the portal. If he had any doubts as to what these two fae were doing, they were erased as black blood sprayed and an eerie chorus of yowling and beastly screams rose in the night.

He didn't hesitate, no mercy given as he pulled his sword free and swung at one of the fae. Flames burst to life in the man's fists, illuminating the barest of features hiding in a hood.

The other fae began gesturing with both hands. Sirius's inner beast had its hackles raised immediately. He dove for his gesturing enemy, killing her in one swift blow. The portal collapsed a moment later. "No! What have you done?" the remaining fae cried. Flames sizzled off Sirius's arm as a fireball grazed his flesh.

He grinned. Despite the pain, he felt more alive in this moment than he had during the countless days of travel and cooling his heels as Izell's Blade. He had a purpose and an enemy. Many enemies. A scorpion as big as he was reached him first, its stinger whipping through the air. Sirius grabbed it at the base, feeling an acid-hot droplet of venom hit his wrist. *A sting like that would make Neala's paralysis look like a blessing,* he thought, severing the scorpion's tail. He dodged another salvo of fire from the fae, ending his life next for fear of what other magic he could cast.

Sirius bent over the male's corpse, rifling his clothes for a quick answer to what allowed him his magic. A metallic gleam caught his eye. The fae man had been holding a bird figurine, and the moment Sirius's fingers closed around it, his inner beast roared in satisfaction.

Freedom!

He pocketed the item and found an orb of magic on the fae woman. His body trembled with potential. He could out-muscle, out-run, or out-think anything in the grass coming to kill him if he shifted into the right animal. If he picked the right shift, he could end this threat without any of the performers above being threatened.

Except none of the animals were coming for him. Even the scorpion without its stinger was scuttling along through the grass, heading for the main road and the mass of fae who wouldn't put up as much of a fight.

He ran after them, dispatching a few stragglers. What he really needed was to get one of these objects to the circus healer and the other to a fae with considerable magic. His sensitive hearing already picked up the echo of screams.

A handful of fae beat at the walls, calling for the guards up top to let them into Ironhold. From his vantage, Sirius saw something far worse than apathy. The guards and other cloaked figures were fighting one another, ignoring the plight of the performers down below.

The camp was overrun with beasts. He chopped a path to the healer's tent, bursting in to find the healer defending her charges against an alligator that had to be twelve feet head to tail. Sirius put it out of its misery for her. "Take this." He shoved the magic orb at her, which she nearly fumbled the moment it touched her skin.

"Her first," he demanded, pointing the tip of his black-slicked sword at Neala.

"Of course." She didn't sound the least bit rattled. *That healer's nerve,* he thought. Neala seemed to be sleeping, but her body writhed in agony the moment the fae clasped her arm and pulsed magic through her. "Get me a bucket," she ordered him.

He grabbed one from another's bedside in time for Neala to be sick into it. He held her hair, heart thudding hard in eagerness to return to the fighting.

"Never again," Neala rasped. She sat up in short, jerky movements. Each pulse of light from the healer made it seem like Neala's motions became smoother and more natural.

Sirius breathed a sigh of relief and helped her to her feet. "Can you fight?"

"Where is Faebane?" She cracked her knuckles and rolled her neck in anticipation.

He cursed because he'd left it with her elk, assuming she wouldn't need it. "Take the next best thing," he said, offering her the pommel of his own weapon. He grew out his fingernails into talons courtesy of a partial shift, otherwise known as a demi-shift. His inner beast growled impatiently, ready to do so much more.

They emerged into the night and the chaos therein. Neala didn't hesitate, so he didn't either, the two of them clearing the area of oversized beasts. "Just like old times," Neala grunted.

"They don't put up as much fight as the Fell." Despite himself, he was disappointed.

Neala scoffed. "Bloodthirsty cur."

He grinned. "Guilty."

One of the circus tents collapsed as they fought, its heavy folds of fabric deflating into one of several campfires still burning. It went up like dry tinder, flames spreading uncontrollably. He branched off from Neala, lifting a flap of tent. "Any survivors?" he shouted.

A peculiar sight greeted him from the depths of the tent. A hummingbird zoomed up to his face. It was a tiny thing, harmless, but insistent. His brow furrowed as he sharpened his hearing, picking up the sound of a woman's faint call. "I hear her," he said to the little bird as if it would understand. It released a plaintive peep, following him as he lifted more of the tent, fighting the fabric as it smoldered and filled what little air was underneath with cloying smoke.

"Help!"

The bird helped him locate her weak voice. She was trapped under the carcass of a fallen beast, a tent peg having spelled its demise. He wondered if that was the reason for the collapse, as several more littered the area. Hefting the creature off of her, he came face-to-face with an aether fae as delicate as spun sugar, her little oval face creased with pain.

A funny feeling tugged at his stomach, but now wasn't the right time to explore it. "I've got you," he said, hefting her over his shoulder. She smelled like blood. His fangs came unsheathed because, despite the tang of monster, her own wounds smelled appetizing after the overexertion of the last couple days.

They both gasped for air as he pulled her free from the tent. He helped her sit down, and as she parted her legs, he saw the wound that'd hobbled her. Deep scratches marred one of her thighs, dangerously close to a main artery. The hummingbird hovered nearby, the picture of anxious concern as it peeped over her.

"Miss, the healer is probably very busy. May I seal your wounds?" he asked, gesturing to her leg. She stared up at him, her blue face pale with shock and blood loss. No answer was forthcoming.

He stripped off one of his gloves and knelt by her side. "Vampire saliva closes wounds," he told her, sticking two of his fingers in his mouth. "I know it seems odd. I'm only doing this to help you." Her stormy gray eyes watched as he swiped her wounds. It was about as much triage as he was capable of until she saw a real healer.

He was tempted to walk her there, but the fighting was continuing without him as the straggler beasts continued attacking their prey. His inner beast came to attention, and he glanced up at the city walls in time to see a wave of magic pass. It looked like it peeled a layer off the sky and ground, everything suddenly sharpening, including his mind as his magic kicked in fully. A fae a few yards away threw a lightning bolt at one of the creatures, frying it on the spot. Flashes and bursts echoed up on the city walls as well.

Sirius realized quickly that, with magic, the fae here were no longer helpless. "Let me get you to that healer," he told the aether fae. He supported her around the back, the touch of her cloud-like wings merely a tickle. Something about her kept drawing his eye. As his adrenaline faded, other feelings seeped in.

Such as how his inner beast *purred* when their gazes met.

Mate, it said. But it was not content with the label, immediately flushing Sirius with possessive thoughts. It wanted to claim her then and there. Lick up her blood in a much more intimate way.

He shuddered at how deep and powerful those urges went, disgusted with his beast. This woman had nearly died! *Shut up,* he ordered it, shocked when it cowered back and ceased its urges.

He did what he had to. Once they were to the healer's tent, he pushed his lifemate into the arms of a helpful volunteer. "Her thigh," he grunted before turning to take out his frustrations on the few creatures that remained.

Chapter 26
Neala

By the time the fighting was finished, Neala was so exhausted she could barely swing Sirius's sword. She found him to give it back. They both turned to view the wall and the magic being thrown around just out of their reach.

"What do you think is going on?" she asked. The camp bustled on without them, escorting the wounded and putting out fires.

Sirius had his teeth set, his voice a mere growl. "Too soon to tell." He told her of the two fae portaling in this set of overgrown animals. Unfortunately, they were dead, and the creatures they'd summoned weren't telling about how they'd encountered demon taint.

Sirius's explanation was cut short as a flaming figure shouted far above them. "Stop!" Ash hollered. "In the name of the crown, stop!"

If Ash was here...where was Cedric? Neala watched shadows retreat up on the wall, a few tossing themselves off of Ironhold's ramparts and flying away swiftly. Some guards either gave chase or retreated with them. With little to distinguish the sides, Neala could only guess.

The gates to the city started to trundle open as Ash continued issuing orders. Wary glances were exchanged around the camp until the princess landed amongst them, her blazing wings lighting up the night like an extra bonfire. "In my sister's absence, I welcome you all to Ironhold." She followed the statement up with a rub of her nose. "I have personally provided for safe lodgings for you all."

"What of our injured?" shouted a terran fae.

"Filthy Unseelie! We needed into the city days ago!"

Mutters of discontent spread through the crowd. Seelie and Unseelie parting into two separate groups, one planting their feet and the other filtering past their princess to the safety of the walled city carrying what remained of their belongings.

"We haven't a special place for the wounded," Ash answered those who remained. "I may also have an extraordinary offer for your healer. The Queen, my sister, may have need of her."

A flight of fae landed behind her. Two individuals held medical kits, and the rest went to work helping clear the camp. They wore the guard uniform as well, but Ash watched them with an approving nod.

There was no need for them to linger. Neala was the next person to walk past Ash, heading for the city. She glanced over her shoulder. "A warm bed for us away from this mess. What could be better?"

Sirius caught up with her with a set of elk better rested than the ones they'd ridden to Ironhold. "How did our mounts fare?" she asked.

His tight expression only ratcheted up further. "Let's just say they weren't the primary targets of the attack. Most of our stuff is okay as well."

The elk seemed to know where they were going better than either Blood Prince. They rode toward the palace, following the streaks of light left by the magical wings of the fae. As Neala sagged forward on her mount, she reached out with a mental probe, searching for Cedric. Upon feeling a connection, she demanded, *Are you all right?*

"Are you?" he asked right back. *"Do you know what's going on? I've been barricaded in this room for hours."*

"Ash must've ended the dead zone. I'm...okay." It was hard to give herself a better rating when her vampiric regeneration was only starting to soothe the ache of a day of muscle-clenching agony. *"Healed. Moving. Coming your way."*

"Thank the stars," he breathed. *"Oh, Ash is here! With the healer who was looking after you?"*

They compared notes as Neala rode. She shared some of it with Sirius, how two guards had turned on Ash and implied that someone else would be a better ruler than her or her sister. And how the royal healer wasn't able to answer questions or even admit to knowing how to treat the Queen's injuries. "A coup, then," he said grimly.

She sneered. "A joke of one, perhaps."

"We're spoiled from our experiences. Lucia overthrew us in one day."

"Must you mention her?" She turned a scowl his way.

"Yes. Like it or not, Lucia had the same magic as the fae here. If they had one bad actor as determined and talented as her, this is a probe of the people's loyalty. What do you think the common folk will think when they learn a group was attacked right outside the gates?" His gaze was unfocused on the palace coming up. She wondered if he saw white stone instead of dark gray, a place he'd helped his brother maintain politically.

She had to admit that, despite his temper, Sirius understood the game better than her. "You're right."

"Public opinion is very important." He sighed, running a hand through his hair. "And it is a fickle beast."

There was a mass of guards at the gate to the palace and another at the steps. At least they seemed helpful—stable hands retrieved their mounts. "Princess Ashaela told us not to expect two human-born," one told them after pointing out how to reach the royal quarters.

It was nice to be expected. They were ushered into the royal wing with due haste. The only signs of a struggle in the hall outside the Queen's chambers were a few scuffs and the lingering smell of blood. Standing by the door was Cedric, plucking his instrument idly. He wavered on his feet, looking as tired as she felt.

Her breath caught as her gaze roved him, seeking out any sign of injury. Thankfully, he was unharmed, with just an awed little smile to see her on her feet again. She closed the gap between them and pulled the lute from his shoulders. Placing it aside, she swept him up into a bone-crushing hug. Sirius put his back to them with a huff.

Free reign to smother Cedric's face with kisses, then. She allowed herself a moment of contentment to hold her new mate, feeling him solid and hale. He laughed, eyes closing in simple pleasure. "I'm glad you're okay," he whispered.

"Only thanks to you," she murmured. "I might be moving, but I don't think I'll be singing for days."

He pressed his forehead to hers, his star-flecked gaze searching. "No regrets?" he asked.

The same thing he'd asked while she held the most valuable gift he could ever give her—his heart. Like she could grow tired of his energy and enthusiasm. Or the way he looked at her as if she were his sunrise to start the perfect morning.

His doubts ran deep, though, to ask this so soon after binding himself to her. And she had the sinking suspicion of why that was. There was a conversation they had to have, but not at this moment. She kissed him instead, stuffing her passion and gratitude into a few moments to leave him breathless. "No regrets," she answered firmly.

She turned to Sirius, just to catch him rubbing his cheek against the wall. He froze. "What? It's soft."

"I did the same thing," Cedric admitted.

Neala parted from him to rub the wall, humming at its velvet-like texture. "Fae," she decided, "are very strange."

"You get used to it," Cedric said with a hint of his usual cheer. "Ash wanted me to knock when you got here. You know, for a chat."

About the last thing Neala wanted to do right now was to have a "chat," but she nodded anyway. Ash opened the door after they knocked a few times. Gone was the princess façade she'd put on to get the performers into the city. She was pale, waving them in with a troubled frown.

"Know what's bad? Not trusting a stranger with your sister over the palace physician." Ash went straight for a cabinet in the richly furnished living room and pulled out a number of bottles. "Wine? Absinthe?"

Neala laid her tired bones on one of the couches before realizing it was placed crookedly in the arrangement of the room. Oh well. She wasn't about to get up again. "Any whiskey?" She turned her nose up at wine and assumed the posh Queen of Faerie didn't have beer anywhere near her personal chambers. She accepted some whiskey in its place, ready to use the amber liquid as a nightcap.

"Will your sister be okay?" Cedric asked. He leaned against Neala's side when she put an arm around his shoulders.

Ash sat across from them, leaning her elbows against her knees. Her head sagged. "I'm...unsure she will be fine, given time," she said. "But before that time, I haven't taken charge to ensure things run as they should. The men I don't know personally have captured a couple of tonight's attackers, on top of the two guards who turned on me. Would you like to be a part of interrogation efforts in the morning?"

Neala cut a glance to Sirius. They'd both seen this posture before, heard the silent plea of a royal in over their head. "Of course," she answered. "We can piece together a better plan once we know what we're up against. If you have your loyal men overseeing operations, it would do you well to rest."

"That's the thing." Ash sighed. "How do I tell who's loyal and who's not?"

"We'll find out tomorrow. Together," Neala promised.

Chapter 27
Cedric

After they were all shown to different rooms close to the royal suites, Cedric found Neala's room and they passed out together with little preamble. Insistent knocking came far too early for his liking. His eyelids were sticky and his body stiff.

Yet he sensed Neala was in worse shape. She barely stirred while he got too annoyed and rolled to his feet. He was still wearing the same clothes from the day before, rumpled from rest.

At the door was Ash herself, dark half-moons starting to bloom below her eyes. She was dressed in a gown that hugged her slim waist before belling out. The material was a deep crimson, trimmed in layers of black lace and tulle in the skirts. With matching elbow-length gloves and rubies glittering in her white hair, she was more prepared for a ball than an interrogation.

"Breakfast isn't in an hour or anything," she said, eyeing him. "Come to my sister's quarters."

"Okay, great." He closed the door and trudged his way to the bathroom. He wasn't terribly surprised to see a shower. His stay in the Shifting Wood's manor had taught him that fae knew how to emulate the more useful of human advancements. They just used magic when their knowledge of the technology grew murky.

He turned the water up extra hot, letting it soak into his sore muscles. Stars above, he'd only taken a fraction of Neala's pain, but the echo of it and their hard ride to Ironhold had worn him down. No wonder Neala was still asleep. It'd probably take an earthquake to...wake...her.

The curtains were drawn aside, and there she was, naked. All the moisture in his mouth evaporated. "Room for another?" she asked quietly. She may be his mate, but their relationship was still new. Boundaries had to be tested.

"Come on in," he said, moving aside for her to join him under the stream. Butterflies quivered in his belly. She was close enough to touch, yet it was her calloused hands that settled on his shoulders first.

"You're tense." Her strong fingers curled and stroked, spreading relief in their wake.

He watched her out of the corner of his eye, noting her expression and posture. Deeper, his connection with her hummed with hints of emotion and thoughts. But one thing was missing. "And you're...better?" he asked incredulously.

"Perks of being a Blood Prince," she said.

"Princess," he corrected.

A twinge of something passed through her feelings. A memory there. Had someone else tried to break tradition and change her title to the proper gender?

"Marcus would tease me about this," she admitted, her hands drifting down his back. Her thumbs were a slice of heaven, pressing knots and working on them as she found them. "'Prince' was one of his pet names for me."

How remarkably unromantic, he thought.

It was the most information he'd gotten out of her about Marcus, though, other than that he was her first lifemate and had betrayed her horribly. Also, the last thing he wanted to do was talk about Marcus.

"We have less than an hour, hmm?" she continued.

"I thought you were asleep."

"I'm a light sleeper." Her lips grazed the column of his throat. He shivered despite the heat of the water.

The soft mounds of her breasts pressed to his back as she drew him in close. He felt like a clueless virgin again as he wondered if they were about to continue where they'd left off a couple days ago. Her arms wrapped around his middle, and pressure suggested she'd rested her chin on his head.

Maybe not. He leaned back into her hold, feeling what she didn't say. Flickers of tenderness and appreciation rose from their bond, softer than words could describe. This wasn't passionate Neala ripping his clothes from his back, melting him with a stare.

No, it was the Neala who'd nearly lost herself to her worst nightmare. Silence. He knew some of the moisture soaking into his hair wasn't from the shower. Her sobs could've been hiccups. She knew how to hide this sort of thing.

He didn't say a word about it. If his presence was a comfort, he was happy as her living teddy bear. Soon, she was grabbing the soap and massaging it into his arms and chest. When it was his turn to do the same for her, he found where they'd left off with a different subject. She was unglamored. So, he traced her battle scars with soapy fingers, each one a story to coax from her someday.

They had time.

BREAKFAST WAS A SMALL AND WELCOME FEAST AFTER THEIR time on the road. The spirits in the room tempered his enthusiasm as Ash picked at her meal and continued to glance toward the closed door, behind which her sister rested, and Sirius glared down at a flaky pastry like it'd insulted his honor.

"Are we still doing an interrogation today?" Neala prompted.

It was just the four of them in this richly appointed living room. Ash had waved off any servants trying to linger and fuss over them for refills or seconds. She sighed and turned her attention to the other woman. "No. The men aren't in our dungeons awaiting their interrogations."

Neala's red gaze flashed over her face, a sense of sympathy echoing to Cedric over their one-way mating bond. "I will take care of the interrogating."

"But—"

She spoke over the Unseelie. "I have illusions, and Cedric.

Sirius has experience with the task. While we do this, someone needs to call for our allies, Izell and Sondus."

Ash chewed on her lip thoughtfully as Cedric said, "I would be a terrible interrogator, actually."

Neala flashed him a fond smile. "All you have to do is play a song to soften them up for me."

"That isn't what truth serum is for," Ash interjected. "And what do you intend for me to do while you take this duty?" The answer was obvious as the fae's attention drifted back to the doorway to her sister's inner chambers. "Okay...fine. I won't contact Sondus, and he can have a message passed to Izell within the hour."

Neala pushed her plate away and stood. "Then I am ready to shake some information out of your prisoners."

Ash personally took them to the interrogation rooms down in the basement of the palace. He already found it disconcerting, a box of white-painted walls and floor, with a shackled-down pair of chairs and a table between them. The table was stocked with pens and paper on one side, hidden from the other side by a thick screen.

Neala laid an illusion over herself, becoming a spot-on destruction fae. At her instruction, Cedric sat in the corner with his lute, where the fae she'd be questioning would have their back to him. He started up a tune meant to disarm and beguile. They were combining that with a serum that would force an Unseelie into a dreamlike state where they'd be forced to tell the truth.

Cedric was still nervous despite knowing this winning combination wouldn't result in any violence. The part of him that was a timid little bird knew that Sirius wouldn't be so gentle with the charges he'd been assigned. But what did it matter? These were bad people. Two of them had tried to murder Ash in front of him last night, and no doubt, he would've been next.

He drew his shoulders in when the first fae was escorted in. The man was a blight fae dragging heavy chains and walking like he was one drink from passing out. Two guards forced him into the seat across from Neala and departed once his restraints were secured to a hook in the floor.

Cedric pulled out the compact that could connect him with the Unseen Council and tapped the mirror inside. It lit up with blue light. Having someone on the other side taking notes would help them from having to repeat everything back to Sondus once the latter was made aware of everything happening.

"What business do you have to share, operative?" a feminine voice asked as an aether fae's visage glimmered on the other side of the mirror.

"Can you hear this?" Cedric propped the compact up so it was facing the interrogation. He pushed it toward the other two with his toes as he resumed plucking a melody.

"Affirmative."

Cedric could hear the scratching of a quill on paper in two places. Neala was already asking questions, and he'd missed what the other fae was saying. However, his voice was familiar—the same guard who'd so boldly swung at Ash first last night.

"...not personal," he was saying with a slur to his words. If circumstances were different, Cedric would be pitying him. "The Queen wanted all threats to her rule removed. I like Princess Ashaela, but she was in the way."

Neala frowned down at her notes. "I was under the impression that Queen Kalimea had a great relationship with her sister."

"Oh!" The former guard giggled like a little girl. "Wrong person."

"Who are you talking about, then?"

At her cue, Cedric increased the intensity of his song. The fae practically melted, listing sideways in his seat as his giggles tapered off with a dreamy sigh. "*My* Queen, of course. Lilith, Queen of Hell. Come to purge this land of the Seelie and to return..."

Cedric's song faltered. Queen of *Hell?* Here? He sensed Neala's attention and returned to strumming quickly.

"To...return...Unseelie to their proper glory. No longer must we pretend we're not made to rule Faerie and Earth. We want to crush Seelie and eat human hearts. Don't you?" he asked Neala's Unseelie illusion earnestly. "Aren't you tired of serving a weak queen who sullied herself by marrying a Seelie? Who acts like one at every turn?"

He missed her response as a flurry of activity hit his ears from the other side of the enchanted mirror. *"Go get the Master,"* the aether fae was shouting. *"Urgently!"*

"No, I haven't seen her," the former guard was saying when he turned his attention back to the interrogation. "I wish! All I've done so far is drunk of her essence."

Neala frowned. "Her blood?"

He nodded, giggling once more. "It was delicious. I felt so strong. But Princess Ashaela was still stronger than me..."

"You stupid man," she muttered.

She continued to probe about Lilith—where she was, what she wanted. Unfortunately, the answers were drying up. But a familiar voice in Cedric's ears brought a measure of hope.

"This had best be good."

"The notes are here, Master Sondus. And the questioning is still ongoing."

Papers shuffled, and the spymaster sucked in a hard breath. *"I hear a lute. Cedric?"*

"Yes," he said over his music.

"I've had the strangest reports since last night. Giant monsters, infighting, all centered around Ironhold. Your report from this interrogation shows that it's a demon causing it. Is that correct?"

"Y-yes." He still didn't know what to do with that information. A notable demon amongst demons, no less.

"I will be answering Ashaela's request after all. I'll be seeing you soon, Cedric," Sondus continued.

"...And these beasts, the ones that've been attacking us. How were they created?" Neala was saying. He perked up, wanting to hear the answer to this one.

"The same way Queen Lilith made me," the former guard answered dreamily. "She gave them her blood. She wants an army of beasts and fae by her side when the time comes."

Chapter 28
Neala

Despite their best efforts, the rest of the interrogations went nowhere. There was no when or how in the brains of any of the demon's misguided servants. Just the ominous warning of a coming army of twisted beasts tainted by demon blood.

Now that they knew to look for demon taint, Ash's loyal friends cobbled together a spell sensitive enough to detect the extra demonic energy in those who served Lilith. Since Unseelie were already demon-tainted to a tiny degree, the test had to be more accurate. Neala tired of watching them tinker and retired to a quiet alcove overlooking the palace gardens with Cedric.

A green-tinged lesser fae clipped the hedges while another weeded the flowerbeds. Even though turmoil lingered on the inside of the palace, outside its walls, things were as normal as ever. Her mind was full of everything they'd discovered.

Cedric laced his arm around her, leaning against her strong chest. "At least we know what's going on now."

"Knowing is one thing. But stopping it is another." Troubled thoughts pulled at her attention. "How did a demon get here?"

"Same way the angel did?" he suggested.

"Soren's presence is a trade-off for Lucia's return." Another problem still in need of solving. But for a time, the only way Lucia could hurt them was with the scars of her deeds. She was a scrap of soul on the wind somewhere, helpless until she regenerated a body.

"So, if we acquire another angel, then we know why," he mused aloud.

Neala's shoulders tensed as a new voice added, "Who says anything about angels?" She whipped around to glare, but the eavesdropper was Sondus with the illusion of wings on his back and more stars in his skin. He released a weary sigh. "As always, Lady Neala, we must expect to be alone in this world with only our wits and talents about us."

What a ray of sunshine, she thought. "You came running," she remarked instead.

"Some things require a more personal touch. Besides, I've heard the most excellent parties have graced these halls recently." His gaze twinkled. "Shall we peruse them?"

He turned without hearing her response, sweeping into the depths of the palace within two turns. The halls were empty, all but the most essential or trusted servants asked to stay in their rooms. "Where are we going?" Cedric asked.

"Nowhere. I figured you two haven't seen everything Iron-hold Keep has to offer. You just arrived after all," the spymaster said mildly. "My room is this way. The people here are still kind to Seelie nobility despite what I overheard earlier."

We want to crush Seelie and eat human hearts. Don't you? Neala couldn't forget those gruesome goals stated so plainly, the fae looking so hungry and eager for the chaos that would lead there.

"It really is too bad about the Unseelie Queen. I understand the blade was poisoned," Sondus continued.

"No one would tell me what they'd poisoned it with. But apparently, the attacker also met a grisly fate for daring to strike Queen Kalimea," she said, shooting him a curious look. If anyone knew what had coated the blade, it would be him.

"I brought two of my best healers to assist with the task," he answered with a minute shake of his head.

Cedric burst out, "But what else can we do to help? There has to be something she needs!"

Sondus tried a door at the end of the hall with a curious hum. It opened to the back of a library, the smell of old pages and ink rolling in. The spymaster inhaled deeply. "There's always something more to be done, young man," he said. "But first, I want to commend you on a job well done. Your group has already averted one disaster."

A starry blush crept up Cedric's neck. "Aww, but I didn't do anything."

Neala nudged him. "Sure you did. You saved me." She didn't hear anyone about in this side of the library, so she told Sondus of their half-bond and Cedric's swift rescue of her voice. The other man listened intently, smiling as she finished her tale.

"Indeed, as I was saying. Always something more," he said, gesturing between them. "You two will work yourselves too hard today and leave another task unfinished. Until Queen Kalimea awakens, you have some time."

He paused, waiting for it to sink in. Cedric twitched first, grabbing Neala's arm. "Go," the spymaster laughed. "Take a personal moment. I will be here, doing what I do best...reading and listening."

"Thank you." Cedric wasn't ready to turn him down, tugging Neala out the way they'd come. She didn't fight it, looking to retrace their steps and head into the royal suites, where their room waited.

Swallowing a stone in her throat, she realized she'd been putting off what they needed to talk about. It was time for them to break down the last barrier between them, one that loomed in her past like a vengeful specter.

They walked past a group of fae conducting a test on a random fae in palace livery. It glowed green, so they nodded and sent that maid on her way. "We didn't figure it out!" one Unseelie called to her cheerfully.

"Then I don't congratulate you!" she called back. When his face crumpled in confusion, she laughed and flashed him a thumbs up.

"You'd think they'd be used to not-congratulations," Cedric said when they were out of earshot.

"They'd better get used to it. I'm starting to think backward the more we talk to Unseelie." She shook her head at the idea, knowing how many people she was going to confuse when they returned home.

When they were close to the golden door that separated them from the royal suites, she practically felt the excitement blazing from Cedric. Could he sense that she had something to say first? If he could, it didn't seem to dissuade him.

Their room was in its same disheveled state as when they'd left it. She immediately went to the bed, sitting on its unmade edge and patting the space next to it for Cedric. He put his lute away and snuggled into her with little hesitation. It would be so easy to set aside her worries—and his clothes—to sink into his embrace there and then.

She wet her lips. "Cedric, I..." His earnest gaze seemed to sparkle up at her. "Before we finish the mating bond, I have to tell you a few things about me."

Finally, it seemed he noticed the nerves pulling at her belly and her reluctance to delve into these memories. "Do you *have* to?" he whispered.

"No secrets between us." She breathed a sigh as she steeled herself. "No regrets."

"No regrets," he echoed, eyeing her like he was afraid she'd reveal she was secretly a monstrous Fell all along.

You can do this. You can talk about it, she told herself. Something she hadn't even done with Nyah yet, despite the offer.

"I haven't told you the full truth about what happened with Marcus and Lucia," she began. He knew the same thing everyone else did.

He left me for Lucia.

It was all she ever said of Marcus anymore. And also the only thing most people needed to know about that relationship.

Cedric sighed, folding his arms tightly like a barrier. But he waited as she struggled to find the place to start. "I had a short time with Marcus," she finally said. "He was the commander of a group of vampire mercenaries. At the time, the only army-for-hire in Europe that was comprised of all vampires, and they were deadly. Originally, I came to Marcus with an interest in purchasing the Hartson Company long enough to storm Nyixa and part Lucia from her head."

Her mind's eye was a thousand years away, remembering a man larger and stronger than her, with a belly laugh and a shrewd mind for battle tactics. Their romance had been as quick as their relationship. "We wed along the way there, and he helped me with young Keegan and Sorsha. He was the father figure they'd never had. Then we arrived at Nyixa, and it all fell apart."

Cedric's expression shaded to discomfort, and she wasn't even to the worst of it. It looked like he was struggling against saying something, his lips firmly clamped on an interruption.

She decided to forge on quickly before it escaped anyway, as it usually did with him. "You see, the worst part about Lucia was that she could see the future. She knew exactly what our plan was and saw a weakness to make it all come crashing down. That flaw was...it was Marcus himself. I know now that she lured him away and forced him to take a potion that made him think *she* was his lifemate instead of me. She cut our connection and inserted herself between us."

Even now, talking to the man who'd risked his heart for her, her gut twisted into painful knots at the memory. "I am the first and last vampire I've ever met whose mate has done this," she admitted quietly. "But that's not the worst part. Lucia made sure I wouldn't protest by using the Mind Key against me. She punched her way into my mind and erased my memories of Marcus. All of them. So, when he realized what she'd done and came back to me, I was the one who rejected him, thinking he was coming on to me out of turn."

"How did you get your memories back?" Cedric murmured.

"A thousand years and a lot of magic later. I'm whole and remember everything about my past...everything I've lost. Marcus is long dead. He gained a touch of the Fell Madness himself, replaced me with a harem, and had a huge family that he drove to ruin. He only has a son and grandson who survived it all."

Her eyes stung. She wiped at the corners, looking up to prevent them from watering. "You've prevented one of my nightmares from happening. I just thought...you may as well know the other one before we bond." Damn it, her voice was betraying her instead with a warble.

"I would *never* do that to you!" he burst out, hugging fiercely to her side. "And you didn't deserve a moment of it. Not him leaving you for her, not her smashing your memories, none of it." She turned to hold him, letting her tears run into his hair when they stubbornly descended.

He caught her cheeks, tugging until they were eye to eye. "You believe me, right?" he asked, tenderly wiping away the trails in her skin.

"Of course. It's just...he hadn't really had a choice. And if he had..." Well, that would make it all the worse, if there'd been a moment for Marcus to stop their headlong plunge into tragedy.

"There's always a choice, Neala. And I choose you. You already know it." He placed a hand over his heart, where it beat to the rhythm of hers.

"Then...I regret Marcus Hartson. He is gone." She made a motion like brushing the memory away. "But I don't regret you. You're a different man than him in all ways."

His laugh sounded nervous. "Not a big, strong guy like him."

"I was surprised that you weren't when I first realized what you were to me." She laced her leg between his, scooting closer. "Now, I understand. I needed someone who could help me heal and bring out a better version of myself." Her breath was shallow as she pressed her forehead to his. Why couldn't she have his way with words to express what her heart was bursting to say?

She looked into his eyes and told the truth. "I need you as my mate. I love you." And she'd never meant it more. They'd agreed to take this journey together slowly, and thus, her affection had crept in unnoticed until it'd surrounded her, impossible to deny.

They breathed the same air as his gaze sparkled from the admission. "I love you too," he said, bringing their lips together at last. They fell back onto the bed to seal themselves as mates with the first joining of their bodies, as slow and tender as their courtship.

Chapter 29
Neala

Neala's blissful sleep was interrupted sometime in the dark of night when someone pounded on the door with a heavy fist. Her new mate was curled up with his back to her as the little spoon, uttering an unhappy groan as he woke as well.

She went to see who it was this time, leaving Cedric in a warm nest of blankets. Dressed hastily in her tunic and pants and little else, she answered barefoot and found Sirius on the other end, looking especially tired and bedraggled. "Queen's awake. Ash wants us right away," he grumbled.

"Want a wake-up slap with that?" she offered.

"Slap me. I dare you."

Wham!

Sirius muttered a curse. She hadn't even hit him that hard when he regenerated in a blink.

"What? You dared me," she said innocently.

"Next time, I'll let you sleep through the meeting," he sighed, stomping off.

Part of her wished he had when she gently prodded Cedric awake despite his requests for five more minutes. "No more minutes. Didn't you want to play for Kalimea?"

"Not right now," he complained.

Despite his grumblings, both of them became presentable within minutes when reality set in. The Unseelie Queen would set her wayward kingdom to rights. The demon plotting against them was using her absence as a sign of weakness. Soon, it would have to come up with a new ploy.

Cedric donned his brightest clothes and placed his hat at a careful sideways angle so his smile sparkled just right. The new bond between them helped Neala understand that he'd practiced everything about his act down to when to wear the hat. "Meeting royalty definitely requires a bow with it," he explained once he realized she was watching with a knowing smile.

He took a bow, sweeping the hat out and replacing it on his head with a fancy doff. "See?"

"Yes, very entertaining." She pinched his rear on her way by, grinning from his yelp.

They went across the hall to the queen's chambers, where Sirius, Ash, and Sondus were already seated and a fourth person stood at the windows overlooking the city. Neala's first thought was wondering why the woman had four wings. They burned behind her, one set at the standard angle like all fae wings, while the other set arched up higher and filled her back with flames like a warm halo. An occultarus floated between her wings, the dark and smoky orb hiding its presence.

"Is that all of us, then?" Her voice was husky and low, reminiscent of Ash's womanly alto.

"Still missing Izell, if she's really coming, Your Majesty," Sondus replied.

The monarch sighed and turned toward them. If Neala hadn't known she was Ash's sister, she couldn't have guessed it. Kalimea's hair was a deep scarlet, falling around her face in careless ringlets. She wasn't as tall as Ash and wore a simple, sky-blue gown to offset her fire. It clung to her curves while a slit up the side exposed the arch of her leg.

Something about her made the hair lift on Neala's arms. Kalimea was beautiful in the same way a jaguar was, as polished as a cat with all the predatory gleam that came from it.

Neala glanced to Cedric, and they bowed together while Ash did the introductions. "My sister's taste in friends grows more eccentric every time she visits," Kalimea said.

Neala's brow furrowed as she tried to find the lie in that sentence. Did she think a vampire and half-fae were somehow less peculiar than usual?

"Sondus." The spymaster's posture sharpened immediately as Kalimea inspected her nails. "They will believe you over me if you explain my peculiarities."

He turned to them obediently. "She can tell the truth and lie. The mantle of monarch is not symbolic—it grants powers to do things ordinary fae cannot."

"What else does it do?" Cedric asked, putting off waves of curiosity Neala could feel.

"An inquisitive mind. Be careful with that," Kalimea interrupted. "Ash was just telling me of the great debt of gratitude I owe you all."

"Something we were all glad to do without compensation," Sirius said, his sigh implying this had been stated more than once.

Kalimea returned to gazing out the window. "To tell a fae that they do not have to repay a debt is a foolish thing. If it's all the same to you, I would prefer to stand. I've been lying in bed for far too long," she said to her reflection. "You may sit if you like."

Neala and Cedric claimed a loveseat together. She shot Sirius a look. *"There is something she can repay us with,"* she said privately.

"There is?"

"The Fell Key she has!"

Thankfully, the Unseelie Queen didn't see it when he covered his face with his palm.

"Despite that, I am quite fatigued, as I imagine you all are at this terrible hour," Kalimea continued. "But Ash has brought me up to speed on everything. Some things take precedence over our own comfort. Are you sure Izell is coming, spymaster, or can we get on with this?"

"I believe it is wise to wait," he said.

"That was neither a yes nor a no, good sir."

Sondus's lips quirked. "She stated that she was coming. But it's also Izell, so..."

"Can we judge the Izell we know by her old behavior when it's been so long?" she mused.

Ash snorted in amusement. "No. You absolutely cannot."

The door opened, and Izell poked her head into the room. "You cannot what?" She had herself heavily glamored as she walked in, locking the door behind her.

Then she let the magic go and revealed herself in her scaly glory. Kalimea turned, and their gazes met for a prolonged moment. Neala tensed, wondering how the monarch would react to an open *mort loci* right there in her chambers.

Instead, she watched in shock as Kalimea crossed the room and embraced Izell, scales and all. "You're back, you old dame. You proved everyone wrong," she murmured.

"I keep my word," the old fae grumbled. She drew back with her hands on Kalimea's shoulders, inspecting her closely. "Are you all right?"

"The wound will heal, but I'm to have a terrible scar." She placed a hand over her side. "It'll be a surprise for Orin."

Izell chuckled. "We must always endeavor to surprise our mates."

As soon as the two of them parted ways, Izell was waylaid by Sondus, whom she hugged more carefully. By the way she lined up her forearms on his shoulders, she was avoiding touching what remained of his wings. "And you! Lord of the Shifting Wood." She grinned with all her fangs. "I was hoping to find an ally in the Unseen Council, but I never expected one of my brightest students at the helm."

"And I'm happy to see you're back, just as you promised," he said, cracking a smile and motioning for her to sit with him.

"You notice how no one's saying anything about her being part dragon?" Now that they were bonded as mates, Cedric's mental voice drifted to her clearly.

"As I understand it, she was a 'mort loci' before she came to Adrun. She must be hiding it from everyone else," she said.

He shrugged, dozing against her shoulder as they waited for the conversation to shift. Smiles quickly turned serious as Kalimea paced the fine rug in front of them. "There is a demon in my kingdom," she began. "One who is corrupting Unseelie and beast alike with her blood." She worried her lip. "Spymaster, how badly has she shaken the confidence in my rule?"

"We are still assessing that, Your Majesty. I will have a report to you by tomorrow," Sondus answered crisply.

"What can you tell me now?"

He produced a book from a small stack laying at his feet. "I researched the claims of those we interrogated for mention of a demon by the name of Lilith. There's a team scouring the Library of Faerie for further references to give us a more complete picture of her." He opened to a dog-eared page and passed it to Kalimea, who stopped to read.

While she did, Sondus narrated, "The book says that Lilith is one of the seven Lords of Hell, akin to a queen. She is a succubus, a demon aligned to the sin of lust, but many demons that ascend as far as she has adopt other qualities of the lesser sins. Lilith in particular is portrayed as a battle maiden who collects the skulls of those who attempt to unseat her."

"Brutal," Cedric murmured.

The spymaster nodded in agreement. "Her blood has corruptive potential. However, the book is incomplete information from thousands of years ago. We still don't know who summoned her and what they sacrificed to do so. A demon of Lilith's caliber is no beginner conjuration. The Unseen Council has stopped summoners in the past, but none have been powerful enough to perform such a spell, let alone practice to get to that point."

"Well, she didn't appear out of thin air," Ash said acidly.

Kalimea passed the book to Ash, who let it circulate around the room. "How do you know all this?" Cedric asked as they waited for a peek at what he was referencing.

He smiled proudly. "I have what mortals refer to as a photographic memory. I don't forget what I read."

The news was like a burst of excitement in Cedric's mind. Neala had to smile as he exclaimed, "I knew it had to be something! You know so much."

Meanwhile, she kept her thoughts to herself. If he truly had a memory that potent, Sondus was the perfect fit for his job. She was just glad he was on their side. When the book finally passed into her hands, she scanned the information on the page. It was almost exactly what Sondus had said aloud, accompanied by a sketch of the demon in question. Despite holding two battleaxes large enough to split a man in two, Lilith was more alluring than monstrous.

The greater demon Jazrach had been a bat-like creature that hulked forward onto its knuckles like a gorilla. It'd been a horror to witness, with wet mouths covering its skin, all working together to produce the chilling chorus of whispers all of its victims had been subjected to. Neala's brief brush with it had been plenty. She was more than glad it was dead.

She had no doubt that Lilith was just as vile as Jazrach despite having an hourglass figure and a face that would make vain Lucia weep with envy. The only things that said "demon" about her were a pair of leathery wings and four horns that sprouted at angles that drew the eye to her face. Neala memorized the image while heaving a sigh.

No doubt if she ever crossed blades with Lilith, the first thing the demon would do was sneer at Neala's appearance. The hyper-beautiful always did so. Hopefully, it would allow her the opening to send this creature back where she belonged.

"After the attack, Lilith appeared in my dreams," Kalimea said, instantly commanding everyone's attention. She took the book back and stared at the sketch. "She tried to sway me to her side. I suspect my would-be assassin coated his blade with her blood to give her access to me. Naturally, I made her believe I was her humble servant."

Ash sucked in a breath, her knuckles whitening.

"She didn't really look like this in my dreams. I just remember the shape of her and her wings," the monarch mused, tracing a finger down the page. "She probably knows I am not under her sway. I'm going to send a message to prove it."

"What did she want you to do?" Ash asked.

"Stop the parties. Assemble the army." Kalimea shrugged. "So, we are having the biggest party we can plan on short notice.

How better to get Lilith to attack me again? I will be the bait, and this time, we will be ready for her."

Neala leaned in, focusing on the shift here, the "we" that she was a part of.

"Absolutely! We will definitely use the one and only Queen Kalimea as bait!" Ash exclaimed, glaring.

"Do I need to remind you of my power?"

"Do you need to be reminded that you almost *died*?" her sister demanded.

"A lucky strike from a cowardly man. Lilith will need to do better than that...especially now that two vampire Blood Princes, my esteemed Spellbreaker sister, Archfae Izell Firebrand, and my cunning spymaster are all in the same room and know an attack is coming." Kalimea smirked, the picture of confidence as she weighed them together like a shield for her wellbeing.

Sirius sat back, his eyebrows close to his hairline. "You think a powerful demon will attack you again if you throw a party."

"Guaranteed. She threatened my life if I even considered not allying the Unseelie as a whole to the demonic invasion of Earth. I'll let you know a secret, vampire. I hate being considered evil because of what I am." Kalimea folded her arms behind her back, her eyes blazing with conviction. "I, like most Unseelie, have never been to Earth. The midwinter crossing is a myth, blocked by the same barrier that blocks demons. Unseelie are labeled as demon-worshippers and treated as such."

Sondus raised a finger. "But you have seen how quickly even your most loyal men have turned on you the moment a demon surfaced."

She turned a cross expression his way. "I will show them the error of their ways personally. Lilith's converts will hang."

"What if they are forced to drink her blood?" Sondus steepled his fingers. "What if the majority of your people turn from you when Lilith's presence becomes public knowledge? Will you go from the Queen who funds soup kitchens and personally raises orphans to the one who bathes in the blood of her people?"

He maintained a poker face as she stared at him hard enough

to burn holes through his skull. "It will not come to that," she said through gritted teeth.

"Won't it?" he asked quietly. "Unseelie began as demon worshippers."

"Many generations ago. Save for a select few, that old guard is gone. We educate our youth on the follies of that time." Her shoulders sagged as she turned to Ash. "We know we are cursed by our lying tongues. I raised my sister without once being able to tell her aloud that I loved her."

"It's okay, I didn't know," Ash murmured.

"How can any Unseelie look at the way we live and say, 'Yes, I want this to be my eternity'?" Kalimea continued.

Izell spoke up. "There is no other option, Kali. Unless you can offer your people something more attractive than Lilith's whispers, you will lose those most disenfranchised by the status quo."

The monarch straightened, her lips moving to repeat those words to herself. "Something to keep me awake at night," she remarked. "In the meantime, I am about to invite the groups left out in the cold outside of Ironhold the honor of performing at the next event. I'm thinking a carnival by day and a masquerade by night. I'll leave the specifics to my master of ceremonies."

"And you expect an attack on yourself during this time, Your Majesty?" Neala asked.

The Unseelie Queen grinned. "I welcome it. Any public display to put down this movement is ideal. What are your specialties?" she asked Neala directly, her fiery gaze roaming over her form.

"Fighting and illusions, mostly."

"Oh? Can you see under my glamor?" She rotated one of her rings as she asked, tilting her head coyly. Neala had no doubt the invitation was a challenge of sorts.

Pulling away a glamor or illusion was usually a simple task. When she tried it on Kalimea, however, it felt like the magic pulled itself back into place the moment it gave her a glimpse of the woman underneath. Kalimea frowned over at Izell. "Stop helping her."

The elder fae lifted her hands. "I'm not doing anything."

Neala's brow furrowed, and she tried harder until she finally ripped the illusion off so she alone could see the woman underneath. "Are you a demon too?" she asked plainly.

"No," the monarch snapped. She was different in shades of her glamored self, sporting small fangs like Neala had seen on her death fae tutor. She also had claws that gleamed like obsidian, and her wings burned hotter and redder than her glamor suggested.

"Destruction fae inherited the power to make things explode. The more one uses that power, the more demonic they appear," Kalimea admitted. She hid her claws in balled fists. "Sometimes, such things are necessary. Especially as Unseelie Queen."

Shows of strength, Neala thought, blinking rapidly to dispel Kalimea's sharper features. "I understand." She may not approve, but she could see how the leader of the Unseelie had to be more Unseelie than the rest.

Despite this, Kalimea was the least Unseelie-like fae she'd met in her short time here.

"I wonder how much more powerful your mind would be with this. Try it out." Kalimea wiggled a ring free from her finger and tossed it to Neala.

With a sinking feeling in her stomach, she turned it over, instantly recognizing the design and the magic that lurked below its glittering surface. "If you can strip me of my illusion, you may borrow it to run security on my next party," the monarch continued as Neala stared at it.

On Lucia's hand, this little piece of jewelry had ripped away Neala's most intimate memories. It was an abhorrent tool. Her breath came short as she wrestled with the offer. Her hold trembled while she rolled the band between her thumb and forefinger. *Just put it on,* she thought. *It can't harm you if you're the one using it.*

Her gaze lifted, meeting the cloudy nebulae in Izell's eyes. The fae mimed placing a ring on her finger. *"Claim it. The Mind Key is your legacy,"* she said privately.

The ring sized itself perfectly to her finger as she slipped it on. The gemstone flashed in acknowledgement of a new wielder.

She reached out and ripped the illusion from Kalimea's form as easily as splitting paper in half.

"You are its true wielder," Izell whispered.

Neala's stomach rolled in complaint. She curled her hand to hide the ring from sight as they were quickly dismissed for the night. Ash stayed behind to argue, her voice white noise as Neala left the room in a daze, only coming to once she emptied the contents of her stomach into the toilet in her room.

Cedric held her hair, concern radiating from him.

"I'll get used to it," she said. She rotated the band so the gemstone no longer taunted her. "Let's look on the bright side. It's another item from my past that I've reclaimed from Lucia."

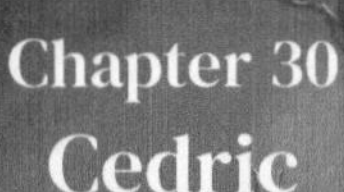

Chapter 30
Cedric

"She didn't want the Fell Key, did she?" Sondus asked over breakfast. Neala stayed in bed, probably to throw the semi-unbreakable Mind Key against the wall with none the wiser about its abuse.

"It's what we came here for, so…" Cedric shrugged.

The two of them dined with Miles and the other bards he'd traveled with, joining the bustle of the palace dining hall with the other residents. Their conversation carried away with the murmur of hundreds of other voices as servants and visitors gathered together to gossip.

"You also came here to perform, did you not?" Sondus soaked up egg yolk with his toast as he spoke. He dressed like he wasn't a nobleman himself, fitting in with the drab colors most Unseelie seemed to wear. Cedric felt like a peacock here with his royal blue suit, more prepared for an upscale performance than breakfast.

He thought he'd perform for Queen Kalimea, since Ash had originally asked him to, just to find that they'd both started their days with a backlog of meetings and diplomacy that had no place for a strutting bard.

"I haven't really performed in days," he said. Other than helping maintain Neala's voice, he'd barely plucked his lute. It lay heavy against his back, a reminder of the sweet music they could make together.

"How do you feel about going out with us today?" Miles offered.

"It would be helpful if you could listen to the laypeople," Sondus murmured around a bite of toast.

"Oh, for your..." he glanced around, lowering his voice. "...for the report you promised?"

The spymaster nodded once in confirmation.

It seemed as good a time as any to keep his ears open. Especially since word was already circulating about the blowout event Kalimea was hosting in the palace the day after tomorrow. She had to have an army of party planners and servants to make it happen, but he was sure she'd announced such a tight timeline to thwart Ash's protests. Whether Ash wanted it or not, Kalimea was going to bait out another attack as soon as possible.

"Anything we should be spreading?" Miles offered.

Sondus inclined his head to the two Unseelie bards. "I believe sentiments will be more honest when whispered in your ears. Cedric, Miles, you would best serve by inviting trustworthy folk to the upcoming party."

"Got it," Cedric said. His heart fluttered faster to be doing real spy work *and* getting to know this new city all at the same time.

The group parted ways to prepare, and he went straight to Neala, walking into their room to find everything not bolted to the floor floating. He poked a plate hovering nearby, sending it into a slow spin before it bounced off the wall with a brittle clatter.

"Oops." He quick-walked past it, pretending he hadn't seen a thing.

His feet left the ground just as he caught sight of Neala sitting cross-legged, floating above the bed. Nowhere near as graceful, he pinwheeled his arms as he fell in slow motion, missing an acquaintance with the ground because whatever was going on slowed his momentum to a stop inches from it.

"*Welcome back, chicken.*" Neala sounded like she was grinning, even though her real expression was creased with intense concentration.

"You're doing this?" he yelped.

"Just an experiment. How is it going?"

"Everything is floating! Including me," he protested.

Her eyes flew open. The magic tapered off to gently lower him and everything else to the ground. It was a mess, plates on the floor, curtains and sheets shrouding upturned dressers. He took it in with a hum.

"Want to go out on the town?" he asked.

She laughed incredulously. "Now?"

"Maybe you could levitate everything back into place first."

She lifted her right hand, where the Mind Key glimmered from its own lighting. Anything within her gaze righted itself on its own.

"What's the occasion?" she asked like she wasn't exerting incredible psychic power with a flick of her wrist.

He watched the curtains reattach themselves to their supports. "Um..." What could she do with that Fell Key if she was really trying?

"I won't abuse it. Not like she did," she murmured to answer his thoughts.

"Of course not. I didn't think you would," he said quickly. He told her about his new mission from Sondus to wipe that concerned frown from her face as she twisted the Mind Key around again so it looked like she was wearing a plain gold band.

"Maybe you could sing," he suggested at the end, which she nodded to absently.

"If I know the songs. And if you eclectic bunch even sound good as a quartet," she hedged.

"Oh! We're probably not playing together." He laughed as he escorted her from the room. He started tuning his lute as he steered her toward the palace entrance. "If a group of individuals like us meets at a bar, we usually take turns, and those not playing interact with the crowd. That way, you get more money...and booze!"

"Which is practically money as well," she said.

"Exactly!"

She glanced down at herself. "Do you think I should put on an illusion for this? We are much more noticeable because I'm a vampire."

"I mean, probably." He was reluctant to see her features wash away as she transformed herself into an astral fae with a sequined dress to twinkle like the stars in her skin. It felt odd to look at a stranger and sense his mate hiding in plain sight.

They joined up with the other bards and walked into the city. The front gates were flung open, flurries of fae coming in with cartloads of favors and fresh ingredients for the kitchens. It was still early, the main marketplace full as various fae shopped for the day's fresh offerings.

"Isn't it a little early to go tavern hopping?" Neala suggested.

"Too true, milady." Miles still hadn't recognized her and instead regarded her with a warm smile that lingered seconds too long for Cedric's liking. "We may as well split up. It's a big city." He tugged his ear in meaning.

Cedric scanned the road and spotted the perfect place. "What's the best tavern in town?" he asked Daron, who named the Battleaxe Pub.

"It's not named for the one who runs it," the Unseelie said.

Neala lifted a brow. "A warrior woman?"

"Or maybe her favorite cleaver!" He snickered.

"Why don't we meet there for the noonday meal?" Cedric suggested, struggling not to laugh when he realized how little Neala was amused by this.

As the others agreed and ventured further into the city, Cedric took Neala's hand and pulled her toward a street corner. "Don't worry, you can be my battleaxe." He winked.

"Oh, I feel so much better." She punctuated it with a roll of her eyes.

"You've been around Ash too long."

The corner was already occupied by a lesser fae begging with a metal cup. A single coin rattled as it shook its taloned hand. They earned a glare from its shriveled face as Cedric strummed his instrument beside it.

"This place is mine! Get your own," it hissed.

"Put your cup down, good..." He hesitated. "Good sir."

The creature eyed him as it did. A forked tongue flicked out. Cedric did his best to ignore that stare and began to sing, plucking his lute to a tune Neala would recognize.

She swayed to the beat, but her voice didn't join his. There was uncertainty over their bond as a crowd of Unseelie trickled by. Some stopped to listen.

When Cedric was done, he bowed and angled the hat in his hand toward the beggar's cup. Coins chimed as they bounced into the metal. "Thank you, folks. Biggest tip picks the next song," he proclaimed.

He just hoped that person didn't choose a song he didn't know. When a coin glimmering gold joined the pot and a song was named, though, Cedric relaxed into a new tune. He looked over at Neala hopefully. They'd sung this duet together while she was learning her voice.

Her mouth opened, and Cedric's heart soared. It wasn't just to hear her share the joy of music with him—there was magic weaving into her tone like she'd never harnessed before. The blessing of the *drasonii*, music that could move emotion. And with her eyes tightly shut, she didn't realize what she was doing until the coins came, falling like rain while the lesser fae watched in awe.

"Neala, that was amazing," he murmured under the call of a growing crowd for more.

She startled from the attention once she realized how much was focused on her. *"I didn't do anything different,"* she said privately.

His gaze fell to the Mind Key on her finger, illusioned into a plain silver band. *"It's the only thing that's different,"* he said.

She lifted her hand with a hum. *"We are bonded now."*

"I can make noises like a lyrebird, not sing with such emotion," he said, convinced.

She pressed her lips together and refused an encore. "The lady is shy of her gifts, you see," Cedric said for her, softening the crowd's disappointed jeer.

His talents alone had most of the crowd moving on after the novelty wore off. He turned his attention to the lesser fae, who was counting its new coins in orderly stacks. Cedric knew what he was doing. He knew there were few folk in any city as invisible at those who begged for their keep.

"Hey. Could you do me a favor?" he asked it quietly. The lesser fae lifted its head, the membranes over its eyes blinking independently of each other.

It threw an arm around the coins like a dragon guarding its treasure. "Mine," it hissed.

"Yes, yours." Cedric bit back a sigh. It was a gift after all. "I want to know if you've heard anything about a demon lately."

The creature alternated its blinks more rapidly. "Are you talking about Lilith?" it whispered.

"...Some fae here speak openly about her, the demon," Cedric finished in a hush. They sat together in the back of Battleaxe Pub, with a clear view of the "cleaver" hanging on the wall. The owner could slice off an ogre's head with the thing, double-bladed and gleaming from a recent polish.

The lesser fae he'd spoken to was their best lead so far, knowing exactly what was going on from catching snippets of conversation from random passersby. Not only had it overheard who Lilith was, it'd caught many fae debating whether or not Kalimea should step down and simply offer the demon her throne.

"About as troublesome as it comes," Neala remarked. She nursed a mug of ale, the stars in her illusion fading the further into the drink she went. He could feel how her thoughts revolved around their song and the emotions she'd invoked with it.

"*Maybe you could perform again with the ring off. See what happens?*" he suggested privately.

"*A good idea,*" she mused, pocketing it under the table.

"Add in how the people already know the Queen is trying to

distract and soften them up for something, and there's distrust," Cedric finished.

"I didn't meet a few sympathizers," Daron said quietly, affecting some familiar sarcasm. "They aren't zealous about their cause or anything."

"Is it an all or nothing thing?" Miles asked.

"Doesn't seem that way," the Unseelie confirmed.

"I imagine we already have enough to report," Miles sighed. "Why don't we do that and own this place tonight for anything we've missed?"

Cedric had to agree while also slanting a look Neala's way. He knew how they could spend a few hours. Her knowing smile echoed agreement. They left Daron to hold their place in the pub and keep his ears open, the rest of them finding their way around the city.

Cedric walked hand-in-hand with Neala, wishing they had less cares to enjoy the moment with. "The last time we wanted that, you suggested placing the past aside for two weeks," Neala said off of his thoughts.

He played a chord on his lute. "Why don't we try a bit of that now?" he suggested. "Sing a little something for me."

Try as she might, without the Mind Key, her voice missed achieving the fever pitch of emotions she'd captured earlier. But when she placed it back on and tried again, Cedric's eyes watered with emotion.

He sniffled and swept the tears away. "Incredible," he whispered. "It's like your voice channels the Key. Maybe it was made for this?"

Neala's back went rigid at the suggestion.

Chapter 31
Neala

Her first night performing was a blur. Fun and terrifying and exhilarating as only a string of songs and the emotions within could be. She practiced with the Mind Key to feel how it worked through her voice, giving her the last boost of talent she'd otherwise need years of specialized practice with a fae tutor to achieve.

Lady Iridia would be so proud.

While she and Cedric performed, the other bards canvassed the crowd. Miles took shots with a bored Unseelie wearing clothes too fine for the establishment. Daron rubbed elbows with dozens of fae, lingering only with a blight fae woman Neala caught staring at her more than once. The blight fae lifted a drink to her once with a smile and a wink. It wasn't terribly unusual, considering how Neala continued tinkering with the strength of her voice through the night. Her performances had everyone's attention.

The next day, on the eve before the big event, Cedric presented her with a little wooden box. "I asked Sondus if he could get me one," he blurted before she'd even opened it. His heart pattered eagerly as she lifted the lid to find a flat, gray stone on a silver cord.

"And I never thought I'd need one," she said, recognizing it as the same kind of rock he wore on his wrist to block out the emotions of his performances on himself.

He helped her fasten it around her neck, where the stone hung just below her collarbone. "Thank you," she said, stealing a quick kiss. "Now, play something for me!"

Cedric retrieved his lute for a familiar song, one that allowed for her to belt the chorus. It was a harsher chorus, one full of rage and swearing revenge on an ex-lover. As her voice built toward that crescendo, her mate trembled from whatever emotions she sang. She couldn't feel them anymore. She nailed the chorus with feeling, exalting in herself until something shattered in the bathroom.

"Oh, shit." She rushed over to find their bathroom mirror pulverized into shards over the basin and floor.

Not even a minute later, the front door opened, and Ash's scowling face peered in. "What was that?" she demanded, motioning they come outside.

"I thought I locked that door," Cedric murmured. He backed away slowly from the shattered mirror, rubbing goosebumps from his arms. The Unseelie Princess brought them into her sister's sitting room, where Kalimea stood next to a red stain in the carpet, holding the neck of a wine bottle with the bottom broken into jagged shards.

Neala felt an uncomfortable surge of heat as she realized this must also be her doing. "My apologies, Your Majesty," she said immediately. "I had no idea..."

The moment Kalimea began to laugh, Neala drifted off uncertainly. "What did you *do*?" the Queen cackled. "It's the only one broken. My favorite vintage, but there are plenty more."

"I was just singing," she said, still not sure how she'd hit a glass-shattering note that'd reached this far. She named the song, and Kalimea hummed. While they pondered the lyrics, the Queen must've called for Izell, as the woman arrived and immediately clucked her tongue.

She gestured to the floor. "Looks like a bloodstain."

"Thankfully it's not this time," Kalimea said primly.

"This time?" Cedric echoed. He'd clutched Izell's sleeve,

already rushing to tell her what she'd missed and how it'd happened.

The elder fae dropped her illusion and fixed him with an annoyed look. "Slow down. You gave her a focus?"

"And I sang and shattered glass," Neala finished for him abruptly. "The Mind Key is affecting my singing voice."

Izell's smile was too knowing. "You don't say."

"You've seen this with your future sight—"

"I don't have future sight anymore," the elder fae sighed.

"—so explain what's going on," Neala finished, unperturbed.

Izell shrugged, her scaly fingers moving through a few intricate gestures. Shards of glass lifted from the floor, fitting themselves together like puzzle pieces until Kalimea was left holding an intact wine bottle. "Not really a mystery. The Mind domain of fae magic has power over anything our brains perceive. Illusions, emotions, memories, psychic powers. Your brain was already strong with how you used to only communicate mentally. Now, you could probably do anything an Archfae could with this one domain of magic."

Neala's lips pinched from that news. It seemed too easy to put on a ring and suddenly experience such a powerful augmentation. "The Fell Keys are all meant for someone specifically," Izell continued. "Like that one zealot and the Light Key. It bound itself to him despite him not understanding where it truly came from."

She pulled on the Mind Key, relieved to feel it slipping off her first knuckle. "I have no intentions of keeping this thing permanently."

Kalimea and Ash exchanged a glance. "It's clearly responding well to you," the Queen said. "Why protest it? Wear it. Experiment. Just go far away from my quarters so you don't break something worth more than a bottle of wine."

"And our mirror," Cedric pitched in.

Neala sighed and practically dragged Izell into the hall for a moment alone. "You knew this would happen," she said, flashing the ring on her hand. Izell was quickly hiding under a glamor again, just in time for a servant to pass them by, none the wiser.

"Sure. I didn't pick you and your companions out of a hat," Izell snarked. "Most of you were meant to carry a Fell Key home."

"Why didn't you *tell me?*" Neala demanded.

Izell's eyes flashed. "I'm very sorry you don't like having complete control over one of the most powerful schools of fae magic."

"It's not that!" She was sorely tempted to bounce her fist off of one of the soft velvet walls to see if it was as cushiony as it looked. "I hate the secrets. Why couldn't you just tell me you wanted me for the Mind Key?"

Some of the irritation bled from Izell's stance. She rubbed the bridge of her nose between two fingers. "Do you really think you'd have come to Faerie if I told you what was ahead? You kicked and screamed your way to your new voice. When you held the Mind Key for the first time, you nearly cried." She clasped Neala's hands between both of hers and leaned in, whispering. "It's okay, Neala. It's *yours* now. You hold the power to crush Lucia's memories like stomping on a watermelon."

Neala wanted to drag herself away, feeling terribly exposed. Izell's hold was like iron clamps, clinging until her words were heard. "But I know you won't. That, above anything else, is why the Mind Key made its way to you."

"How can you be so sure?" Lucia more than deserved to feel the same hollow pain, to experience probing her memories knowing person-sized chunks were missing.

The elder fae smiled and lifted one shoulder. "Some things, I can see. Some things, Cossette has told me."

Neala worried her bottom lip. "What can you tell me of the future?"

"You'll have to be more specific. What do you want to know?"

She wanted to gesture broadly and ask for everything. But that wasn't how Izell worked. She'd be lucky if she got a nibble of useful information despite wanting a flood of everything. "Fine. Tell me a little something for each of our companions. Will they be getting what they came for?"

Izell released her, rearing back with a hint of offense. "I

wouldn't extend the invitation without being sure I can guide everyone to their deepest desires."

"You promised Cedric family."

"And he has you now, and the fae family you adopted long ago."

Neala figured that was a creative interpretation of the wording, but one couldn't argue that her new mate was a beacon of happiness at how things were going, even though she could sense him eavesdropping on her emotions during this conversation.

"As for everyone else, their feet are set in the right direction," Izell continued. "Jaromir will receive the Mending Key from King Orin once we can get an audience. Cossette's mind grows more and more ready for her transformation by the day...and before you ask, turning her into an adult is beyond my magic. But I know someone with the capabilities."

She ticked them off on her fingers. "Who does that leave? Sirius. His path will be the hardest to walk." She tilted her head in consideration. "In fact, you should be saying your goodbyes to him soon. He has an important decision to make tomorrow."

"What...?" Neala reconsidered her question as it formed in her mouth. She dropped her voice. "What did you even offer him?"

"Ah. Sirius suffers the same way his brother does. He is his own worst enemy."

That almost didn't answer her question. But then again, Neala thought, maybe it had. She weighed it and set it aside for further study later. If he had to make a decision so soon, she was determined to help him make the right one. "What of Ash? What did you offer her?" she whispered.

Izell snorted. "Nothing. I told her I required her, and she came."

"All right." She struggled to believe that, even delivered from the tongue of a Seelie fae. "And what of yourself?"

The elder fae stiffened. All this time, and Neala had never questioned whether Izell was receiving any extra benefit from visiting Faerie once more. "Success is its own reward."

"But Jaromir."

"He is a good friend." Her face broke with a tender smile. It was fleeting and bittersweet, but Neala wanted to seize the memory of it and crow. The elder fae rarely ever smiled except to bare her teeth. There was something real there between her and stoic old Jaromir. Maybe it would be enough to save him from the pit he was digging for himself. "...I intend to return Jaromir to you ready to endure the ages, of course."

"What do you mean, 'return'?" Neala echoed.

Izell's expression pinched. "I'm not ready to talk about it," she murmured. "But we have the rest of today to teach you how to use the Mind Key to its fullest for the trials of tomorrow. Are you prepared?"

Neala was balanced on that knife's edge of demanding answers verses gobbling up any knowledge that would help her hone the Mind Key down to something she could use. At the same time, she needed the precision to respect the boundaries of others. Because she wasn't another Lucia, and she'd rather see the Mind Key destroyed for good rather than have it exploit one more person.

"I just need you to do one thing for me first," Neala said.

"Hmm?"

"Can you repair my bathroom mirror?"

Chapter 32
Sirius

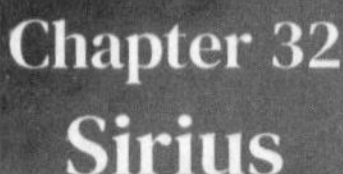

Sirius spent his time helping to set up the main event, putting his muscles to work to distract the beast pacing in his brain.

She was mine, it whined on occasion. *She could've been mine.*

Peeling potatoes and prepping other foods was the best, safest distraction. He avoided Izell, taking to camping out in a spare room in the servant's quarters when he wasn't working. The anger in him was too real. He didn't want to do anything he might regret.

If he saw Izell, he would ask about Jaromir. Their doctor, the man who should've been there when Neala was bitten. He couldn't take another melee mouthed response from their so-called leader. Why hadn't they come to Ironhold together as one group? Where was Jaromir now? Did he know what he'd missed?

One thing was certain—the kitchen was more than ready for the feast that night, with Sirius's knife skills put to good use on defenseless fruits and vegetables. He diced and minced and mashed, convincing his inner beast it was revenge they were having. He didn't notice the way the chefs and servants whispered behind his back, but they were respectful and kept a safe distance.

Soon, Sirius had nothing else to do and was shooed from the kitchens at last to "enjoy the festivities." He went outside and saw it was already well into the day. Somewhere close by, children screamed with glee.

The festivities had begun sometime in the early morning, dominated by the traveling circus that'd camped outside Ironhold's walls for nearly a week. At the top of the palace steps, he saw the tops of several tents, some brand new and still smelling of dye, while others were the worn survivors of that midnight battle.

Somewhere in the massive crowd of multicolored fae was his lifemate.

He locked his legs as his inner beast snarled. *Find her!*

Behave. He shut his eyes tightly to ward off a wave of fury from the beast. This time, its anger was aimed straight at him. With him irritated at its lack of decency, they were stuck in a self-hating spiral until a cool voice washed over him.

"There you are."

The tension in him broke, released in a long sigh. "Hello, Neala."

He nearly did a double take as he cracked his eyes open and focused on her. Neala had covered herself in a glamor to make herself a different person. The only sign that it was her was her red gaze through the face of a gold filigree mask. She was a study in the colors of an open flame, with an understated scarlet gown as the centerpiece.

"The masquerade isn't until later," he pointed out, tweaking the edge of her mask so it hung askew on her nose. It was real. *An expensive gift*, he thought.

Her glare was evident even with her brows covered. "I'm just a pretty placeholder. This is my post for today."

"Here?" There was a slight breeze, the chill of autumn and the wild scent of turning leaves carried upon it. They stood before the wide-open doors to the palace.

"Security," she said. She adjusted the mask to set it on her face just right. "This is the only entry or exit to the palace tonight. Ash is making sure Queen Kalimea won't encounter the trouble she's hoping for."

He snorted contemptuously. "There's never one entrance to a

place this large. Or to a race that can make portals anywhere they like."

"I asked about that, actually." She clasped her hands behind her back, a cautious eye turning to a pair of fae who passed them to head into the palace. "Any important place like the palaces or the Library of Faerie have anti-portal artifacts. Anyone who wants to enter Ironhold Keep has to walk in the old-fashioned way."

"And you're supposed to rebuff any would-be attackers while wearing a dress?" A warrior down to her blood and bones, he had seen Neala in a dress maybe twice in his life.

She smiled under the edge of her mask. "That's what Ash is for. I take a glance under the illusions; she alerts the guards if someone needs to spend the night in the dungeon rather than the ballroom."

"You've thought this out."

"While you were off sulking, yes."

His hands balled into fists as his inner beast snarled. "I do not *sulk*," he hissed.

For once, Neala did not needle him further. Her gaze traveled over the rigid line of his body, and for a pregnant pause, she said nothing at all. He scrubbed at his face, fighting the instinct to stare and challenge.

We like Neala. We respect Neala, he reminded his beast.

"What happened to you?" she asked at last. "Ever since we woke up, you've been so...*ill-tempered*. The breeze blows wrong, and you snarl at it."

He worked his jaw. Could he even begin to voice the truth? "Adrius. Gwendolyn. Lucia." He ticked them off on his fingers. "Need I mention our betrayers, Elandros and Qin?"

"Old news." She tilted her head. "Didn't you forgive Adrius and Gwendolyn?"

"That doesn't mean I can't blame them for wasting most of my immortal existence," he muttered.

"So, looking after your brother was a waste."

This time, he didn't stifle his growl. "What are you getting at?"

"I'm saying that he's your brother," she said evenly, meeting his gaze deliberately in challenge. "You should not hate him."

"He's…" What? He had nothing to say. He didn't hate his brother, but it was too complicated to put into words.

She held up a hand. "Or Gwendolyn, for she did what she thought was best. We were not put to the sword as Fell Mad because of her decision."

"I don't care about that. She still took a thousand years of our lives." He leaned in, heated.

"Mmm. I understand now." Turning away, she let a larger group of fae pass. Neither wanted to argue in front of the guests. He was ready to stalk off and ignore her, lest his beast convince him that taking a bite out of her was the next best option.

He made it three steps before they were alone again. "I know what your problem really is," Neala said to his back. Pausing, tensed, he waited for her to call out his anger, his beast, his lack of control. Which meant he wasn't prepared for her words. "You're selfish."

He snapped around so she couldn't stick another figurative knife into him. She was the picture of calm as he stomped right up to her. "Tell me I'm wrong," she stated when his face was inches from hers.

"You, over anyone else, know exactly what's been done to me." His voice was a low rumble, promising violence should she push him one more inch.

"I do," she agreed quietly.

"Yet *I'm* the selfish one?" he demanded.

Anyone else would've backed down by now, but not her. Her spine was steel, unbending no matter how close he crowded her. She stared him down so fiercely he backed away, his beast cowed into listening.

"Yes. Your anger is an issue, but in the bigger picture, you take no responsibility for it. You inflict your anger on others and expect them to deal with it." She shook her head slowly.

"I saved your sorry ass," he growled. "Was *that* selfish?"

"No, but coming to blows with Ash certainly was." At his

look, she smiled grimly. "I heard about it. Is that how this conversation ends? Are you going to take a swipe at me too?"

He drew back, blowing out a breath as his hands flexed at his side. They were dangerously close to that kind of ending, but her calling him on it was like fresh air on his overheated skin. He had to walk away. She didn't know his inner beast was ravening for a fight, demanding one. No one insulted his honor without consequences.

"Maybe I should just go." He took a step away, breathing like a bellows. "If I'm such a selfish hothead, maybe you all will do better without me."

"You would just be proving me right," she murmured.

"You *are* right!" he snapped. "I am a bastard, okay? I know! *I can't help it! I can't control it!*" His claws dug into the flesh of his palms as he finally admitted it out loud. "I can't control my magic."

Her expression said it all. She already knew.

"That's why you're here. I came to Faerie for my voice, and you traveled all this way to master yourself once more," she said. "Was it really that hard to admit it out loud?"

He scowled. "Don't patronize me."

"Why don't you go find Izell? Maybe she can help you. *Really* help you," she suggested, gesturing to the carnival going on and a huge crowd of fae blissfully unaware of their near-fight.

He turned away, fatigue weighing on his shoulders already. His beast would relive every word of this conversation. Whatever they were even fighting over, he knew he'd lost. "What can Izell do for me?" he sighed.

"More than you can do for yourself."

He muttered uncharitably and stomped off. It was only because he had the sharpened hearing of a predator that he even picked up some of her last words. A good luck and something about a hard path to walk. Whatever. He got himself lost in the crowd, trying to find any distraction so he could calm himself down.

A hand slipped into his, and he turned a sharp look at...nothing. Looking down, he realized it was Cossette who was tugging on his fingers. She turned a sunny smile up at him, for all intents a happy kid at a carnival.

It felt like his inner beast had run full-pelt into a wall. His anger blunted instantly in the presence of a child. Whether or not she was actually of Ancient age didn't matter.

"This way, Mister Fabron," she said, leading him into the crowd.

"How do you know my surname?" It was nearly surreal. He'd been Prince Sirius, the Dawn for as long as he could remember, even though he'd been born a normal village boy to an ordinary, if impoverished, family.

"I was at your brother's wedding," she giggled. "Don't you remember?"

His mouth twisted with guilt. Not because he hadn't noticed her, but because he remembered being so proud of his brother and everything he'd overcome. Yet moments ago, he'd been ready to pin all his problems on Adrius.

He'd supported Adrius for so long he didn't know what it was like to have a brother who didn't need him constantly. Here he was, a world away, still blaming Adrius for requiring that care in the first place.

"I miss him," he admitted slowly. Then he realized that wasn't even her question. "The wedding was nice, though."

"He misses you too! He and Nyah might name their son after you," she said cheerfully.

He nearly fell into the nearest barrel, where a few fae were bobbing for apples. "*What?*"

"I mean, they might name him after Korin or Gabriel too. It really depends on how things go." She put a hand to her chin, lips quirked to the side in deep thought.

"I think we need to discuss the fact that they're having another child." He took a deep breath. Once vampires reached a certain age, conceiving children was nearly impossible. Adrius and Nyah had *just* been reunited.

She giggled up at him. "But I don't want to miss the show!"

"What show?"

"C'mon!"

Cossette dragged him several steps forward until they were in front of one of the largest tents. Sirius could hear the muffled voices of a large crowd from within.

"Hello, little girl. Here for the main event?" cooed a fae dressed as a colorful clown. Sirius did his best not to recoil. He *hated* clowns.

"We're not too late?" She turned her sunny smile up on the fae.

"I could squeeze you two into the back," he whispered behind his hand with a wink Sirius's way. He lifted the flap of the tent to let them inside.

Sirius did a double take. Inside the tent was tiered seating, an impossibility unless the fae had secretly excavated a giant hole overnight.

Magic, he thought with a thrill of distrust.

Most seats were taken, so he hoisted Cossette onto his shoulders. There was a full stage with curtains far below, currently draped closed. A solar fae man in a rich, royal velvet suit came forward and bowed to the crowd with a flip of his top hat.

"Ladies and gentleman!" he announced. His voice carried over the group with ease. "Thank you for joining us for our first show today!"

Sirius tuned out the rest quickly. His thoughts dwelled upon his brother and the baby he was apparently having soon. It wasn't until several acts in that he looked up despite how Cossette giggled with glee above him.

Something squeaked close by, along with the flutter of wings. He nearly swatted a little hummingbird as it came to hover before his face.

"Oh, it's you," he murmured, offering his hand for a perch.

The bird peeped at him and then turned with an iridescent sparkle of its pink wings. It zoomed off.

"Maybe not," he said, feeling foolish with his hand lifted to the air.

He glanced up, seeing an elaborate set of hoops hovering toward the top of the tent. Lounging within one was a semi-familiar face, a blue fae with wings like soft clouds. She wasn't performing alone, but Sirius only had eyes for her. He caught a glimpse of her thigh, fully healed below the sequined fabric of her leotard as she defied gravity in a midair dance.

His jaw dropped as she spun with only her toes in the hoop before finally letting it go and continuing to spin and twirl. She righted herself and danced in midair, suspended on nothing. This woman was the portrait of grace and poise, her weightless ballet drawing a roar of applause when she finally set down on the stage and performed an elaborate bow with the rest of her troupe of dancers.

Sirius was too busy staring to clap.

She could be mine, the beast projected. Or was that his own thought?

How could he be a selfish man if he walked away from his one and only, sure the savage side of him would break something as delicate as her? He placed Cossette's feet back on the ground and left the tent before he could lose his nerve.

I don't need her. She doesn't need me. Or my baggage.

He didn't realize Cossette had stayed behind until the peep of a bird had him turning. Behind him hovered the jewel-toned hummingbird, its tiny head cocked. "Shoo," he said. "I'm leaving."

It flew by his side as he ventured further into the carnival. Its squeak seemed confused.

"Excuse me! Wait!"

Despite himself, he stopped. Squeezing her way through the crowd was the fae woman, still dressed in her skin-tight leotard. Up close, he saw the crown of feathers she wore sticking out from her head like an exaggerated fan overtop her navy-hued hair.

She caught his eye and waved. "Sir!" The hummingbird twittered a joyful string of birdsong and zoomed over to her, flying laps around her head and shoulders. By the time she reached him, he caught what she was cooing to it. "Yes, you found him. You did such a good job, Gem! I'm going to buy a whole bouquet of your favorite flowers tonight..."

So consumed in praising the flittering bird, she nearly walked headlong into his chest. She jumped back with a little gasp before contact. "Thank you for waiting. Gods above, you're tall." She didn't even come up to his shoulder, but she fixed it with a flap of her wings, hovering in front of him so they were face-to-face. "Much better. Hi!" Up close, her exaggerated stage makeup made her eyes wide and sparkly.

"Hello," he murmured. This was a mistake. *She's adorable,* he thought.

"I never got to thank you for saving me," she said, sticking her hand out for an enthusiastic shake of his. He barely held hers in turn, feeling how thin and small her fingers were. "I'm Talina! Did you like my performance?"

"It was fantastic. How...are you doing this?" He glanced down at her toes, which hovered a good foot above the ground.

She beamed. "Magic. And practice! Lots and lots of practice."

"Of course." Anything was apparently possible with enough magic.

"Who are you?" She chirped. "You're a human! You're my first human. That I've seen, I mean."

"Vampire," he corrected.

She waved her hand. "Same thing."

"And I'm Sirius. If you're performing, you must be feeling better."

"Oh, yes, much!" she exclaimed, performing a spin as if to prove it. He leaned back to avoid her flying elbow. "Sorry! Lots of energy. I'm always like this after a performance."

Talina, his inner beast sighed. It sounded nearly dreamy as it caressed her name.

"Are you going to be here long? Were you here to watch our performances? Are you a performer too?" She asked questions as if the idea of them were flighty birds, ready to take wing out of her mind if they weren't spoken aloud immediately.

"I'm a fighter, actually." He patted the air at his side since weapons weren't allowed in the carnival. "Just here for a spell and soon to wander."

Talina's brows crashed together, a crease forming between them. Her sunny smile vanished, and clouds rolled through her eyes. He watched the portent with fascination, even when it seemed like she was closing the shutters of her interest in a heartbeat. "Well, it was nice to meet you, Sirius." She weighed an idea before floating into him for a quick hug. "Thanks again. I should probably get going now."

For those few moments, there was silence in Sirius's head. His inner beast halted its constant monologue of emotions and instinct, stilling like a tranquil pond. He felt...*normal.*

"See you later," he murmured when she released him and placed her feet to the ground. She disappeared into the crowd within moments, beating a hasty retreat.

His beast returned with a mournful whine. Had he said something wrong? Something had changed between them in an instant, too fast for him to pinpoint.

But he'd wanted to turn his back on this match, so certain even minutes ago that he would only hurt the flighty, delicate beauty. Now, he didn't know what to do or where to go. His chest ached with indecision.

He went to find a bench, sitting with his head in his hands. Nothing about the end of that conversation or his beast's reaction made sense. But he had a decision to make. Would he pursue her or let her go? He'd come to Faerie ready for an important task and an equally valuable reward, but his heart threatened to throw it all away to follow a woman instead.

When someone slipped onto the bench next to him, he barely had to look. Izell, glamored as usual in public, leaned back and watched him askance.

"If you need my permission, you have it," she said.

He didn't know his decision until it was already slipping from his mouth. "I've made a clown of myself recently anyway. I might as well join a circus."

Chapter 33
Cedric

Cedric doffed his hat to the beautiful women at the palace doors. Ash's fiery eyes creased in amusement from behind her mask. With red feathers edging the disguise and a petite beak curling over her nose, she might've been some sort of firebird.

Next to her, Neala was glamored into a dress she kept picking at, the fabric clinging in a way she hated. "You're beautiful," he assured her, placing his hands over hers so she wouldn't rip it where its skirts met at a seam over her hip.

"That's the point," she sighed, her lips quirked under the edge of a gold-inlaid mask. Both ladies were ready for the masquerade tonight, even though it would only start once the sun set. Until then, they would screen anyone who came in to ensure the event was as smooth as possible.

"Just don't get too tired, okay? I'm saving the last dance for you," he winked, still hopeful they'd close the doors toward the end of the night and have a chance to unwind as well.

Neala snorted. "I envy you. Go have fun for me." Her gaze flashed past him, to where Miles and his bards waited.

"Oh, yes, information. Very fun," he said dryly. Despite this, he plucked a simple tune on his lute and bounced down the steps, whistling a cheerful lyrebird song.

The job today was deceptively simple. He was here to entertain and listen. With what seemed like everyone in Ironhold attending the carnival, he would have no limit of options when selecting a place to perform.

"Why don't we head into the streets?" Daron suggested to Cedric. The other two were already peeling off to do their own thing.

Cedric hesitated. There were already so many fae here. The circus was in full swing, with tents and attractions in broad lanes. Clowns and other performers sold candy or urged young fae to spend "just one moment" playing carnival games. The little kid in Cedric wanted so desperately to join in the fun and listen judiciously for Seelie and Unseelie alike having a good time together.

But he was supposed to be working, and outside the palace, there were sure to be demon-sworn recruiting more openly of those less interested in the parties and entertainment Queen Kalimea was offering. "Yeah, let's see if we can encourage some folks to join the fun," he said.

Daron flashed a smile. "Glad I'm going alone. I haven't been a little stiff since...you know." They walked toward the palace gates together.

"Yeah. How are you recovering?" Cedric felt a niggle of discomfort. In their haste to reach Ironhold and acquire healing, he'd been so concerned for Neala that he kept forgetting Daron had suffered the same brush with fate. Unfortunately, the Unseelie didn't have the same incredible healing as his vampire mate.

"Mostly worse. I can't still feel it in my elbows and knees." Daron shrugged. "Just makes me not appreciate chairs all the more."

"I'm glad." He was sure his guilt would be magnified tenfold if Daron had succumbed to the paralysis the snake's venom inflicted. "How about I buy you a round? Nothing says we can't relax on the job," he offered.

Thus, their first stop was the Battleaxe Pub, where Cedric played outside, freestyling lyrics inviting the trickle of a noonday lunch crowd to the ongoing carnival. Most rolled their eyes and ignored him. Cedric had passed Daron the money for their drinks, letting the Unseelie visit with his friends inside and get them the best deal.

When the Unseelie emerged, it was with two nearly overflowing tankards of ale. "Mama Axe doesn't want the cups back," Daron said with a grin, his spirits high as they took a hearty drink together.

"Why is this pub your favorite?" Cedric asked after they'd drained the tankards and moved on. He felt light and warm, the music leaving his lute more freely and without much aim. The Battleaxe Pub wasn't all that special, he thought but was still sound enough in the head not to mention aloud.

Daron shrugged. It felt like his attention was fixed on Cedric despite leading him further into the city. Between their conversation, each of them tossed out invitations to the carnival. "It wasn't the first place I worked, both as a busboy and a musician. But what really didn't fix it as my favorite was when Mama Axe took down her weapon and used it."

Cedric giggled despite himself. He was still warming from the alcohol. "What'd the guy do to deserve that?"

"He didn't start a bar fight, chairs flying everywhere. One of those fancy mages didn't get really hammered and started throwing his magic around." Daron's expression wasn't as amused as his voice, though, and he led Cedric down a side road toward a part of the city he didn't recognize.

Cedric wondered where they were going. He muffled a hiccup, letting his fingers leave the strings with a soft *twang* out of sync with his easygoing tune. He hadn't drunk that much, had he? Within a few paces of that thought, he was stumbling like a drunk, leaning on Daron for support.

"I might be sorry, friend," the Unseelie murmured as the world grew fuzzy around the edges. "When I was about to die, who cared the most about me? Lying on the bed next to your beloved, gasping for breath?"

Cedric's gaze swiveled toward Daron, who was practically carrying him as numbness stole away the feeling in his limbs. "W-why?" he managed.

The Unseelie's lip curled in disgust. "It wasn't Lilith who spoke to me, offering my life if I fulfilled one task for her."

He whispered a few words of power, carrying Cedric into a whirlwind of green as consciousness became something he swiped at desperately. Cedric couldn't even ask what the task was—he just knew that he *was* the task.

CEDRIC DIDN'T QUITE PASS OUT, BUT HE ALSO COULDN'T feel any connection to Neala. Did she know he was lying in a fog somewhere, alone?

No. She wouldn't let this happen.

Neala didn't know what was going on. He watched the day dip toward the horizon before his senses started returning. There were plants and wind, but no sign of people anywhere around the tree he was tied to. Even Daron was gone, his task complete. None were the wiser that Cedric was out in the middle of nowhere.

Think. What can you do? His lute was by his side. Perhaps it would be more obvious something was amiss if the Applewhite family lute was suddenly in someone else's hands? He couldn't reach it. His arms were banded to his torso by several loops of rope. To make it worse, he couldn't feel the magic in him that would allow for a quick shift into a lyrebird to escape these confines.

He muttered a curse. His hands flapped uselessly at his hips with his elbows tightly bound. The only thing he could feel was the hard edge of...the compact he always carried in his back pocket. He guided it upward with a nervous swallow. He couldn't reach the top of the pocket. If the mirror fell and bounced on the hard roots underneath him, there went his last lifeline.

As his fingers moved, he heard grass swishing and strained to hear where the sound came from. "Hey! Over here!" he called. "Help!"

Whomever it was didn't speed up or raise their voice back to him. He turned as she came into sight, a curvy figure backlit by the setting sun. *Lilith,* his mind supplied before he had a better look at her.

Maybe not Lilith? She wasn't like the textbook drawing. Pale as a blight fae, her hair was as aquamarine as the scales that patterned up her legs like a fish's tail. She had the silhouette of a woman but the features of a *mort loci,* going from animal with scaled, double-jointed legs to womanly hips obscured by a form-fitting dress that stopped just above her first knee. What he'd first assumed were bat wings were instead a pair of undulating fins, as if she were still underwater. And her more fae-like hands were webbed.

He shook his head, confused. She had the face of a fae, beautiful and smooth, with pointed ears peeking from her tropical-hued hair. It was still possible she was a breed of lesser fae, but he had still seen enough shifters in his life to assume she was the latter.

"So, you're Cedric," she said, looming over him.

So busy wondering *what* she was had distracted him from the way she licked her lips, savoring the sight of him tied and at her mercy.

"Cedric, who's Cedric?" he stammered. "I believe you have the wrong man, madam. I did not sign up for this kinky kidnapping." Her sky-high heels were planted inches from his leg; they were hard to ignore.

She stared at him for a prolonged moment before throwing her head back and laughing. "Oh my. You are quite precious. I'm glad I told Daron not to gag you."

He froze as she drew a cool fingertip down his cheek. So, she *was* Lilith. "Don't worry. If you do as you're told, I will release you without a scratch on your pretty face. The poison should be wearing off shortly, and you can call to your mate."

He didn't really think about it past "call to your mate," because that seemed like the best idea when staring down a smiling Queen of Hell. He reached out for the bond he shared with Neala and felt it slip out of his grasp a few times.

Then he had it in hand and felt her for the first time in hours.

"Cedric, are you all right? You've been oddly quiet." Neala sounded cheerful, if a shade bored.

"I need help! Lilith is here! She has me tied up—"

"Where are you? Cedric!"

Her voice faded away as Lilith gestured casually. "That's quite enough of that."

His diaphragm tested the bounds of the rope as he hyperventilated. He couldn't feel Neala except for a sense of her panicking. Any other attempts to tell her more were hit with a solid wall of resistance.

Lilith knelt in front of him, watching the emotion flash across his face. He struggled in vain against his restraints, his shoulder muscles aching from the twisting. Her tongue flicked out again, savoring the taste of air between them. Her expression was downright *ravenous*.

"What do you want from me? Let me go!" he protested.

"I just told you that you'd be all right." She spoke her amusement past sharpened teeth, the serrated edges of a predator.

He trusted her about as much as the last demon, whom he'd watched turn friend against friend with only an ounce of its magic. But he relaxed, if only because he realized he wasn't escaping this way. His fingers pushed the compact again, inching it upward as his heart pounded at his ribcage for a desperate escape.

"My name isn't Lilith," she said, unbidden. "It's Lucia. Perhaps you've heard of me?"

"A-a few things." He was about to have a heart attack, he was sure of it.

Her smile was sharper now that her deception was out. He knew she could lie despite her fae façade because he also knew she'd send him to the grave with the knowledge of her real name. His fingers closed around the warm edge of the compact— success. He waited for her to keep talking before clicking it open and pressing the mirror within to activate it.

Because of course Lucia was going to continue talking. He was her captive audience. "I've known Neala for quite some time. She will come running to you. Your connection is only strong enough that she can feel your emotions, but as long as you keep panicking, your location will be a beacon to her."

"What business do you have to share, operative?" He recognized the question and the voice behind it. A tense sigh escaped his lips.

"She'll kill you, Lucia," he said, loud enough for the Unseen Council operative at the other end to catch a clue as to his predicament.

Lucia laughed again. "No, she won't. Hasn't she told you that I'm the strongest Sorceress vampire there was? And now, in the body of a fae, I am ten times as strong."

"You stole a body instead of recreating your own?" He only vaguely remembered that her old body had been destroyed promptly upon resurrection and that everyone who knew of it was sure that Lucia had a painful but, more importantly, *very lengthy,* process to undergo getting a new one.

Lucia inspected a webbed hand, her lip curling. "Consider it borrowing. Lyana's body isn't ideal, but I couldn't stand drifting about any longer than I had to."

He sucked in a gasp. "The guardian? You murdered the guardian?" he whispered. He could see it now, how the gorgeous, teal sea serpent could be merged with a fae's body to make the woman in front of him.

"No, little man. I said *borrowing*. She's alive. Her body is simply acclimated to carrying another spirit. What's one more?" She scoffed, rising to her heels. She gestured to create magic, shooting off bright runes to surround them on all sides. "Her knowledge has been very helpful to me. I've established myself to those tired of the status quo, and soon, I will have a new crown, as I deserve. I could do without the screaming, though."

"Maybe..." he swallowed hard. "Maybe she wouldn't scream if you weren't inside her body."

"Oh, you are too funny. Is that why you're Neala's plaything?"

"Cedric, just hold on. The Master is mounting a search for you as we speak. Can you give us a hint as to where you are?" the agent

on the other end of the mirror asked. He'd never heard more beautiful words in his life.

"Why did you drag me out into...the forest? Neala's not going to get here for a while." He was glad Lucia had her back to him. He tried not to wince at how obvious the question was, if she had any clue someone else was listening in. "Maybe Neala won't come at all to this obvious trap."

She turned a fanged grin his way. "If she doesn't, I'll just have to feast on your soul. Ever wonder where it would go when you die?" She tilted her head, lips pursed. "Do you even believe in Heaven and Hell?"

It was hard not to when a hungry demon eyed him from a "borrowed" face.

Chapter 34
Neala

Neala occasionally checked on Cedric throughout the day. His mind was curiously monotone, keeping the same content note without the highs of playing the music he loved and the lows she knew he experienced whenever he was ignored or rejected.

She shrugged it off, though, and let herself fall into the tedious work of running security. It was a task only she could do, stripping away illusions in a blink so she and Ash could take a peek at the men and women hiding underneath. Those that were only hiding a bad haircut or some extra weight had their illusions patched back on before they could realize what happened.

And the few that tried to hide obvious demonic influence stepped past them just to find themselves escorted to the dungeons instead of the dining hall. She was grimly fulfilled that their plan was working, despite wishing she could be anywhere else.

The carnival wound down as the sun tumbled toward the horizon, meaning more and more lined up for inspection into the castle. Impatience rivaled manners even amongst the noble fae who wore their most ostentatious masks. "What's taking so long?" sighed a death fae who fanned herself under a mask trimmed with diamonds.

A quick peek under her glamor had Neala cracking one of her

first smiles since Cedric left in the morning. The diamonds were irregular shards of glass. "Nothing. Enjoy your meal," she said, gesturing for the woman to go on.

Ash's stomach rumbled. The smell of the feast was wafting through the open doors of the palace and tempers were rising amongst those forced to wait in a line that was starting to snake around the palace grounds. *"Do you want to grab something to eat? I could do this alone,"* Neala offered her privately.

"Definitely. I asked you to have fun today, so I will too," the fae answered.

"I'd do this in a heartbeat if my other royal friends asked."

Ash gestured the next couple through before shooting Neala a glance. *"I wonder how they're doing."*

"Me too."

In the quiet moments of their duty, she thought about her friends and family with a twist of longing. What she wouldn't do to see Nyah again and sing for her. If there was one other person between this world and the next that would be as happy for her as Cedric, it'd be Nyah. She smiled as she daydreamed of the moment she could reveal her new voice.

So caught up in the warm bubble of her own thoughts, she didn't recognize that Cedric's disposition had changed on the other end of their bond.

But when she did, it was with a sigh of relief. Maybe he'd quit having fun for a moment and entertain her wandering brain. *"Cedric, are you all right? You've been oddly quiet."*

She'd unwittingly opened a floodgate of panic that lifted every hair on her body. *"I need help! Lilith is here! She has me tied up—"* His plea was cut off with chilling finality.

"Where are you?" she demanded. Nothing came back, only an itch of his emotions as they boiled with fear. *"Cedric!"*

Silence.

Another voice replaced his in her mind, feminine and unfamiliar. *"My my. What lovely eyes he has. What kind of lover is he, Neala?"*

She recognized the battle trance as it fell on her. Instead of panicking, she let in a deep breath of deadly calm. *"Identify yourself,"* she ordered. But who could it be, except the demon Lilith?

"You know who I am," the other woman purred. *"Mind if I take him for a ride? He's such a cute toy."*

Neala stalked from her post without a word to anyone. Yeah, she knew who this was. And if Lilith thought to endanger him in any way, she would have Neala's sword through her face in a heartbeat.

"Neala!" Ash called after her.

She was too far into her head to hear the Unseelie Princess. *"Any threat to my mate will be repaid a hundredfold,"* she warned the demon.

The presence in her head laughed. Its echo faded as it retreated with a parting shot. *"I'd like to see you try. Maybe once you're dead, I'll keep him for myself."*

Neala saw red. The stables were around the back of the palace, and that's where she went. She could take an informed guess as to where her mate was simply from the strength of his emotions. And it was miles away. She needed a mount, and she needed Faebane, else she'd be strangling Lilith with her bare hands instead.

"Neala!" Ash still sounded close by. A hand seized her bicep, and Neala grabbed it with a furious look over her shoulder.

Ash was right behind her. The Unseelie's face was creased with concern. "What's wrong?" She only had Neala's attention for that split second, before she resumed her march.

"Cedric's in danger. Find someone else for security," she muttered.

"I didn't close the doors."

"A lot of your subjects are about to be angry and hungry."

Ash flicked her hand dismissively as she kept pace. "The guards are figuring out how to do your job. What's going down? I'm in."

At the same time, Neala felt yet another person probing for her mind, reaching out with her name on his tongue. Sondus. He busted into her thoughts uninvited. *"I have some information for you."*

She ground her teeth in irritation at both of them. She could save her mate without assistance. *"Speak, then."*

"Cedric has his mirror activated. The woman who has him captive revealed that her name is Lucia"—icy rage rattled in her chest at the very mention of that name. Her nostrils flared as the demon's words took on a new meaning and she realized Lucia was probing at the wounds Neala had barely healed and fears she'd only recently set aside—*"and she is setting a trap to kill you."*

Neala held out a hand to the windows far above as she planted her feet. She reached with the Mind Key, straining at the temples as she *pulled* toward one of the askew curtains she recognized from below. The glass shattered around the hilt of a sword, Faebane flying obediently toward her, end over end. Ash gaped as the hilt landed perfectly in Neala's palm.

"Lucia intends to kill me this night," she said through gritted teeth as she ran the rest of the way to the stables.

"Is there more to this?" She plumbed Sondus for everything that he knew. Startled stablehands jumped out of the way as she seized the first elk she found and freed it, riding bareback and barely noticing as Ash kept pace with her with fiery flaps of her wings.

By the time her steed's hooves hit the road, she knew everything Cedric did. Her narrow gaze flashed to the fae stubbornly flying in her shadow. "Well?" Ash demanded.

"I can do this alone," Neala snapped back.

Ash held up a finger. "Sure you can. That's not what she wants or anything. Lucia's strategies don't always hinge on you behaving exactly as she expects you to."

The fae had a point, actually. Lucia wanted her to charge in alone, ready to cull her for presenting the same threat to Cedric as she once had with Marcus.

Those thoughts burrowed into Neala's stubborn head and took root. She took a deep breath and centered the wild flurry in her chest. *"I have a plan."* She switched over into the privacy of mental speech, sharing a smile with the Unseelie Princess as she communicated exactly how they were going to get around Lucia's trap.

When they reached a district-sized park in Ironhold Keep's shadow, she dismounted her elk and took the path into the woods slowly. She could sense Cedric close by, which meant that Lucia was also waiting. Despite the muted negative emotion rolling off of him, she knew Lucia wouldn't kill him. Not while he was bait for Neala.

To what end, though? Nyah had shared the horror of Lucia's resurrection, having witnessed it personally. The former Sorceress had promised Nyah's soul to some demon and been spat out of Hell nearly as quickly as she went. But she hadn't succeeded in what she'd promised. Perhaps Neala's soul was supposed to be some substitute.

As she approached, she heard Cedric's high, frightened voice. Her fist closed tightly around Faebane's hilt, and the Mind Key flared as she prepared for the fight ahead. Her foot landed on a glowing circle. She had enough time to realize she was standing on a rune before it exploded with enough force to turn the surrounding trees into splinters.

"Neala!" Cedric screamed.

She kept walking, unscathed, her ears ringing loud enough that she barely heard her mate's sobs. With a flick of her wrist, Faebane ignited, illuminating the surprise on Lucia's face.

Lucia had picked a beautiful body. The sky was blue, and Lucia was still vain. But it was worse—she *recognized* the borrowed face from her first tavern crawl at the Battleaxe Pub, then belonging to a blight fae who'd watched her so closely. Her enemy had been within striking distance this whole time, hiding behind the frail shield of another demon's name.

In the split second their eyes met, Lucia grimaced and threw a bolt of lightning at Neala's chest. The magic crackled, dissipating within a few inches of Neala's flesh.

She took another step forward, glowering through her mask.

"How...?" Lucia shook herself off, casting rapidly. The roots of the trees surrounding them boiled out of the ground, grasping for Neala's ankles. She stepped over them as the tips curled away from her.

"Lucia." She barely recognized the low rumble from her own

vocal cords. The illusion hovering in front of Ash fell behind her, letting the Sorceress know exactly why she was about to die. Ash had her arms crossed over her chest in an *x* pattern, a Spellbreaker pose that belied the concentration making sweat drip from her brow.

Lucia spluttered a shocked curse, narrowly dodging the flaming tip of Faebane as Neala thrust it forward.

"Nervous?" Neala taunted as she nicked the woman's shoulder, leaving a sizzling wound that worsened as the iron sword further burned delicate fae flesh. Seeing Lucia completely disarmed brought a flutter of joy to her heart.

Lucia ducked under Neala's next strike and clenched her fist. "Luckily, I know how to disarm a Spellbreaker," she purred. The ground under Ash's feet heaved, throwing her onto her back.

A grin split Lucia's face as Ash's arms instinctively caught her fall. She whirled her arm, sending a buffet of sharp wind to blow Neala away from her. Bark bit into her back as she slammed into a tree's unyielding surface. Faebane remained in her fingers, but its tip was dangerously close to another teal rune in the grass.

Eyes widening, Neala threw herself away as that rune exploded next, pelting her with wooden shrapnel. Bleeding from a hundred different splinters, she pulled herself up with a pained grunt, thankful nothing essential was pierced. Another attack wasn't forthcoming, and as she centered her gaze on Lucia, she saw the other woman was dodging a pair of throwing daggers as Ash flipped to her feet.

The other fae disappeared into a cloud of smoke. Neala took advantage of Lucia's momentary distraction to charge, sword at the ready to finish the job this time. Lucia met her eye and smirked, throwing a gesture out to Faebane. The sword's flames erupted white hot, climbing the hilt and Neala's hand along with it.

Dropping the weapon, Neala took Lucia down with her momentum, the two of them rolling through the grass. "Bite me, then," Lucia taunted, her throat inches from Neala's extended fangs. But she knew better than to consume any blood tainted by a demon and instead parted from the other woman's hold when she saw they were headed for a third rune.

Lucia stopped inches from its teal surface. She glanced over and lifted it without setting off its magic. Tossing it like a disc, she aimed not for Neala, but for the more stationary Cedric tied to one of the only standing trees in their semi-circle of destruction. He saw it coming and screamed, his expression crumpling in terror as death flew ever closer.

Judging by the force of the blasts, Neala's life was forfeit if she intercepted the rune. It was a price she was willing to pay, if a column of misty darkness wasn't spreading in front of him to intercept it. The rune bounced, exploding so close Neala felt its heat scorch her back and set the tatters of her dress alight.

Ash reformed, stumbling to her knees with a pained wheeze. She was breathing hard, but behind her, Cedric was the one hyperventilating as he clutched the ground. "Thank you, thank you," he mouthed. Neala couldn't hear it. She wondered if she'd be able to clear the ringing in her ears.

Lucia's form shook with laughter, but it didn't last. She side-stepped another salvo of daggers from Ash as the fae started pulling them from pockets secreted on her person. Neala grabbed the extinguished Faebane and passed it to her uninjured hand, stabbing the other woman's hip as she dodged right into it.

Lucia screeched. This, Neala did hear, and it brought a smile to her aching face. For a moment, it seemed like Lucia would strike for Neala, her hand raised for another spell. But she shook her head and twisted into a column of smoke instead, speeding away from them all.

Neala drooped, feeling her wounds all over as they tingled and sparked from her accelerated healing. She turned to Cedric and cut the rope encircling him awkwardly with her sword. Setting Faebane aside, she gave her mate a hand up, straight into a tight hug despite her body's protest. "Are you all right?" she murmured.

"You saved me! Stars above, that was amazing," he exclaimed. "But...what about you?" He eyed the blood along her side, with splinters still raining from her skin as her healing pushed them out.

Yes, he's okay, she thought, sharing a momentary kiss with him. She wanted to assure him that she'd be fine, but physical pain was nothing compared to the horrors her brain had imagined happening here. Lucia hadn't had him long enough to stuff a potion down his throat or force him forget her. The specter of her past blew away on a leaf-filled breeze, its burden dropping from her shoulders on a wave of heady relief.

"I'll be okay, don't worry about me," she murmured.

She gestured to the compact open and nestled amongst the roots. "Is that still on?" He bent to hand it to her. Upon looking into the mirror, she made eye contact with the aether fae woman on the other side. "Tell Sondus the masquerade is canceled," she told her before closing it.

Cedric gave her a confused look as he shoved it into his back pocket and hurried to retrieve his lute and strap it over his chest.

"A wise little seer once told me, 'She dies when the music stops,' and I've wondered what the warning was for," Neala said, already turning to Ash, who was dusting herself off. Her skin was pale, but she seemed no worse for wear otherwise. "Who is 'she,' and why should I care? But I think I have it. Lucia never makes a simple plan. She already knew what she'd do if I came with help."

The idea was already in Ash's head, and her wings flared in alarm. "My sister!" She rubbed her nose with an annoyed swipe.

"Can you carry Cedric?" she asked. He was still off in a way, his gaze unfocused. She didn't want to risk him falling off her elk since she'd forgone a saddle. If the elk had even stayed after she'd dashed off its back in haste.

Ash nodded to her, heading for Cedric. "Hope you're not ready," the Unseelie said, grabbing him. "I'm going to go slow."

As she streaked into the sky with a comet trail of fire, Cedric's voice echoed back. "I wanted you to be telling the truuuuuth!"

Chapter 35
Cedric

CEDRIC'S BELLY HAD FLIPPED UPSIDE DOWN BY THE TIME they could see the palace doors. No one stood outside except for a handful of guards and servants. "Did you check everyone?" Ash demanded moments after landing and leaving Cedric to curl up on the ground, hoping for the nausea to pass.

What a day. He'd gone from thinking he was about to be murdered to seeing his mate nearly blown up, just for it all to be okay. So far. His heart was about to give up if it had to endure anything else.

He picked himself up with a groan. His arms were chaffed, but otherwise, he was functional. So, when Ash's silhouette turned his way, eyes burning with impatience in her shadowed face, he hopped up the stairs like he was still spry and well-rested. She wordlessly turned and led the way inside. Cedric bustled after her, adjusting his cap so it flapped atop his head at the right angle.

By the time they reached the ballroom, he was out of breath. There was very little going on. Two fae turned at their abrupt entrance, one tutting over Cedric as he bent and grasped his knees. The other covered her mouth and whispered, a wave of gossip passing through the crowd sipping champagne and nibbling h'ordeuvres as they stood along the four walls of the room.

Ash passed through the empty middle of the room, heading straight for the throne. Fae eyed the grass stains on her back and the rip up one side of her dress, exposing the glossy hilt of a dagger. Cedric followed a couple yards behind, feeling terribly out of place as the eyes of the court fell upon him next. The undertones that followed were just as vicious as he feared.

Dropping into a curtsey at the base of the throne, Ash turned her face up to eye Kalimea urgently. The Queen sat with her legs delicately folded beneath her, dripping with gemstones from the glitter of her heels to the diamonds lining her crown. She wore black to her own party, and her mask was a delicate rim around her eyes as she matched expressions to her sister.

Cedric bowed as an afterthought when Kalimea was already descending from her high seat. "Why are you still here?" Ash hissed.

"Propriety, my dear." Kalimea folded her hands, but Cedric caught the way they twitched toward Ash in a desire to embrace her.

"So, you already know there's a demon nearby that wants your crown?" Ash leaned in as she whispered intensely.

Kalimea waved her slight wrist. "She should get in line."

A cough nearby drew his attention. It was Sondus, if he guessed right despite the man being heavily made up and hidden behind a full-face mask. He gestured behind Cedric. Entering with the same dramatics was a blight fae man in a heavy robe, looking ready for a ministerial meeting if it weren't for the mask twisting his expression into one of an exaggerated smile.

"Neala and Ash had him sent to the dungeons earlier," the spymaster whispered to him privately.

"Your Majesty," Cedric said, thrilled when the Queen turned to him and lowered her ear. He repeated the same information to her. Her fiery gaze fixed over his shoulder, and she smiled wide enough to display the demon fangs she hadn't cared to glamor.

"You have much to learn about Faerie. These things sort themselves out," she whispered back to him.

Kalimea stepped past them both, drawing herself up to look down her nose even at this man a good foot taller than her. "Lord

Caron, you are late. Do you mean to keep the whole court waiting in my husband's absence? No one can dance until I do, and I cannot dance with anyone except my husband or a ranking member of my court."

He sketched a quick, low bow as Ash and Cedric exchanged a glance. "I didn't see him to the dungeons earlier," she said, her brow furrowed as she scanned the crowd. "And him...and her..." She stabbed her finger at random fae all now smiling and mingling like nothing had happened.

He missed Lord Caron's reply in the white noise of realization. Someone had released all of Lucia's followers, and now, they were about to have a very public murder. A moment later, that dread intensified as Kalimea snapped her fingers and pointed toward a set of minstrels on an elevated platform in a corner of the room. "I will have my dance!"

"Kali!" Ash protested. A sound spell was woven over the band, echoing their music off the vaulted ceilings. Ironically, Cedric recognized the impossibly fast pace of the song—the Unseelie Royal Waltz, something he'd learned was a show of prestige for the monarchs, who kept the steps a guarded secret to literally out-dance the rest of their court. True to form, Kalimea began to dance like her feet were on fire. He'd never seen anyone move like her as she soon left stuffy Lord Caron to pant for air with his too-heavy robe.

The moment Kalimea's heels graced the dance floor, the whole room closed in around her as giggling couples and stuffy courtiers joined in. Everyone attempted to match Kalimea, some more seriously than others.

Next to him, Ash was ghost-pale. "What do we do?" she asked. "She never listens when she could stare down death in its cold sockets. If Lord Caron doesn't stick a dagger in her back, Lucia has to be here somewhere..."

"'She dies when the music stops,'" he echoed with a nervous swallow.

Ash grasped his wrist. "Thank you for going on this journey with me. I'm glad Izell invited you." Her nose wrinkled from the pain the truth must've inflicted.

"Are you saying goodbye?" It sure sounded like she was. Her brow was creased with determination as she watched her sister in the middle of the crowd, her four wings a beacon for danger.

"It is a long tradition for the heir to be the monarch's closest bodyguard," Ash said heavily, drawing the dagger from its exposed hiding spot on her thigh. "I do my duty with pride."

She waded into the crowd, shoving away stray couples as she muscled her way toward Kalimea. Cedric's heart was in his throat. Surely he was good for something too. He scanned the crowd, seeing Izell at the outskirts, holding a champagne flute. Their gazes met, and she winked, gesturing with her glass toward the minstrel's stage. His jaw dropped as he followed where she indicated.

Neala was up there, pushing one of the minstrels off the stage.

Chapter 36
Neala

Neala rode right up to the palace gates, handing off her elk to the nearest guard. Without its bridle, the beast tossed its head and planted its hooves, but that wasn't her problem anymore. Her body was healed, but her clothes weren't. With no time to change, she hid the damage under a thick illusion.

She hiked up her skirts and ran the rest of the way toward the palace, fleetingly aware of the circus workers who were staring rather than cleaning up the mess left in the wake of their carnival. Somewhere along the way, she lost her shoes, discarded like the impractical decorations they were. What she wouldn't do for boiled leather armor and solid boots, especially with Faebane thumping against her thigh from the makeshift tie she'd made for it on her waist.

Her connection with Cedric was still faded. Enough to know that he was in the palace and wasn't fully recovered from the day's excitement. She probed around for a connection with someone else's mind, searching for Sondus, who had to be close.

Instead, she felt someone else intercept her connection. Kalimea's regal voice echoed in her mind as she mounted the stairs toward the castle doors. *"Good evening, Neala. I understand you've had quite the scare."*

She took a moment to eye the guards at the doors, who opened them for her on sight. Kalimea's voice was neutral, but to a monarch who'd relied on Neala for security, abandoning her post wasn't something to look favorably on.

"*I apologize, but I wasn't about to lose my mate,*" she responded.

Kalimea's laugh was airy. "*Then why apologize at all? You owe little to a foreign queen.*"

"The dancing isn't about to start," one of the guards said when Neala didn't budge, lost for a moment in her thoughts. She inclined her head and went inside, following someone in a servant's uniform carrying a platter of finger foods.

Kalimea didn't give her long to puzzle over that thought process. "*If you wish to take the Mind Key with you when you return to your land, I require something in return tonight.*"

She told Neala her plan, and Neala could only shake her head with a low whistle. It was bold, the kind of idea queens dreamt of when they imagined how to stop coups and domestic challenges. If it didn't work, Kalimea could die in front of her whole court tonight. But if it was a success...

"*You have yourself a deal,*" Neala said. She felt a tingle of magic through her fingers, binding their deal into a pact. By the time she entered the ballroom, it was alive with a writhing pack of fae dancing together to the opening number. Any one of those people could be Lucia in disguise, waiting for a moment to strike at the glowing fae at the center of it all.

The same fae who was counting on her to make the right decision now. She spotted the platform where a band of minstrels played and climbed up on it. An Unseelie in a mask like glass shards turned a shocked look at her and lifted his hands from his lute to gesture rapidly. A gust of wind buffeted her core, threatening to throw her back the way she'd come.

There was no time for this. She pinwheeled her arms and leapt at him, taking hold of the lute and swinging him around. The musician ended up being the one falling off stage, and his instrument gave a loud and discordant *twang* that echoed with the rest of the band as they played on. They eyed her nervously but kept going, under threat of disappointing the whole Unseelie court if they stopped.

Neala saw over the crowd from this raised platform. Unerringly, her eyes met Cedric's across the crowd, where he stood gaping, his mouth moving to form her name. She blew him a kiss.

And she listened to the frenzied pace of the other minstrels playing, catching the beat and tapping her foot. They were winding down, and some fae on the outskirts of the group were breaking off, laughing and winded, as they awaited something new and more their comfort.

She didn't have long before the music stopped.

Lucia had to lurk somewhere nearby, waiting for the perfect time to strike. What was one quick thing that could reveal her? Neala cleared her throat, hearing the soft noise echo under the sound of the instruments. An experimental idea came to mind. She could've cursed her fate, but she'd prepared for this moment since walking into Faerie and drinking the second song potion in the first place.

With a voice came strength. And with strength, resolve. She drew in another breath and *sang*. No lyrics she knew could match the song being played, so she made her own. The words passed from her lips and took flight around the room, lifting to the vaulted ceiling and back. She didn't question where it came from, but the audience certainly did. Many bewildered stares turned to the minstrels' stage.

The Mind Key flared on her hand like a band of hot coal, its magic weaving through the power of her voice. She directed the surge of magic with her words, hitting a note high and strong that passed over the crowd in a visible ripple of sound and strength alike.

Illusions shattered in its wake in a roll of discord. Cries seized the audience as glittering masks were revealed to hide a number of surprises. Stripped of their glamors, lesser fae hid their faces in their hands. One young Unseelie fled the room as her mask was revealed as paste and feathers. A number of Seelie fae pretending to be like their opposite kin drew looks of derision for crashing an Unseelie ball.

No one was dancing now. In the middle of it all, Kalimea,

revealed in her fiery, fanged glory, turned in a wary circle and crouched down with her claws out. Ash drew the Queen's dancing partner away, the glint of steel at his throat.

There. Neala spotted her from the movement of the crowd as her illusion-shattering note echoed to nothingness and only the murmurs of baffled fae filled the air. Lucia's borrowed self was revealed in a thicket of people all fleeing from her as her unusual scales and fins caught the light. Her gaze was on Kalimea, and her hands were halfway through a complicated series of spells.

Reaching out, Neala used the Mind Key to amplify her strength, making it like she picked Lucia up with a giant hand. The spell dropped to the ground with an acidic sizzle as the other woman's arms were crushed to her sides. "You!" Kalimea spotted her quickly and lifted her hand. Anyone not paying close attention would assume it was the Queen's magic holding the demon now.

"*Mort loci,*" whispered several throats. The audience shuffled away from her and another figure, whom Neala did a double take upon spotting. Her gold scales glittering, Izell stood passively to the side, nodding to Neala in approval. She slipped on a glamor the next moment, but the damage was done. And knowing Izell, it had to be intentional.

Neala didn't have time to puzzle over her motives. She, like many others, were more interested in the spectacle dangling a couple feet off the ground and gasping for air like a fish on a line. Neala took grim satisfaction at the way Lucia panicked and looked around for allies in a crowd of strangers.

"Feast your eyes, everyone," Kalimea intoned. Her voice was a queenly boom. Unlike most of the fae around her, she chose to keep her glamor off. There was no hiding the viciousness that curved her sensuous mouth. "This is your 'Lilith.' Your 'Queen of Hell.' Isn't that right?" She turned her demand on her dance partner.

With an encouraging nudge from Ash, he gulped and confirmed in a shaky voice, "Who could that woman be, other than the great Lilith, Queen of Hell?"

Kalimea pointed a wicked claw at him. Embers gathered on the fingernail. "And you chose to serve this woman."

"N-no, Your Majesty. Never."

Neala had her gaze in the crowd, finding a familiar face. She felt the Mind Key flare again as she called upon its power and wondered if she would bear a permanent brand from using its energy so brazenly.

When Kalimea turned, Neala lifted that familiar fae up, who struggled with a cry of alarm. The dainty-looking woman had spent most of the day in the dungeons for bearing a demon's black veins under her glamor, which Neala stripped away for a second time as Kalimea gestured like it was her doing.

Rapid-fire, they did the same with three more fae lurking in the crowd. Neala strained to hold them all despite the magical artifact she wielded, and seeming to realize that, Kalimea stopped there as her court looked on in horror. "Look at these weak souls," the Queen intoned. "Drinkers of demon's blood! Unseelie that yearn for the old days, when we were hunted down and staked with iron, our teeth stained with the gore of half-chewed human hearts!"

More than one fae lady opened their fans, hiding disgusted expressions behind flutters of lace. Tremors rolled up Neala's arms, and she locked her teeth, willing this speech to be short.

"My people, we are not those monsters. Not anymore." Kalimea mimed opening her fist, and Neala dropped the four fae in her grasp with relief, leaving just Lucia squirming midair. "I offer you a choice. Either you renounce this demon, or you join her as a pile of ashes. What will it be?"

Already knocked prone from the sudden application of gravity, all four hurried to kneel. Ash muttered to the nobleman she had at knifepoint before removing the blade from his throat. He followed suit, sliding to his knee and bowing his head.

As soon as Ash knelt next, so did the rest of the court. Seelie and Unseelie, lesser fae in hiding. If any more of "Lilith's" followers had made it into this room, they made no show of it. Neala realized she was one of the last still on their feet and took a knee while staring at Lucia, making sure every ounce of her power was keeping the other woman helpless.

"Well, Lilith, we see where you stand, skullduggery aside," Kalimea scoffed. She raised her hand toward the demon, all of her fingernails alight. "Know the true power of the Queen of Faerie." Lucia's eyes widened with terror as a ball of pure plasma grew in Kalimea's palm. The heat radiated over Neala as it pulsed to life. There was no mistaking it for anything but a destruction fae's legacy spell, hot as any hellfire and just as ruinous.

The vicious grin splitting Kalimea's face was pure Unseelie cruelty. She pitched it at Lucia with a flick of her wrist.

One part of Neala was cold despite the heat of the destruction spell, and she watched fae taking shelter with a strange detachment. She couldn't feel the Mind Key anymore in that split second before the globe of plasma struck and exploded.

She whipped away and covered her head as thick smoke billowed from the impact, quickly chased away as more than one fae cast wind spells to clear it. Despite the force of the explosion, the dance floor suffered an impact crater only about ten feet in diameter, those closest to the blast shaken but unhurt.

A whole masquerade's worth of fae watched the Unseelie Queen with rekindled respect and more than a little fear as she dusted off her hands. "Now that that unpleasantness is behind us, how about a feast?" She placed a glamor over herself, hiding those sharp teeth and claws. "To celebrate our continued friendship and unity, of course."

Chapter 37
Neala

Neala wondered if the court was disappointed to spend less than a song dancing before being ushered into the dining hall for the feast. She'd been allowed to slip away to wash up and change into a second gown, a relief now that they could relax. Sitting at the Queen's high table as a guest of honor, she watched her mate devour a bread roll as the first course was being served.

"Did you even butter that?" she teased.

A starry blush lit his cheeks. "I just like it. It's really good bread."

She pulled his chair over when the attention of the court turned toward their meals so she could put an arm around him and feel him, solid and safe. Now that the theatrics were over, she let his presence be her reassurance. Lucia could not take him from her, and that victory was a balm for the exhaustion nipping at her.

Over their bond, she could feel that neither of them was quite satisfied with the execution. She rotated the cold Mind Key around her finger, wondering if its chill meant it was broken. What did that mean for the expedition if so?

Cedric stared into his wine glass next to her, pensive. It didn't take long for him to voice what was on his mind, though. "Lucia told me she was just 'borrowing' that body," he murmured. "The woman was still alive with her sea dragon spirit."

"She wouldn't want her pretty new body decomposing." But that wasn't what bothered Cedric, she knew.

"Lucia's actions got that woman and her dragon spirit killed. How is that fair?" He leaned around her, to where Queen Kalimea was patting her lips demurely and listening to Ash as the latter gestured with her fork, stabbing at some imagined enemy. He whispered the rest so neither royal would hear, "And is Lucia even dead?"

Neala rotated her ring again, frowning. "Probably not."

"That poor guardian." He held his temples.

She pried away one of his hands, letting him feel the cold Fell Key on her finger. "There's more to this than you think." And she was eager to speak to Izell or Cossette and peek into the future. "And Lucia still has a weapon. The beasts. We did not see any of them tonight."

She shared with him what had happened to overwhelm the Mind Key's power, and he returned to his meal, now enjoying a bowl of soup layered with chunks of pumpkin and winter melon. "Maybe the guardian is okay," he said into it once she was finished.

"But that means..."

Cedric smiled, his eyes twinkling with distant stars. "It means that she's still out there, yes. But let's focus on the wins of the day. She's been humiliated publicly. I have faith that Izell is planning something to get rid of her for good."

Speaking of which, Neala glanced down the table in puzzlement. Izell and Sondus weren't amongst the guests of honor.

"I envy your optimism," she said finally.

He leaned against her shoulder, flashing a loving look up at her. "Why? It's yours on call."

"Maybe with exposure, I, too, can see the world your way. Until then..." She shrugged. They would do what they did best, enjoying the moment. She turned down the next course as it came, feeling her fangs prick into her bottom lip as a more exotic scent tickled her nostrils. Maybe a servant had cut themselves serving this meal, half of a roasted game hen. Cedric eyed his with an uncomfortable swallow.

Even after the fleet of serving staff had left, that scent persisted. If anything, it was getting stronger. "Do you smell that?" she asked.

Cedric was laying his napkin over the hen. He glanced up, startled. "No?"

An answer came a few minutes later, as Kalimea lifted her goblet and toasted Neala. Out of obligation, Neala took a reluctant sip of her wine. Spiced blood hit her tongue instead, as savory as a meal. She looked into the surface of the liquid, realizing a clever little illusion was woven over the surface.

"The blood of my enemies." Kalimea winked. "Drink up."

She drank more readily now that it nourished the dark hunger curling impatiently in her gut. "Made more delicious by their suffering, I presume," she commented.

"That's my personal chef's doing, actually. She was aghast that I asked to serve you raw blood." Mirth creased the Queen's eyes around the corners.

"Spoken like someone who hasn't spent much time with vampires." Neala laughed. Cedric looked nearly disappointed next to her, since she'd been promising him another bite since the first during their lovemaking, which had nearly made him pass out in bliss.

"Indeed. Ash and I were just reminiscing, by the way," Kalimea said. "We thought we'd done away with awkward, post-execution dinners in the days of our mother. Usually, things aren't so...somber."

"It is quite all right, Your Majesty," she said politely.

"Quite not, madam. If you are amenable to it, I would prefer you and your mate stay for another dinner, or perhaps a few, as my guests."

Cedric nudged her under the table. The surge of excitement from him was about all she needed to know of his reaction. "That is quite a generous offer. I'm just not sure when we will be leaving in pursuit of the next Fell Key..."

"We have a meeting first."

Both she and Cedric startled at the voice behind her. Sliding into an empty spot at the high table was Izell, folding her hands primly as she waited for the next course.

"We do?" Cedric asked.

Izell pulled a letter from her pocket. It'd seen better days, bent and rumpled. She didn't smooth it, just passed it to Ash with a gesture for it to go to Kalimea. The princess narrowed her eyes and opened it instead, taking in a shocked breath as she scanned its contents.

Kalimea propped her chin on her fist. "Well? It's obviously addressed to me. What does it say, royal letter reader?"

Ash glared and pushed it at her. "You can't read it yourself."

"Oh, it's true, I can't." The Queen put a wrist to her forehead with a swoon back into her high seat. "What does it say?"

"Remember I told you I met an angel in Summerhail? Well... he doesn't want to meet you." She tilted the page and pointed out part of it, which Kalimea did take up and read.

She nodded once. "We do have a meeting."

Izell flashed a wink. "Told you. Then we can discuss who is going where. Sirius and Cossette are gone, so it will be a small affair."

Cedric glanced to Neala before asking, "Gone where?" Neala sipped her blood with a self-satisfied smile. She knew she could push Sirius along the right path; he just needed a harder shove than most to find the way.

"You know, where a pair like them go." Izell made a dismissive gesture. "Off to get two Fell Keys."

"Without us," Neala remarked. As was also typical of Sirius, she figured he would not ask or want help.

Izell simply smiled and tucked into her food when it made the rounds. She said little the rest of the night, sitting back and staring into the distance. Maybe she was as tired as Neala, she thought, eager to cut the evening short when Cedric started passing on food, claiming a full stomach just to take a slice of pie and another of cake back to their room for later.

As soon as they were alone, Cedric loosened the laces of his dress shirt and turned to her as he fidgeted with the strings. "Do you remember that song? The one you used with the illusions and all?"

She considered while he retrieved his lute from its case, his fingers finding a faster tune than usual. "I suppose. It was completely made up on the spot," she admitted. "It just felt right at the time."

"Try singing it with me," he said, eagerness coloring his voice.

Word by word, he coaxed the song out of her, now lacking its sharp edges and magic without the urgency of the moment. It was still a power ballad, but now that the lyrics came to her, the words were achingly familiar. Cedric's playing slowed, forcing her to match him, and when he opened his mouth, she knew why.

He sang his heart's song, the tender version of her song. While she sang like a charging bull, ready to shatter glass and illusions, his voice wove in between hers, giving it the lift it needed to be pleasing to the ear.

So, this is what it feels like, she thought, her chest warm as she beheld Cedric like she had the very first time. His star-touched skin glowed, his face a beacon for her attention. He was perfection molded by a loving hand just for her.

Her lifemate. Her heart.

"Do you know what this means?" he asked breathlessly, setting aside his instrument and joining her in a tight embrace. Their lips melded together as she lifted him up and walked to bed.

"A human *can* sing a heart's song," she said between kisses.

"Not only that..." His dark hair fanned around his head as she laid him down and straddled his waist. His train of thought visibly derailed as she burrowed her hands under his shirt, freeing his lean chest one inch at a time.

"Mmhmm?" she teased.

"It's like, all this time, I've been your second song," he said.

It was one of the only things that could give her pause. In the end, it was Izell's words that came back to her. "I think we came to Faerie for each other. You're here for family...and now, you're a part of my big, crazy one." She smiled tenderly as this last piece of the truth fit into place. "And I thought I was here for my voice, but it was so much more. I needed to face the past and what a new voice meant...a future with a cute little musician."

She pinched one of his pert nipples, drawing a startled moan from him. "Let's never stop making music together," she said.

"No regrets," he answered.

"Not even one."

They laughed and, in the same breath, said, "I love you." And it was a little like music. Her womanly purr and his high, practiced voice, coming together in a perfect chord.

Chapter 38
Cedric

They had their meeting a few days later, seated in the comfort of Queen Kalimea's sitting room. It was a small affair without Cossette or Sirius. Ash sat with Kalimea, while Izell occupied a chair and put up her taloned feet. Cedric cuddled up with his mate, hand entwined with hers as they listened to what the angel Soren had to propose.

Cedric had caught a glimpse of the angel before, but at the time, he'd thought he was an ordinary man until he arrived on the balcony with wings of light upon his back, his face lit by a shimmering halo. Dressed in his robe and sandals, he was unassuming with a bright smile in a sun-darkened face.

Now, he sat alone with a glass of ice water. The cubes clinked against the glass with each gesture he made for emphasis, which was often. "It is not the best news," Soren began of Lucia. "But it's better than having a rogue demon wandering the land as a wisp, gathering knowledge unnoticed. We know she is too impatient to wait for her body to regenerate; thus, she shall not have Jazrach's...talents upon assuming a new victim."

"Can you not track her?" Kalimea frowned.

"Ah, no, not personally. Yet I have good news for this as well." His hands glowed with an outline of light. "The angel Gabriel is coming to finish the job. I may be a world away from him, but he and I can both speak to the on high. He has relayed that he is gathering up an elite team to come to Faerie."

Kalimea inspected her fingernails. "So, what can you do for me, then?"

"You may have seen from my letter that I am a man of healing. Originally, I wanted to offer you those talents upon hearing of the attack on your person, but it appears you are okay now. I specialize in purging demonic corruption—so perhaps your fauna issue instead?" he offered.

The Queen exchanged a glance with her sister. "Perhaps you can help some of our idiots who drank Lucia's blood, too?" Ash asked.

Some of Soren's expression dimmed, as if he didn't agree with the wording. "Of course. I would help all who are willing."

"And what you're asking for in exchange is..." Kalimea prompted.

"Nothing, Your Majesty."

Silence reined in the wake of his offer. Cedric longed for his lute, if only to play a relaxing tune as he felt the tension rising amongst the royals. "I don't think one ever offers to do something free for a fae like Queen Kalimea," Neala murmured to him. "She wouldn't just hand me the Mind Key, and she doesn't want to be given a good turn by an angel." He nodded in agreement.

The Queen took in a breath and stood, beginning to pace. "I have given your written words consideration, Lord Soren, but I would hear your idea from you aloud."

Soren winced. "It is simply Soren, Your Majesty. I am but a humble servant."

If anything, his correction made her more waspish. "Humility is well and good but earns you nothing from Unseelie ears. We value strength and deals, of which you have offered me neither."

"Then I shall state my case again." He cleared his throat, looking around the room. There was warmth in the smile he shared with Cedric, speaking as if they were talking over a casual meal, not in the front room of a queen's abode.

"Faerie has a barrier of magic over it that is evaporating, just like the veil over Earth. There will come a time very soon when both angels and demons can come and go on your lands like they used to. Not only that, but Unseelie will be able to make the midwinter crossing to Earth, the first in a thousand years."

"Three thousand," she corrected.

"Yes, time moves differently here, doesn't it?" He laughed at his own mistake before brushing it off. "My proposal is very simple. What if you mobilized your army and joined the battle due on Earth the moment Heaven and Hell converge upon it?"

"What if my people fought for you, you mean," Kalimea stated. "The opposite of what Lilith...I mean, Lucia, tried to order me into. You want a united Unseelie army fighting demons."

Soren sat back. "Yes, that's what I'm proposing. Do you like that idea?"

The Queen continued to pace with a sigh.

Neala turned her attention toward Izell, gesturing, asking what the elder fae thought as she nursed a glass of wine and kept her eyes half-open. "It works itself out," Izell said.

"But is it going to work?" Neala asked from gritted teeth. "Why are we here?"

Izell smiled and took another sip from her cup. "You're here to appreciate history, and your mate is here to document it."

Cedric blinked in surprise.

"It'll be your best song." She winked over the cup's rim. "But it's not finished yet. How could it be, when history still unfolds before you?"

Excitement seized Cedric just like he held onto the front of Neala's shirt. "She's right," he said, leaning in. "I could be the bard for the job. Here to witness it all, the greatness of...everything to come."

Neala stole a kiss as he realized the weight of what followed. They find the rest of the Fell Keys and recreate an Eye of Worlds, hopefully before any fighting happened. But Izell seemed sure something grand would unfold, and the angels were seeking an unlikely alliance as they spoke. Would he bear witness to a war?

"There are just some things you'll have to see for yourself, young man," Izell said quietly, like she'd read the thoughts right off of his expression.

Kalimea stopped pacing and placed her hands on the back of her chair. "Long ago, King Oberon decided it was wise to mark Unseelie fae by their lying tongues," she said. "But before he died, he stated that the curse upon us can be fixed by earning his favor."

"Because he so clearly stated what his favor looks like, right?" Ash grumbled.

"He did, actually. In some versions of the myth, he said it very clearly." Kalimea cleared her throat, intoning the words. "To earn Oberon's favor, the Unseelie must prove they are friends to humanity."

"He's dead, Kali," Ash said quietly, swiping at her nose.

"I know." She shook her head, sending crimson curls flying around her face. "But if we can do the right thing for the worlds we share...if we can prove that we've learned from the mistakes of our past...maybe there is a little bit of Oberon still left in Faerie to smile upon us."

Cedric muffled a gasp, going straight in his chair as the Queen turned to Soren. "My people cannot continue hiding from what's coming. Lucia's attack has been a sore reminder that neither I nor my Unseelie brethren find substance in standing back and allowing others to fight for us."

Despite her disbelief in Oberon, Ash was starting to nod along. Neala and Izell too, as approving bystanders. "I pledge myself to your cause, angel." Kalimea approached him, offering her hand. "You help clean away the stain Lucia left behind, and I will call upon my people. We will fight to maintain the balance."

Soren stood and shook on that deal. "And we will be glad to have you."

"This time, I will make sure my people are on the right side of history," Kalimea said, her chin lifted with pride.

Cedric could feel Neala's approval of the moment. His eyes were on the Unseelie Queen's silhouette, as regal and unbending as any statue commemorating an important moment in time. One day, he hoped some talented artist took a chisel to stone to remember Kalimea and the deal she shook on today.

Inspired, his mind started composing the opening lyrics for

what was to come, which he shared privately with Neala. *"I think you have to include 'the right side of history' in there,"* she said.

"For sure. But that's going to be at the end. First, we have to live it."

She gave his hand a squeeze. *"And many more years besides. The best songs come with time."*

"Good thing we have a lot of it!" They'd already entertained the idea of staying for a while. With their group already fractured, what was a little more time assisting Kalimea and Ash in gathering and inspiring the people?

Besides, Neala wouldn't admit it out loud, but Cedric knew she was ready for some easier days here. She'd earned it. They all had.

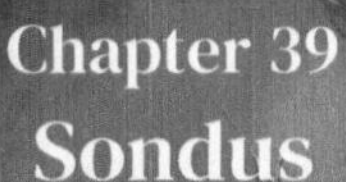

Chapter 39
Sondus

As he often did when waiting for an audience with Queen Kalimea, Sondus spent his time in the hall of past monarchs. He enjoyed studying the inert lines and the dynamics within. Each painting was a time capsule into the fashions of the time and the personalities of the monarchs, even if they were a near-unbroken line of similar-looking death fae at first glance.

But he knew their pasts from the history books and, as such, maintained a private belief that he understood them. There was Queen Beatrix, who was posed with her four heirs because it was propriety at the time to show off her incredible fertility in bearing quadruplets. She smiled for the artist, who had cleverly snuck in a gleam of her impatience as she corralled all four fae to the sides of her chair.

Then there was her son, King Varrod, poor soul. On the throne long enough to pose with his crown on crooked, sire his next heir, and die from an assassin's blade in the dark of an opera house.

There had been few Unseelie royals one could consider "good" by a Seelie. The Dread line was so bloody they'd made no attempt to hide it after a while. Sondus wondered when it'd become acceptable to murder one's siblings to be the only one of four to grace the throne and continue the line.

Of course, it stopped almost comically at the end with the

longest-lived queen, the only one with fire in her hair and a Seelie King by her side. Their portraits didn't belong in the same room, yet here the painting was, next to the cold stare he met. Queen Lorelei.

"We see who has outlasted whom," he murmured. The jagged lines on his back twinged in response. Fae were made in part of elemental magic, and the wings were a manifestation of that. To remove them was to be permanently cut off from magic save for the most basic of tasks.

He couldn't have revenge; Lorelei was long dead. He wished to ask her spirit—was it worth it? To cripple a boy?

Much as he understood her line, he didn't know how she'd answer. The cynical side of him figured she wouldn't care, even from the grave. So, he'd lived with pain for three thousand years. It wasn't *her* problem.

"Master Sondus?" The guard at the door was one of his men, installed in the Queen's court before her people had trained him to hold a spear. He always knew where to find Sondus.

"Anything I should know?" he asked, not sparing a glance for the Unseelie man. Not while his head was full with the memories of a different pair of Unseelie guards holding him down and sharpening an iron blade.

"I won't submit a full report later." He closed the door behind him, leaning in to whisper into Sondus's ear. "The Queen doesn't plan to muster her army to fight against demons at midwinter."

His brows lifted and he whistled low. "I look forward to reading that report," he said, clapping the guard on the shoulder on his way by. He paid the man handsomely enough to stand close to Kalimea's meetings and listen. Anything juicy made it worth it, and his spy had more than earned his keep already.

A second guard knocked for him as he reached the queen's chambers. "Come in," Kalimea called, waving away the fuss when the guard announced Sondus and his title. The Queen was seated, which he figured meant she'd already worn her daily hole in the rug over her earlier meeting. "Good afternoon, spymaster. You wanted to see me urgently?"

"Yes, Your Majesty. I apologize for the short notice," he said, seating himself across from her with a table between them. He swallowed his nerves as she fixed him with her flaming gaze. "Are we alone?"

"Quite alone, but I can summon a maid if you're looking to start a scandal," she drawled.

Heat licked his cheeks as he took out a triangular crystal and set it on the table between them. "Not necessary at all. I just have some confidential information for you." She waved him on with an indolent flick of her wrist.

"You may recall, the night of Lucia's execution, I was in the crowd along with Izell. Well, I noticed her acting strangely after you had Lucia in your psychic grasp." He mimed holding up air in a nearly-closed fist, and her eyes narrowed.

"Strangely how?"

"She was staring quite intently at Lucia and Neala. I saw her perform a spell, but it was too quick for me to see what it was. But...I thought she was acting off, so I had one of my operatives follow her." Now that the words were coming, his nerves were starting to settle. All he had to do was report the facts, and they were quite clear in this case.

"I had a shapeshifter follow her with this memory crystal just in case something happened. And it finally did...last night."

He gestured for her to use the memory crystal. It was about the size of a fingernail, but when depressed, its angular sides opened like a flower and projected the recorded memory within at a much more reasonable size.

It was the dark of night and the view was partially obscured by grass, but his operative had placed the crystal back from her and at an angle to see Izell's draconic features as she cast a spell with the waving of her hands and a few drops of blood gathered from a cut on her arm.

"I summon thee to my side," she muttered.

Time passed with nothing happening. Kalimea flashed Sondus a concerned glance around the projection, and he inclined his head, echoing that emotion.

They had to wait the several minutes it took in real time for a ball of smoke to appear and coalesce into another woman's figure.

Kalimea gasped in outrage as Lucia's *mort loci* body stood before Izell. "Yes?" the demon demanded.

"She should be *dead!*" Kalimea spat.

Sondus held up his hands, so she didn't miss it as Izell answered just as waspishly in the recording. "Lucia. How dare you? I told you to do two simple things, and you can't even accomplish that."

The demon tilted her head, her voice growing syrupy. "I didn't know I took orders from you, save for the required one." She gestured to her arm. "Besides...I don't remember anything you've ordered of me anyway."

"Stay alive. And stay out of my way," Izell said through gritted teeth.

"And look at that! I've done them both." Lucia's gesture was lost in the dark, but Sondus figured she was showing off her intact self. "I'm alive and doing my own thing. Surely out of your way."

"You great moron! You're only here because *I* saved your sorry ass," Izell shouted.

"Oh?" It sounded like Lucia was smiling. "So, that was you who released me at the last moment. Thank you dearly."

Izell scoffed. "I did it for my friend. Of all the fae in Faerie, did you have to pick Lyana?"

Kalimea glanced toward him again, and he supplied who that was. "The guardian of one of our last back doors. She was a sea serpent *mort loci* who's served for approximately a thousand years."

"I didn't realize you cared so much," Lucia purred. "Well then, if we are such good allies, perhaps you could toss a strong soul my way? I have this awful demon in my head demanding I pay my debts, and it would seem I'm going to leave him disappointed again." She drifted closer to Izell, her voice lowering. "You don't want me to burn in hellfire before I help you make your precious Dark Eye, do you?"

"I tire of you," Izell sighed.

"But you *need* me," the demon said gleefully.

Sondus felt sick to his stomach, already knowing what Izell was about to say. "I just sent off two powerful souls. Perhaps you will have better luck when there's two of them," she said with a touch of her usual venom. "But be careful with your own self. They are heading to the Outer Reaches—and this time, I will not be around to save you should you be trapped."

Lucia cackled. "Then I shall not get caught. Oh, do tell, is one of them Sirius? I have something special for him."

Izell turned away from her. "You may go."

"You don't have a task for me?"

"No," Izell snapped. "Just don't die! You're no use to me otherwise."

"You mean, you don't want Lyana to die. It's okay, I understand," Lucia purred. "Why do you think I picked her? Other than being so knowledgeable of Faerie and its workings. You two are friends." She clasped her hands under her chin. "Soooo sweet."

"You may go," Izell repeated with an edge of annoyance.

Darkness swirled out of the recording, and soon, it ended as Izell stalked away. The little crystal shut its edges tight, at the ready to repeat that damning meeting again and again. Kalimea traced its edges, her lips pressed tight. He didn't blame her; he could barely form a thought after watching it himself.

However, long practice had taught him there was power in speaking first and shaping the conversation, so he ventured some extra thoughts for her to chew on, "I looked into the two souls she spoke of, and they are the vampire, Prince Sirius, and the girl, Cossette, who is an Ancient-aged vampiress in disguise. At your word, I can move resources into the Outer Reaches in anticipation of another demonic attack."

Kalimea nodded slowly. "Of course. Do it." She weaved her fingers into her curls, pulling at them with a groan. "To Izell's credit, she does not seem eager to be working with this demon."

"Yet they are still conspiring together in the dead of night," he pointed out. "With Izell's considerable power, you could assume she can easily capture Lucia for a proper exorcism and execution."

"But she didn't," she sighed.

He understood the Queen's pain too. Izell was the reason for his reminiscing, for long ago, as a broken boy with no wings, it had been Izell who'd recognized his other talents and suggested that he'd be a great match for a secretive organization homed in the Shifting Wood. But that woman obviously wasn't the same one they'd just seen in that recording.

She was a wild card, and that made her dangerous for any reigning monarch. He knew it, and Kalimea struggled with it right in front of him. "What do you suggest, spymaster?" she asked quietly.

"I need your permission to bring her in for questioning, as she is still an Archfae of incredible power and influence," he said. It would be the operation of his lifetime, to disarm and capture her despite the considerable resources at his disposal.

But it was a task he would complete, for the good of Faerie.

Kalimea composed herself and nodded to him. "Granted," she said. "And good luck."

Ready to see Sirius's redemption? Don't miss...
Shadow Dance: Blood Legacy Series Book 5

Also by Elise Hennessy
Altare World

Are you ready for a high-flying adventure on gryphon-back? Join Sivana as she becomes the first female cadet at the highly competitive Gryphon Rider Academy after the blind gryphon Arimus chooses her as his new rider.

Dragon Riders of Pern meets Song of the Lioness in this YA fantasy series in which a pair of underdogs rewrite what's possible in a formerly all-boys military academy.

- See Gryphon Rider Academy on Amazon -

Also by Elise Hennessy

Join an unlikely crew of five misfits and a mouse as they strive to become one of Altare's newest elite spy teams. Heists and adventures await!

The Gilded Wolves meets Six of Crows in this YA fantasy series in which a former thief uses her skills to become a spy. If you like clever heroines, strong friendships, and found family, then you'll love Royal Spy Institute!

- See Royal Spy Institute on Amazon -

About the Author

Elise Hennessy is an author of young adult fantasy full of adventure and found family. She holds a master's degree in journalism and enjoys crafting unique stories. When Elise is not busy writing, she's trying to reduce her prodigious TBR list. She lives in Texas with her family and is owned by two cats.

Find out more about her books at: www.elisehennessy.com

Glossary

Adrun: A section of Faerie submerged under the ocean and shrouded in magic to make it impenetrable. Formerly a prison for the cursed Fell. Queen Nyah renamed it from "The Fell Lands" when she and her shifters reclaimed it and eliminated the Fell curse. It is a place of complete darkness that sustains life through druidic magic.

Alchemyst: An incredibly rare sub-distinction of vampire with golden blood. They can create powerful tonics and potions with one drop of their life essence. They are immortal, but lack the superhuman aspects of vampirism and the bloodlust.

Angel: A being of pure light and a denizen of Heaven. All angels are called to uphold and spread a grace, or positive emotion/trait. Can only be permanently killed by another angel or demonic magic.

Blade: A fae skilled with martial magic and a weapon of choice, usually a sword. Traditionally they serve as bodyguards to Sorcerers.

Blood Prince: A title given to the few Fell Hunters that survived the Fell Crisis. They are the first vampires and each started their own unique bloodlines.

The Crossing: Seelie fae can cross The Veil and travel between Earth and Faerie or vice versa during midsummer in a magical process called The Crossing. The only way to otherwise cross between the two worlds is through one of a handful of well-hidden portals.

Demon: A being of pure darkness and a denizen of Hell. The most common demons represent one of the seven sins, though it's possible to find a demon that represents any negative emotion. Can only be permanently killed by another demon or angelic magic.

Deveaux Accords: A set of laws created by the major covens of New York City and enforced by Ancient vampiress Cossette Deveaux. Covens are required to police their members to keep mortals safe.

Dhampir: A half-human, half-vampire by birth.

Drasonii: Literally "dragon-blessed." Members of a fae orchestra with instruments blessed by the four dragon gods of Faerie. The instruments are peerless and capable of conveying the emotions of a song to a listening crowd.

Druid: A fae or shifter that has manifested the virtue of druidism. They maintain the balance of nature through husbandry and control of the elements. It is possible to be both a Sorcerer and have druidism, but a fae or shifter that has both gifts is considered a druid exclusively. A druid in Faerie serves the four gods and the balance of the elements, while a shifter druid in Adrun keeps the land alive in the absence of sunlight.

The Everlasting War: The conflict between angels and

demons. The Veil was created to keep this eternal war away from Earth and Faerie.

Eyes of Worlds: A pair of giant tools that anchor The Veil into place. One was created by the willing sacrifice of an Archangel— it is the Light Eye located in Faerie. The other was created from an unwilling greater demon and became its prison—it was destroyed during the events of *Dream Walker*.

Faerie: A separate world magically linked to Earth. The place of origin for all magic and mythical creatures.

Fell: A fae afflicted with a curse of eternal hunger. The curse was spread from Fell to fae via a bite and was considered incurable. Fell are twisted creatures known for squat, frog-like legs, sharp and interconnected teeth like a bear trap, black veins, and pitch-black eyes. All Fell were banished from Faerie to The Fell Lands (see Adrun). The Fell Crisis or Fell War occurred when the Fell learned they could create portals to Earth during the Dark Ages and began consuming man and beast alike like a black tide of locusts. After their defeat, all records of the Fell were expunged from mortal record to hide the existence of vampires.

Fell Hunter: The first vampires. Soldiers exposed to Fell blood became strong and fast enough to fight Fell in the service to humanity. Though the first Fell Hunters were turned by accident, many were turned on purpose after the phenomenon was studied. In those days, being a vampire was considered a sacrifice for the greater good. Most Fell Hunters died fighting monsters.

Fell Keys: Thirteen in total, referring to a set of rings with gemstones of pure magic. Each one represents one of the schools of fae magic and grants the wearer great power.

Fell Madness: The boogeyman of vampirism. First manifested in Fell Hunters when they consumed too much Fell blood. Fell

Madness gives vampires black veins, a mouthful of sharp teeth, and endless hunger for blood. Very little is known about the affliction because those that manifested it were swiftly executed. In modern day, the affliction can be cured by an Alchemyst's potion.

The Gift: Some vampires manifest the Gift rather than the abilities of their bloodline. They are capable of healing others from even the worst of mortal wounds. The Gift leaves if a vampire uses it to harm or kill others.

Heartsong: The fae version of a lifemate (see below). Every fae has a unique melody that they create when they come of age, which they refer to as a heart's song. Two fae with harmonizing heart's songs are destined to be mates.

Heaven-Hell Accords: A set of rules agreed on between angels and demons as it concerns their interaction with Earth. As the Everlasting War is based off of balance, if a demon is summoned to Earth, an angel is allowed through The Veil to hunt it down. Resurrections of newly created angels or demons is strictly forbidden. Hell attacks, Heaven defends. Demons historically have bent these rules to the breaking point.

Lifemate: A perfect match to a vampire. It is possible to identify a lifemate on sight and many vampires describe the sensation as being as subtle as a punch to the gut. A lifemate is usually a vampire's perfect opposite. It is possible for a vampire to have more than one lifemate, but the phenomenon is exceedingly rare as most vampires don't survive to an advanced age if they lose their first lifemate.

Mort Loci: Translated to "death speaker." A derogatory term for a person with the soul of an animal inside of them. The fae consider such people possessed or cursed. (See shifter below.)

Nephilim: A person with angel parentage, who is capable of wielding light magic. Nephilim are considered extinct in modern day due to The Veil and the Heaven-Hell Accords.

Nyixa Island: A chunk of The Fell Lands that the Fell managed to drag to Earth. It is a relatively large island with the Dark Eye at its center. After the Fell were defeated, vampires made it their seat of power before it was sunk to the bottom of the ocean in a bid to eradicate Fell Madness. It has only resurfaced recently in modern times and is considered inhabitable.

Occultarus: A tool used by Sorcerers to concentrate their magic. Instead of using complicated gestures to summon magic, a Sorcerer can hold an occultarus and cast spells more quickly. An occultarus is a sphere of glass forged by dragon fire and contains concentrated magic within. The Eyes of Worlds were modeled after occultari and are giant versions of them.

Primordial Fae: The very first denizens of Faerie. They were powerful, but unstable, and evolved into the four sub-races of greater fae, split into the four elements of earth, fire, water, and wind. King Oberon is the most notable Primordial.

Seelie Fae: Greater fae who aligned with angels before The Veil separated Faerie from Heaven and Hell. Their tongues are cursed to utter only the truth. While Faerie is at peace now, Seelie and Unseelie have historically been at war along the same lines as their patrons. Their sub-races are terran fae (earth), solar fae (fire), astral fae (water), and aether fae (wind).

Shifter: A fae or human with the soul of an animal within them. While the fae will refer to a shifter as *mort loci* in a derogatory manner, the denizens of Adrun all became shifters as the Fell curse cannot take root in a body with two souls within it. The creation of a shifter is a partnership and the resulting person can appear fully humanoid or gain physical characteristics of their animal side. Some shifters fully give in to the whims of their animal and never return to humanoid form.

Glossary

Spark: A piece of a demon's soul that can be given to a "willing" person. A spark will slowly corrupt the person's soul until it resembles the same level of darkness as the original demon, twisting their personality in the process. A spark can out-live a demon if they are killed. Powerful demons can "resurrect" by taking over the body of a humanoid afflicted by their spark.

Spellbreaker: A fae skilled in reflecting or mitigating magic. A highly trained Spellbreaker can render a Sorcerer's magic useless.

Sorcerer: Originally a distinction for the rare fae who can control all thirteen schools of magic, this title is also awarded to the sub-class of vampire that has silver blood and the ability to control every school of fae magic. Sorcerers are highly trained and often manifest extra rare abilities called virtues. The five virtues are: true sight, future sight, empathy, druidism, and mediumship.

Unseelie Fae: Greater fae who aligned with demons before The Veil separated Faerie from Heaven and Hell. Their tongues are cursed to utter only lies. While Faerie is at peace now, Seelie and Unseelie have historically been at war along the same lines as their patrons. Their sub-races are curse fae (earth), destruction fae (fire), death fae (water), and blight fae (wind).

Vampire: Descendants of the original Fell Hunters, spread by their cursed blood. The existence of vampires has become a myth to modern mortals as the purpose of vampires has tarnished from war heroes into former mortals trying to avoid their mortal coil. Contrary to popular myth, vampires are not walking corpses; they eat, breathe, and reproduce, though the chance of conception narrows as a vampire ages. Young vampires act a lot like humans with a taste for blood, though as they age they grow more powerful and inhuman. Vampires manifest an aura, which communicate to each other how old and powerful they are.

Glossary

The Veil: A magical barrier that separates Earth and Faerie from the realms of Heaven and Hell. Anchored in place by the Eyes of Worlds, it's been in place for over a thousand Earth years and prevented the worlds from coming to ruin by being battlegrounds for angels and demons.

Cast of Characters

Modern Day Vampires
Residents of New York City's covens.

Alexander Rehnquist

A vampire nearing his five hundredth year. Master of Coven Rehnquist and skilled shapeshifter. He is bitter rivals with Bryant Collins and lost his first lifemate due to the conflict between their covens. Fate crossed him one night and he ended up partnered with a second lifemate, Violet Reynolds.

Violet Reynolds

Formerly a mortal zookeeper, Violet was exposed to vampirism after Lucia secretly turned her into a kind of vampire that hadn't been seen in a thousand years. She became a silver-blooded Sorceress, learned how to master her magic, and captured Alex's love.

Julian Fairfax

One of the officers of Coven Rehnquist. The only vampire who mysteriously manifests an icy cold aura. He searched for his life-mate for hundreds of years until they were united via Lucia's machinations. He was viciously hunted by Lucia due to him killing her obsession. Possesses the Winter Key.

Olivia Cooper

A struggling mortal actress who was kidnapped to New York. She knows of the vampire world due to her best friend, Charlotte, but was quickly over her head after taking in Violet's blood and turning into an Alchemyst. She developed magical empathy and used it to save her Ancient allies from Jazrach's corruption. Due to her blood and quick thinking, she transformed a portal manifesting a connection between Earth and Hell into one that linked Earth to Adrun instead. Possesses the Shadow Key.

Charlotte Smith

Olivia's best friend and the only dhampir around. She is loyal and protective of her friend, joining Coven Rehnquist when Olivia did. She joins the supernatural police and becomes Armando's patrol partner when Julian retires.

Armando Nizzola

Julian's cousin and a member of the supernatural police. He is Charlotte's lifemate and earns her affection in the Christmas special *Dhampir's Wish*.

Bryant Collins

A bitter rival to Alex and Coven Rehnquist. He owns the telecommunications company Haven and thus members of his coven are referred to as Haveners. He is an Ancient and a religious zealot, believing the Light Key is his by his faith. He allied with Lucia thinking he could finally crush Coven Rehnquist with her might and magic, instead realizing his mistake too late after she got his entire coven killed and sacrificed his wife's heart to power a portal. He now seeks repentance for his misguided ideals.

Kim Cox

Bryant Collins's wife, known for her sadistic personality and enjoyment of torturing others. She is deceased as of *The Winter Key*.

<h1 style="text-align:center">Cast of Characters</h1>

Cossette Deveaux

The Ancient leader of the most powerful coven in New York City. She is an albino and a rare vampire who possesses future sight. She is stuck in the body of a little girl due to the twisted ideals of her vampire master. Due to her unique circumstances, her mind is damaged. She usually acts like a cheerful and sweet girl, but sometimes shows hints of her age as she delivers prophecies of the future.

<h1 style="text-align:center">Ancients</h1>

Surviving Fell Hunters whose bloodlines have shaped the vampire world in their absence.

Adrius

King of Adrun

Strongest Fell Hunter and owner of the Shield Key. He fell into a deep pit of depression to be separated from his lifemate, Nyah. Possessed every vampiric ability until he became a shifter by bonding to the spirit of the dragon Zerenth.

Lucia

The first vampire Sorceress. She inherited Jazrach's spark and was slowly driven insane. Nyixa was sunk partially to contain her evil. Upon dying in *Queen's Return,* she was reincarnated as a demon of corruption and now terrorizes her peers as she tries to capture a powerful soul to fulfill the debt of her escape from Hell. Was briefly Queen of Vampires in *Blood Curse.*

Gwendolyn Firetree

A nephilim who represents the grace of duty. Conspired to sink Nyixa in *Blood Curse* to contain Fell Madness and Lucia. She has committed her immortal existence to curbing the damage of old vampires on the brink of Fell Madness by making them mysteriously "disappear."

Sirius

Blood Prince Sirius, the Dawn

Adrius's second-in-command and brother. Was once a kind and giving man, but emerged from his thousand-year rest bitter, angry, and unable to fully control the whims of his inner beast. He is a shapeshifter and possesses the ability to walk in daylight without harm.

Korin

Blood Prince Korin, the Bane
The gentle giant of the Ancients, a steady and quiet personality. He is a blood tracker.

Neala

Blood Princess Neala, the Wraith
A mute orphan raised by Gabriel and Gwendolyn. She defied the odds and survived the Fell Crisis, though she sustained several terrible wounds that scarred her face and chest. Despite being an illusionist, she refuses to hide her scars or make herself more attractive and feminine. Loved and lost her first mate, Marcus Hartson, to Lucia's machinations.

Elandros

Blood Prince Elandros, the Legion
Squire to Gabriel Legion and also his murderer due to unfortunate circumstances. Possessed the ability to make minor illnesses and blights. After being blackmailed for the rest of his life by Lucia, he confessed his crime to Gwendolyn and was forgiven. Deceased as of *The Winter Key*. His soul was delivered to Heaven in *Queen's Return*.

Jaromir

Blood Prince Jaromir, the Mender
The doctor of the surviving Ancients. He was in possession of the Gift until he was briefly afflicted with Fell Madness in *The Winter Key*. He believes himself incomplete without his Gift.

Qin

Blood Prince Qin, the Ascended

He is considered a greedy coward by his peers, as he took a payment from Lucia and went into hiding, never to be seen again.

Taryn
Blood Prince Taryn, the Blade
Lucia's bodyguard due to taking a stage three love potion and being enslaved by his emotions. While he was immediately driven to Fell Madness upon being released from her control, he found his peace and center by becoming a druid as of *Queen's Return*.

Marcus Hartson
A close friend to the Ancients and Neala's former mate. After his mating bond was severed by Lucia, he was poisoned by her cursed blood and grew increasingly insane as the years passed. Died in an honorable duel with his son Julian after he drove the family to the brink of ruin from countless wars with other vampires. Deceased as of *Blood Curse*.

Adrun

A land of shifters and eternal darkness, full of life despite the odds.

Nyah
Queen of Adrun
Banished to the Fell Lands in *Blood Curse* due to Lucia's machinations for her throne. Instead of dying in the desolate land, Nyah used her Alchemyst blood to cure the Fell around her one at a time and establish life with the help of the Spring and Autumn Keys. Once her people discovered they could become shifters to permanently stave off the Fell curse, she was crowned Queen of Adrun and ruled with an empty throne beside her until she was reunited with her lifemate, Adrius. She is a shifter bonded to the greater wolf spirit Night's Howl.

Celeste
Princess of Adrun
A shy druid accustomed to taking the form of her beast, the

greater fox spirit Swift Spirit. Raised believing her father was a great hero, she helped push him out of his depression so he could achieve his destiny and win back her mother's affections.

Izell Firebrand

Considered to be the oldest fae alive. She is King Oberon's grand-daughter and the first Archfae of the astral fae people. She's been through a lot and has learned to keep her true thoughts hidden under a thick layer of cynicism. Bonded to the spirit of her familiar in life, the golden dragon Queldian. She's a distant ancestor to Keegan Firetree, much to his chagrin.

Cedric Applewhite

A half-fae, half-human born in Adrun. He inherited an enchanted lute from his grandfather and became a self-taught musician. He is known for his energy and enthusiasm.

Chandra

Blood Princess Chandra, the Dreamer
The only Ancient locked into the Fell Lands alongside Nyah. She shed her vampirism and bonded to an earth spirit, becoming the head druid of Adrun. She now believes in peace, love, and parties, and gladly helped Taryn escape the grip of his rage.

Caladorn Nightweaver

An astral fae Blade who lost his wife tragically when they were both afflicted by the Fell curse. He surrendered his newborn daughter, Sorsha, to Neala and promised to repay the favor one day. He serves Nyah as her general and has developed an icy façade to endure his immortality alone.

Calinhes Nightweaver

An incredibly powerful Sorcerer who was afflicted with the Fell curse while defending an academy full of fae children. He became the leader of the Fell, crowned the Fell Emperor, and became the reason the Fell came to Earth due to his keen mind and magical prowess surviving the transition. His familiar was Zerenth and the dragon mourned Calinhes's death for an eternity, refusing to believe his master turned into a monster until confronted by the facts. Deceased as of *Blood Curse*.

Faerie
The mythical residents of a secret world.

Orin Lux
King of Faerie
A solar fae who cemented the peace of Faerie by marrying the Unseelie Queen, Kalimea Dread.

Kalimea Dread
Queen of Faerie
A destruction fae said to be soft for an Unseelie due to her efforts to curb homelessness and creation of social welfare programs. She is a forward-thinker amongst a people used to cruelty and callousness from the royals that preceded her.

Talina Evenfall
A circus performer and aether fae who has caught Sirius's eye as a potential lifemate. She is a ballerina who can defy gravity with powerful wind magic. Her familiar is the iridescent pink hummingbird, Gem.

Sorsha Shadestone
An astral fae Sorceress with the true sight ability. She was born in the Fell Lands, but her father gave her to Neala to raise, who adopted her alongside her brother-by-circumstance, Keegan. She is petite, sweet, and still sometimes acts like a teenager when she lets her guard down. Otherwise, she's a diplomat and advisor to King Orin from her position as an Archfae.

Keegan Firetree
An astral fae Blade who comes off tight-lipped and reserved. He was adopted by Neala alongside Sorsha and took on his adoptive

mother's warrior persona. He is considered to be very powerful due to bonding with a fire dragon as his familiar.

Ashaela Dread
Unseelie Princess
Queen Kalimea's destruction fae half-sister. She is a Spellbreaker and trained assassin who relies heavily on her shadow magic. She is cagy and sarcastic, preferring not to be identified by her titles as she does not want to be the heir to her sister's throne.

Theron Shadestone
A powerful terran fae druid who has earned the title of Archdruid due to his skill in training young druids. He is standing in for his mate, Sorsha, in her absence from Faerie. His honest and to-the-point personality is already rubbing the rest of the Archfae the wrong way.

Sondus Arus
A spymaster for the royal family. He lost his wings long ago as a punishment from the last Unseelie Queen and thus has very little magic. His quick mind and photographic memory serve him well in his chosen profession.

Lyana Wavecaller
A guardian of one of the last known portals between Earth and Faerie. She is a sea serpent shifter, bonding to the soul of her familiar when he died. Fae society shunned her for her choice to become a *mort loci* and she was forced into a lonely underwater post.

King Oberon
A Primordial fae who served as the first King of Faerie. He originally welcomed both angels and demons to Faerie before they started infiltrating amongst his people and causing strife. He created The Veil and the Eye of Worlds in a powerful spell that was fueled by his life force. His sacrifice also cursed Seelie and Unseelie alike, but the way he worded the spell suggests that the

Unseelie may one day break it by proving they are "friends to humanity."

Other

Soren
A humble man who is Adrius's guardian angel.

Gabriel Legion
In life, a vampire named for the amount of Fell he killed. In death, an angelic soldier whom has returned to Earth to hunt Jazrach. He was the original commander of the Fell Hunters before his untimely death.

Jazrach
A greater demon of corruption whom was unwillingly sacrificed to create the Dark Eye of Worlds. He plotted to escape his prison and eventually stole a living body to wreak havoc and spread his corruption. He is deceased as of *Queen's Return*, but his spark remains...

Getana
Fae goddess of earth.

Raenith
Fae goddess of fire.

Cyranos
Fae god of water.

Zalice
Fae god of wind.

www.ingramcontent.com/pod-product-compliance
Lightning Source LLC
Chambersburg PA
CBHW061656190726
48289CB00006B/1907